SWEET MADNESS

"You are going to have to find yourself a wife." She smiled. "Unless you want me to take over that task for you."

He put his hands on her shoulders and brushed her cheek with his lips. "There."

"There what?" She looked up at him, hoping her smile hid the flush of warmth that surged through her with his unexpected kiss. "If you were to offer that kiss to a woman you are considering as a potential bride, it would make you the laughingstock of the *ton.*"

"I would think so. That was a thank-you for proffering help, but I would rather that you be my friend who leaves such matters in my hands." He grazed her cheek with another swift kiss. "And thank you, Valeria. You are a good friend."

"Yes," she said rather faintly as he strode away, calling for his man Kirby to order a bath for him and one for her. Her breath caught as she imagined relaxing in a steaming bath while his fingers swept soap through her hair and down her back and . . . She shivered as powerful heat surged through her. Was she mad? Half the time she did not even like Lorenzo Wolfe, who seemed to take pride in annoying her. And hadn't he just said that they were to be friends?

Friends. She wondered if that were possible when, at his most casual touch, heat ricocheted through her, settling in the most secret crevices of her heart.

She must be mad . . . or falling in love with him.

THE CONVENIENT ARRANGEMENT

Jo Ann Ferguson

Zebra Books
Kensington Publishing Corp.
http://www.zebrabooks.com

ZEBRA BOOKS are published by

Kensington Publishing Corp.
850 Third Avenue
New York, NY 10022

Zebra and the Z logo Reg. U.S. Pat. & TM Off.

First Printing: February, 1999
10 9 8 7 6 5 4 3 2 1

Printed in the United States of America

For Michelle Drosos and Terry Pino—
Thanks for your hospitality in Boston last March
and your friendship for so many laugh-filled years.

One

"I tell you. This is insane." Mrs. Ditwiller folded her pudgy hands in her lap and jutted her chin at the men sitting across from her in the crowded carriage. Keeping her voice to a whisper that would not disturb the earl who was sleeping beside her, she said with all the authority of her new station as housekeeper, "No one has ever said or heard a good thing about this horrid place, and now we shall be living there."

"Mayhap not long," suggested the young man by the door. He grimaced as the carriage dropped into yet another chuckhole. "Mayhap Mr. Wolfe—"

"His Lordship. Do not forget that." Mrs. Ditwiller wagged a finger at the lad who was still growing into his full height. "Gil, he has been generous enough to give you a position as his footman. Do not repay him by forgetting that he is now a fine earl."

" 'Tis not easy." Gil shifted on the seat, but his long legs found no place more comfortable. Lord Moorsea was so tall, and Gil did not want to wake the earl who had found little time for sleep in preparing for this journey from Wolfe Abbey to the desolation of Exmoor Forest.

"But you must." Kirby, the lord's valet, patted the lad on the shoulder. "This time, he shall remain a lord for good, and that is the way it should be."

Mrs. Ditwiller gasped, "You would have had Lord Wulfric die in the war?"

Kirby smiled, although he knew the housekeeper could not see his expression in the lengthening shadows that were

claiming the interior of the closed carriage. "You know well
what I mean. No one was happier than—" He gestured toward the sleeping man, afraid that using Lord Moorsea's
name would chance waking him. "—he was to have his
cousin home and alive. The title rightly belongs to the man
who holds it now, but you have to own it was our new earl's
turn to be honored with a title."

"But this one . . ." Mrs. Ditwiller twisted a linen handkerchief in her hands, threatening to shred it. "No one has
spoken of this estate in all the years I was at the Abbey. It
must be beyond horrible."

Kirby glanced out the window. Although many called it
Exmoor Forest, he saw few trees beyond the hedgerows edging the road. The steep hills were covered with heather and
gorse before dropping into bogs where no wise man would
travel without a guide. Now, as night crept out to claim the
bleak land, he longed for the familiar comfort of the kitchen
hearth and a freshly laid fire at Wolfe Abbey. "It is, one
must acknowledge, far from anything else."

"A most fearsome prospect," Mrs. Ditwiller replied.

Or a most convenient one. Lorenzo Wolfe kept his eyes
closed as the conversation continued to swirl in whispers
around him and the carriage bounced beneath him with the
enthusiasm of a child on a bed. He appreciated the concerns
expressed by his loyal staff. They were traveling with him
in the carriage after the fourgon, which should have been
carrying the servants and the boxes, had broken down miles
back near Minehead. To his mind, coming to Moorsea Manor
was the best of all that could have happened. Sometimes, he
wanted to believe, things just had a way of working out quite
conveniently.

"Blast!" he muttered under his breath when his head
banged off the side of the coach as the wheels struck another
cavity along the twisting road. He could not fault the
coachee. This road through Exmoor had more holes than a
sieve.

"Awake, my lord?" asked Mrs. Ditwiller gently.

"Yes." He rubbed his skull. He did not want to arrive at

Moorsea Manor as battered as a gentleman of the fists who had just had his nose introduced to a bunch of fives. "The first thing I shall do upon arriving at Moorsea Manor is find out who is responsible for this road and have it repaired posthaste."

Kirby laughed again. "Probably you, my lord."

"You may be right." Lorenzo folded his arms over his wrinkled coat and smiled at his valet, whose features were lost in the darkness. Thank goodness for Kirby's sense of the absurd. Lorenzo was letting Mrs. Ditwiller's dismay infect him until he was worrying like an old tough watching over her young charge at the beginning of the Season. As lord of Moorsea Manor, he might wish to keep this road in a state of steady disrepair. It would allow him the privacy he craved.

He had not guessed life would lead him in this direction. He never had visited Exmoor, but, before the twilight had cut off his views of the undulating hills and brooklets that appeared and disappeared with the skill of a ginn, he had delighted in the rough and untamed beauty of this land rising from the Bristol Channel. The views brought pretty phrases into his mind, phrases of sunlight and shadows, phrases of the play of the wind through the low-lying shrubs and clumps of trees, phrases he could manipulate into poems.

Now he would be taking up residence here in this grand, forbidding land. Mayhap if he kept telling himself that things would work out quite conveniently he would begin to believe it instead of thinking of his book-room back at Wolfe Abbey where he had withdrawn each evening to enjoy his writing and reading.

"Shan't be much longer, my lord," Kirby said.

Lorenzo's smile became taut. He could not tell his valet how he despised that title which he once before had possessed. Then he had believed, as most others had, that his cousin Corey had been slain on a battlefield in France. Corey had come home, and Lorenzo had gladly relinquished the title to him.

Now he was a peer once more. He had never met his mother's late brother who had cut himself off from the rest of the family long before Lorenzo was born. He guessed the separation had been over some sort of a disagreement, but no one had ever spoken of the matter. The previous Lord Moorsea seldom had wandered far from his estate of Moorsea Manor upon its hilltop in Exmoor, and none of the family had ever called. Lorenzo had not even known of this uncle's existence until only a few years ago when his mother died. Among her papers had been a letter to her only child where she mentioned that she had a brother named Francis who was Lord Moorsea.

"Our arrival shall come none too soon," Lorenzo replied when Gil shifted again on the seat which had grown more uncomfortable with every hour of travel. He moved his legs, so the lad could stretch his out in the narrow space between the seats. When his feet struck a small bag, Lorenzo lifted it on his lap. This bag must arrive undamaged at Moorsea Manor.

"Especially when night is falling." Mrs. Ditwiller cast a fearful glance at the window at the night.

Lorenzo laughed, wanting to ease the housekeeper's dire expression that did not fit well on her round face. "Do not tell me that you believe all those tales stuffed into your head before we left, Mrs. Ditwiller."

"Which tales?" asked Gil eagerly.

"Tales," Kirby replied, his voice dropping to a whisper, "so appalling you would never be able to close your eyes in sleep again. Tales of people who go out into the night and vanish, never to be heard of ever again. Tales of black magic and evil curses. Tales—"

"Enough!" Lorenzo laughed. "Look at them. They believe you."

Mrs. Ditwiller raised her chin. "I know better than to heed Kirby, my lord."

"You are a sensible woman," Lorenzo agreed as she sniffed at Kirby, who was grinning so broadly that Lorenzo could see it in the dim light, "which is why, Mrs. Ditwiller, I asked you to join me here."

"Sense has nothing to do with what might lurk out in the darkness."

"Exmoor may be little traveled even now, but it probably is less dangerous than any other part of England. Few knights of the pad would venture over these precipitous hills when their sole reward for their felonious activities could be a mired mount."

Kirby leaned forward, lowering his voice to a near whisper. "Might be other reasons no one is abroad after dark. We have not met another vehicle or anyone on foot for the past hour."

"Mayhap the folks in these parts are wise enough to keep their journeys short." He resisted the temptation to rub the ache in his back as the carriage dropped into yet another hole in the uneven road.

The trapdoor in the top of the carriage opened, and a cheerful voice called, "See the lights out yer left window? Moorsea Manor be right ahead of us, my lord."

Lorenzo ignored Mrs. Ditwiller's mutter of "Finally!" and peered out the window. Fog coiled like phantasmagorical serpents along the ground, glowing in the dim moonlight with the cold fire of a dragon's breath. Stars glittered with unobtainable light, far beyond any mortal's reach. When a pair of them shifted through the tree branches, he realized they were not stars, but lanterns hung by the stone gates of what must be Moorsea Manor. He was intrigued to see what appeared to be an ancient stone wall leading back from the gates. Even in the dim light, he could see enough to guess the wall must predate the invasion by the Normans.

His smile returned. This could be most interesting. Only his love of writing and quiet contemplation eclipsed his delight in studying history. Mayhap some enlightening and possibly rare tidbits waited to be found on the grounds. He needed to ignore Mrs. Ditwiller's cries of doom and enjoy the good fortune that had brought him to this place.

"Where is the house?" asked Gil, sticking his head out the window as he peered in both directions. "Can't see a dashed thing in this fog."

"Patience."

"You may have patience, my lord." He grimaced as he pulled his head back into the carriage with a yelp. Branches from the hedgerow growing out into the road brushed the sides of the carriage, scratching like a giant cat. "But not me. Been traveling over this feather-bed lane for too long."

Lorenzo rested his elbow on the edge of the window, then pulled it back as more branches struck the carriage. Dash it! This road must not have been trimmed back in his lifetime. He liked privacy, but not to the point that it ruined his carriage. He wished his eyes could sift through the fog to see the house that once had been as familiar to his mother as Wolfe Abbey became when she wed his grandfather's second son. Odd, that she had not reminisced about this house once in his hearing. He was tempted to speak of his curiosity, but Mrs. Ditwiller was certain to see some malevolence in what must have been nothing more than the result of a misunderstanding.

That misunderstanding was now over, because both his mother and her brother were dead. And Moorsea Manor was about to become his new home. He hoped this rough journey augured a good beginning for his new life, for his cousins were now well settled with their own lives. Here he could do as he wished—study and write his beloved poetry about the rugged landscape that surrounded him. He hoped the old house, that he was told by his late uncle's solicitors had been standing since the reign of the first Richard, would be as isolated and peaceful as any he could imagine.

A quiet life. That was what he wanted.

One of the horses whinnied nervously, and Mrs. Ditwiller gasped a prayer against the undead. Lorenzo waited for a teasing comment from Kirby or Gil, but they remained silent. He was amazed, then realized they shared the housekeeper's anxiety.

When daylight returned, they would see that they were allowing the stories they had heard, stories that were most likely untrue and had been devised by the servants at Wolfe Abbey, to unnerve them.

The house loomed out of the trees, a dark block within the fog rising to consume the night. Dozens of windows were lit, but the glow barely reached the road. The walls jutted out at every possible angle. The roof could not be seen through the darkness, but Lorenzo noted something hanging high up under the eaves. He hoped it was not a section of the roof that was in need of repair. On the morrow, he would take a tour of his new property and see what obligations he had inherited along with his title.

When the carriage slowed, Lorenzo shoved the door open, too eager to get out and stretch and explore his new home to worry about ceremony. He gripped the handles of his small bag. The leather struck the door as he climbed out, but it had been battered by many trips along the sea cliffs by Wolfe Abbey, for he took this bag with him everywhere.

Turning, he offered his hand to Mrs. Ditwiller. She giggled like a chit, although she was older than he by nearly a decade, and he realized that once again he was constrained by his new rôle. An earl should not be offering his help to his housekeeper. When he had served as master of Wolfe Abbey until Corey had returned, he found these restraints of propriety and rank irritating. Now he was encased by the strangulating rules again.

But he need not be. He could become as eccentric as his uncle, never leaving Moorsea Manor and living his life in peace and introspection exactly as he wished. A most pleasing prospect.

Leaving the others to tend to the bags and boxes crammed into the boot and stacked atop the carriage, he strode up the steps. The four steps were half-circles with some sort of design engraved into them. He tried to see in the faint light from the carriage lantern, but either the design was so worn by weather and time or the light was just too scanty. He could not discern what the pattern might be.

Tomorrow, he promised himself. Tomorrow he would act like a child with a new toy that was sure to become beloved. He would explore the manor house and then the grounds. It

might take him weeks, but he could envision no better way
to spend his first fortnights here at Moorsea Manor.

When the front door did not swing open to admit him,
Lorenzo frowned. The house was lit inside like a Covent
Garden theater stage. Someone must be within. A chuckle
welled up within him, but he swallowed it. If visitors seldom
called, any footmen who watched this door might have grown
lax at the post. Not, altogether, a bad thing.

"Allow me, my lord." Kirby took the steps two at a time
and reached for the door and gave him a wide grin. "Let
me be the first to welcome you to Moorsea Manor."

Lorenzo freed his chuckle, which was tinged with regret.
This place well-suited him, but he wondered how Kirby
would fare. Here, his short, round valet might find little opportunity to savor his fondness for emoting and poking fun,
at every possible moment. Although his family had ques-
tioned why Lorenzo, who preferred serenity, would want
Kirby serving him, Lorenzo suspected it was simply that they
shared a sense of dry humor few others understood.

"Thank you, Kirby," he said with all the exaggerated gen-
tility that his valet's voice contained. Amazing that they could
still laugh in the wake of this seemingly endless journey from
Wolfe Abbey far north of here near the Lake District.

The light poured out, an unstoppable flood, as the door
opened. Dozens of voices, each of them high with strong
emotion, pounded Lorenzo's ears. As he stepped into the
foyer, he wondered if all the residents of Moorsea Manor
and half the shire were squeezed into the space. It was not
a small area, but choke-full of people who all had their backs
to him.

Even as he tried to sort out the chaos of the voices, he
stared about him. He could not help but admire the rafters
woven in the ceiling three stories above him. He had time
to do little more than give the heavy, oak staircase a cursory
glance. Even the ironwork lanterns hanging from the walls
that were criss-crossed with boards and plaster in a decidedly
Tudor motif earned no more attention than just the corner
of his eye as one voice rose above the others.

A woman's voice.

"Why are you just standing there?" The woman's question was tinged with despair. "Go! Now!"

Kirby back-pedaled, nearly bumping into Lorenzo when someone shoved past and ran through the door at a high speed. The lad tripped on his own feet and stumbled down the steps before recovering. He ignored Lorenzo's half-spoken question as he stared at Mrs. Ditwiller's wide-open mouth and eyes. The lad then vanished into the darkness.

"I have no idea what is going on here," Kirby said and stepped aside to let the housekeeper enter. "Sounds like a goodwife about to give her husband a curtain-lecture."

Lorenzo had no idea what was happening either. He stared at the people filling the foyer. One or two people stared back at him before bending to whisper to one another and point at him, but most of the eyes were focused on a woman standing at the foot of the stairs.

Lorenzo could not blame them for staring at the woman. She was unquestionably beautiful, although her hair was a bold shade of red. Within her heart-shaped face, that was the perfect size to be held between a man's palms, her purple eyes flashed with emotion. Her gown flowed along her lithe curves, its lilac lace and silk flattering to her smooth skin. Across her shoulders, she wore the most outrageously patterned shawl he had ever seen. Its heavy fringe sifted down her arms, changing pattern with every motion.

When silence spread across the foyer as more and more of the people turned to look at him, the woman took note of the inattention to her words. She focused those incredible eyes on him and tapped her slender foot on the stone floor. "It is about time you got here."

"Me? Who are you, madam?" He did not doubt she was of the Polite World, for her gown was well-made, although he could not judge if it were *à la modality*. He had not been to Town in several Seasons. He had no idea what a lady of the Polite World could be doing here about as far from London as she could get and still be within the borders of England.

She gave him no answer. She turned to speak with a woman who was wringing her apron as severely as Mrs. Ditwiller was her handkerchief.

"Does she belong here?" asked Kirby, scratching his head under his cap. With a lecherous grin, he added, "Do you think the old earl left her for you, too, my lord?"

Lorenzo scowled, and the valet's smile vanished. No matter what sort of bumble-bath this was, Kirby should not be speaking so of a lady.

The woman shoved a vagrant strand of red hair back from her face as she pointed at Lorenzo and asked, "You there, why aren't you helping?"

"Madam, I ask again," he said, closing the door behind Gil who was staring, open-mouthed, around them. "Who are you and what is this upshot?"

Valeria Fanning aimed a furious glare at the tall, dark-haired man who refused to give her a direct answer. The old earl had been a warm-hearted man, but she suspected he had made little effort in this horrid house to keep his staff well-trained. This lean man, who must be the butler, for he was not dressed in the light blue livery of the other servants, made no effort to assist her. He carried a battered, black leather bag in one hand. Usually she would be curious what he might be toting about the house, but now she had no time to assuage her curiosity.

She started to turn back to ask a question of the woman she guessed was the housekeeper, but the exasperating man's gaze refused to release hers. For a moment, surely no longer than a single heartbeat, she was captured by that silver-blue gaze in his sharply carved face. His jaw's firm angle warned he was not a man who accepted reprimand well.

Dash it! Why was she worried about the butler when David was missing? Again!

"How can you just stand there?" she gasped, resisting the yearning to take him by the arm and shake him until he gave her a single answer to her questions. "We need to find him."

"Him who?"

Was the man completely bereft of his wits? She had just

described the problem to the manor's household staff. She took a deep breath to keep from flying into a pelter. That would gain her nothing at this point, and she could not fault this household staff for its lack of guidance. That must be changed posthaste. Pointing to the footman who had opened the door for her, she said, "You explain. I do not have the time."

Valeria whirled to rush up the stairs. David had a fondness for high, precarious places. Mayhap this drafty, archaic pile of stones had a tower that he had seen upon their arrival. She dared not consider how unsafe such a place would be for an eight-year-old lad.

A hand on her arm sent a fiery shock through her. Anger burst within her as she was spun to stare up at the man with the pale blue eyes. When he swiftly drew back his hand, astonishment on his face at his own forward behavior, she took a step away.

"Your manners are intolerable for a butler," she snapped. "I have no doubts that you would be dismissed immediately if Lord Moorsea were here to witness this."

"I am sure my manners are quite intolerable for a butler," he said, with a tilt of his head in her direction. "However, madam, I am not the butler."

"Not the butler? Then who are you?"

"Allow me to introduce myself." He bowed more deeply. "I am Lorenzo Wolfe, Lord Moorsea."

"You . . . ?" Her voice came out in a squeak.

When Lord Moorsea put his hand under her elbow, she was grateful to let him assist her to a chair next to the massive staircase whose banister must have been made of oak sturdy enough for a ship's keel. The rickety chair gave a warning creak as she sat on it, but it did not collapse. Dear God, she feared she was about to.

Squaring her shoulders, she clasped her hands primly in her lap. This was not a good beginning, but she must not allow her ill-spoken words to return to daunt her as Lord Moorsea had with his introduction. She was no young miss who could run crying back to her schoolroom in the wake of a *faux pas*. She had left that child behind long ago. She had endured more than she had thought she could in the past few months, and she had survived. Making a May game of herself mattered little when David was still missing in this strange house.

"Do you wish me to send for some *sal volatile?*" asked Lord Moorsea. A wry smile tilted his expressive mouth as his gaze swept the foyer and staircase. "I daresay it might be a scarce commodity here."

Her answer faltered when his compelling gaze settled on her once again. He was not what was commonly considered handsome, but he had a face no woman could ignore. The sharp planes altered with each of his expressions, making him look one minute austere and daunting, the next warm and wondrously kind.

"I am quite well," she whispered. "I shall not swoon."

"I am glad to hear that, Miss—"

"Lady Valeria Fanning." She stood and held out one hand while she gripped the back of the chair with the other. "Forgive me for my double errors of not realizing your identity, my lord, and of not introducing myself as soon as you entered."

Lorenzo took the hand she offered between his and was not surprised when it trembled. Bits of color were returning to her face, but it still resembled carved marble. "You are quite distressed, as I noted upon our arrival. Whatever has unsettled you seems unresolved. Will you tell me what has upset you?"

"David is missing."

"David?"

"My nephew David Blair. He is but eight years old, yet he has a curiosity that is unhampered by his age."

Lorenzo looked over his shoulder. "Kirby? Gil?" When they pushed through the crush to his side, he said quietly, "Search the house without delay and find one eight-year-old lad who answers to the name David."

"He is quite tall for his age," Lady Fanning hurried to

add. "His hair is dark, and he is wearing a forest green coat and brown riding pantaloons."

Kirby gave her a consoling smile. "Don't fret, my lady. No lad has ever been able to stay hidden when I have been seeking him. We shall ferret him out." His smile wavered. "To own the truth, though, that was at Wolfe Abbey."

"Take some of the footmen here with you," Lorenzo said. "They know the house, and you have a way of knowing what might interest lads. Use your keen eyes to spot the lad." As Kirby gathered some helpers and sent Gil on his way to one wing of the house while the valet took another, Lorenzo added, "I think you and I, Lady Fanning, should take this opportunity, while the search is on for young David, to become much better acquainted."

"What do you mean?" She snatched her hand back from his and pressed it to that outrageous shawl.

Lorenzo sighed. He had meant exactly what he said, but he had forgotten that the plain speech of the country did not fall easily on the ears of those who preferred the artifice of Town. If he said that he simply wished to know why she was here at Moorsea Manor, that would be the truth. However, if he had added that he had not realized he was still holding her hand, she would be offended . . . and it would be a prime out-and-outer.

Was he mad? He had no interest in engaging in a flirtation. All he wanted was the tranquillity that these rough walls and the moors should offer him. He would offer Lady Fanning and her missing nephew hospitality for the night before their journey continued. Tomorrow, he could begin his new life.

"Madam," he said quietly, "I hope you are more familiar with this house than I am."

"More familiar than you?"

"I am just arrived for the first time. Does the house have a library or a sitting room where we might speak while we wait for what supper can be prepared for us?"

"I am not sure." She glanced up the stairs.

"My lord," Mrs. Ditwiller intruded before Lorenzo could

ask the questions about Lady Valeria Fanning and her nephew that were burning on his tongue. "One of the lasses told me there is a comfortable room at the top of these stairs and to the left."

"Thank you, Mrs. Ditwiller." He was glad his housekeeper had the wit to know what he wanted before he needed it. Now, he could get the answers to those questions without so many of the household heeding every word they spoke. "Can you see that these people have tasks to do that will keep them busy while I speak with Lady Fanning?"

"Of course, my lord." She smiled, and he knew she relished the opportunity to assume her place as housekeeper.

He motioned toward the stairs. "Lady Fanning?"

The lovely redhead nodded and led the way up the stone stairs that were covered with miniatures of the carpet which had been hidden beneath all the people gathered in the foyer. The slow sway of her hips drew his eyes, but he forced himself to look away. Even if he had wanted to amuse himself with the harmless court-promises of a flirtation, this woman with her snapping violet eyes would not be the one he chose. With her Town *bon ton,* she represented everything he wanted to put out of his life—silly parties and worthless calls where the prattle filled him with *ennui.*

His eyes widened as he stared at the items lining the upper hall. Suits of armor battled for space with dusty portraits and antique vases, many of them chipped and broken, that were stacked four deep on the tables flanking a doorway. A stuffed bear, which stood on its back feet, leaned heavily against the wall by the narrow window, and some plant that he could not name was growing in wild abandon from its pot to curl around the banister leading up to the next floor. He tried to imagine his mother, who had always been so tidy, living with this hodgepodge.

It was impossible both to imagine her here and to wend his way through the jumble.

As she edged toward the door that must lead to the sitting room, Lady Fanning held her gown close to her, offering him a beguiling view. Again he looked hastily away. He yelped when his shin struck something that had been hidden under one of the suits of armor. Bending, he lifted the cracked hilt of what once must have been a broadsword. He set it on the windowsill.

"Mayhap it would look better in the bear's claw," suggested Lady Fanning.

"What?"

She smiled as she slipped, with an ease he could not copy, past the tables to the doorway. "It would be interesting to invite your guests up here and surprise them with a bear armed with a broadsword."

"I have no intention of entertaining here."

"No?" She stared at him with as much amazement as if he had just announced he had been named the next king. "Do you plan to pay only a brief call here?"

"No, I plan to live here."

"All alone?"

He smiled. "From what I saw in the foyer, Moorsea Manor need never worry about a dearth of people."

"But this is such a large house. It would hold many guests for a hunt gathering or simply an assembly here in daisyville."

"I enjoy my own company, madam."

"And no one else's?" She shook her head as she ran her fingers along the bear's upraised front paw. "I swear I would go quite mad if I were not surrounded by friends and gaiety." Throwing out her hands, she said, "My dear Lord Moorsea, this house is made for entertaining."

"I doubt that. My uncle seldom, as I understand it, received anyone here." When she opened her mouth to retort, he edged past her into the large room. "I mean to say, this is much better."

Lorenzo heard her soft gasp when she stepped into the room. He shared her incredulity, for the room was twice the size of the spacious foyer below. Every wall was lined with bookshelves, and others were stuck out in the middle of the floor. It was the largest book-room he had ever seen, and each shelf was stacked, to overflowing in places where books had fallen to the floor, with books and papers and bric-a-brac. This changed his plans. First he would explore this splendid room, then he would acquaint himself with the rest of the house.

Looking up, he saw the ceiling vanished into the shadows that claimed everything beyond the fire someone had thoughtfully laid on the hearth and the single candle that was set on a table between two chairs. Even from where he stood, he could see the chairs were well-worn. He hoped that was a sign of their comfort. One for him to sit upon, the other to balance his feet on while he worked on his writing. That would be just perfect, he decided, as he set his small bag on the floor beside one.

"Quite miserly with the light, I see," Lady Fanning said as she picked up the candle and walked to view the rest of the room. She called, "David?"

"I doubt you will find the boy lurking in a library when it is too dark to read." Lorenzo smiled up at the stacks of books, lying at every angle on the shelves reaching to the ceiling. A man could spend a lifetime trying to read all of them.

He took one from the nearest shelf and open it, tilting the pages toward the fire so he might read the letters printed upon them. He chuckled. He had a fool's own good fortune, for the book was poetry. Scanning the French and then the English translation, he closed it, his nose wrinkling with disgust. He had no use for Marquis de la Cour's sickish-sweet love poems. He set it back on the shelf and reached for another.

"How dare you!"

He turned as Lady Fanning surged around the end of the shelf as if she had been shot at him in a flurry of fireworks. Frowning, he wondered what he had done to disturb her now when, in truth, she was the one disturbing him in his own home.

"How dare I—?"

Her hand striking his cheek echoed through the room. As he stared at her, too stunned to speak, she cried, "Curse you, Lorenzo Wolfe."

Two

Lorenzo put his hand on his stinging cheek and bit back the retort he could not let ring in a lady's ears. "Madam, I have no idea what—"

"Better acquainted?" Lady Fanning sniffed in outrage. "I should have listened to my better sense and stayed downstairs until David was found."

"I do not understand what you are babbling about."

"Babbling?" Her finger trembled as she pointed to the end of the bookcase where she had gone to explore. "You expect me to believe that after—after—"

"After what?" He was trying to be reasonable, but he was hungry and his head had been aching even before she struck him.

"After I saw *that!* I have no idea what kind of woman you think me to be, but I can assure you, I am a lady come in hose and shod."

"Lady Fanning, I have not intimated otherwise."

"Intimated?" Her laugh was sharp. With fear? He could not understand why, when he had been the pattern-card of propriety, save when he had taken her arm to halt her from storming up the stairs. "Odd that you should choose that word."

"Mayhap I would not have chosen it if I had any idea what in the blazes you are prattling on and on about."

Her chin lowered a finger's breadth. Confusion filled her voice. "Are you asking me to believe you are unaware of what is on the other side of this bookcase?"

He did not answer. Reaching through the thick fringe on her shawl to take her gently by the arm that was holding the candle, he steered her around the end of the shelves before she could fire another demure hit at him. She pulled her arm away, but he grasped the candle before she could walk away to leave him in the dark.

In disbelief, he stared at the grand bed set behind the bookshelves. It must be of an age with the house, for its tester was hung by silken cords from the ceiling. The bed curtains were open. The headboard, that was carved with leaping stags and a unicorn, came alive as the candlelight skimmed across it.

"Now I know why you have been lurking in the country," Lady Fanning said coldly. "No decent woman would allow herself to be alone in your company. If you think that you can lure me up here and—"

"Lady Fanning," he said, glad the shadows hid his smile which she was sure to misinterpret, "you must recall several things. First, the whole of this household could burst upon this room at any moment with the tidings that your nephew has been found. Secondly, I am, in spite of your low opinion of me, a gentleman, a fact that is generally known. Lastly, as I informed you in the foyer below, I have only arrived for the first time at Moorsea Manor. I have no knowledge of what is in any of these rooms."

She wrapped her arms and that ridiculous shawl even more tightly around her. "I am not interested in listening to your explanations and apology here. We must speak of this elsewhere."

"Nonsense." He pulled the curtains on the imposing bed and walked to the hearth. He looked back, sure she would follow instead of huddling in the darkness. He was right, but she kept more than an arm's length between them and looked anxiously toward the door. "You cannot leave here until you learn where your nephew might be." Turning the two chairs so they faced the fire, he said, "Please sit."

She hesitated, then nodded. "Very well, but only this once."

A chilly prescience filtered through him, but he could not pounce on each word she spoke. She was quite distraught, and he must treat her with extraordinary gentleness until her nephew was found. He did hope it would be quite soon. He had not realized how exhausted he was from the trip to Moorsea Manor until they chanced upon that bed. He could use a long nap and a longer night's sleep.

"Lady Fanning—"

"I would as lief you call me Valeria."

Lorenzo wanted to ask her why she offered that familiarity when she had accused him, but moments ago, of heinous motives. When he noted how wan she appeared in the candlelight, he silenced the question and said, "As you wish, Valeria."

"Thank you . . . Lorenzo." She closed her eyes and took a deep breath. "I would like to say—"

"So here you are." Another feminine voice, this one not as melodic as Valeria's, came from near the door.

Lorenzo stared at the woman entering the room. The lamp she carried lit her face, making it a macabre mask. As she walked closer, he saw that she was not young. Her face, which once might have been lovely, now resembled the crags on the sea cliffs beyond Wolfe Abbey, worn by time and falling from its former glory. Her gown, even though made of fine fabric, was worn thin and of a style last popular almost thirty years before.

He glanced at Valeria, but she shrugged. For the first time, he wondered how long Valeria had been at the house before he arrived. She seemed as unfamiliar with it as he was.

"You must be the boy," the old woman said as she strode toward them. A cane was hooked over her wrist, but she did not use it.

"The boy we are seeking is—"

She interrupted Lorenzo, "Not the youngster, the boy."

Although he was not quite certain what she meant, he decided to fall back on formality. It might serve him until he could figure out even one of the peculiar denizens of this manor house. "Lorenzo Wolfe, madam." When she held out her hand, freeing it from the heavy lace edging of her sleeve, he bowed over it. "A pleasure."

"Pretty manners. Not that I would expect less from Francis's nephew. I must say that I am glad you are finally here to take care of all of us in this house. The house needs its master." She rested her hand on the back of Valeria's chair and peered at Valeria who drew back from her. "Your wife?"

"No."

"Your convenient?"

"No!" gasped Valeria before he could reply.

He clasped his hands behind his back and smiled coolly at Valeria who had the decency to look embarrassed by her outburst. At least, she shared one opinion with him. The sooner their lives separated again, the better it would be for all concerned.

The old woman chuckled, the sound oddly lyrical when it came out of that ruined face. "Be careful how you speak, young lady. Such fervor often reveals more than one would hope."

"This is Lady Fanning," Lorenzo said quietly. "She and I have just met. She is a guest at this hour at Moorsea Manor." He glanced away from the sudden consternation on Valeria's face as she glanced up at him. One problem at a time, and right now this old woman seemed to be the more pressing one. "And you are?"

"Nina Urquhart." She gave him a wicked grin and poked him in the belly with the cane. "I see your curiosity, my boy, so I will tell you that the late lord was my dear, dear friend."

Valeria pressed her lips together to keep from smiling as Lorenzo stared in dismay at the old woman. Lorenzo looked like a country parson confronting the devil, shocked, horrified, and yet somehow fascinated by the whole. If David were not missing and if the circumstances had not been so intolerable, she doubted if she could have kept from laughing right out loud.

She was impressed when Lorenzo bowed his head again and said evenly, "Forgive me, madam, for being unfamiliar with you and the rest of this household. My uncle and I were not well acquainted."

"You mean," corrected Miss Urquhart, "that you never saw the man." She shook her head as she eyed him up and down. "Too bad. I think you would have enjoyed each other's company far more than you can guess. I suspect you would have found you are two of a kind. I was watching you from the doorway. You seemed delighted with this library. He was, too. We spent many exciting, exhilarating hours here among these bookshelves."

Valeria could not silence her gasp. When the old woman looked down at her, she tried to regain her composure. Lorenzo was wearing that disconcerted expression again, and Miss Urquhart was grinning. Caught between the two of them, she thought it best to be silent.

Miss Urquhart patted her shoulder companionably. "Do not let your mind take you where you should not go, my lady. Saw you give Lord Moorsea here a facer when you thought he had enticed you here for a tryst, but that bed is not here for the reasons you both clearly think. Francis had that bed brought down here when his old legs could no longer manage the stairs. He could not bear to be far from his beloved books."

"That I can understand," Lorenzo replied.

"I thought you might when I saw those heavy boxes on the back of your carriage." Her dark eyes twinkled beneath her gray hair as she poked the bag by his chair.

He shoved it back out of her reach with his foot, but she would not be denied. Bending, she snatched it with surprising speed. She snapped it open and pawed within it.

Lorenzo plucked it from her hands. "The items within are private, Miss Urquhart."

Valeria's curiosity was aroused. She heard the crackle of paper, but could not see within the bag. What might Lorenzo have brought with him? A copy of the will to prove his claim? Absurd. No one would deny him this house when it was rightfully his.

"More books?" the old woman asked. "I saw the like of

your book boxes on the back of Francis's carriage any time he left the manor to . . ."

Valeria pulled back again as the old woman suddenly bent and put her face right in hers. "Is something wrong?" she asked, wondering if Miss Urquhart had an empty garret.

"You are Valeria!" gasped the old woman.

"Yes."

"I thought I recognized you from the miniature that Francis used to carry about. It is long past time that you came to call here at Moorsea Manor." She straightened and stared at Lorenzo again. "Odd that you should choose this time to pay us a call here, child." Not giving anyone a chance to reply, she continued to mumble to herself as she went toward the door, "Odd. Most odd."

Valeria had no chance to compose her thoughts before Lorenzo asked, "How does she know you? Have you met her before?"

"No, this is the first I have ever seen her."

He took the chair facing hers and let his hands hang between his knees as he leaned toward her. Bafflement ruffled his brow, tossing his hair aside as if upon a wild sea. "Yet she knows you."

Glancing toward the door, she said, "My lord—"

"Lorenzo."

"Lorenzo, I am very worried about David. He knows nothing about this house, and—"

"That is something else that puzzles me. Miss Urquhart knows you well, but you do not seem to know her or this house. How is that?"

"Lorenzo, I should go and see if David—"

His hand clamped over hers on the worn arm of the chair and kept her from rising. "We need to get some of this muddle sorted out."

"*You* need to stop interrupting me." She drew her fingers out from beneath his which were warm. Deliciously warm. She shook that thought from her head. She must be fatigued if she let such fanciful thoughts form in her mind, especially about this impossible man.

"My apologies."

She blinked, startled. Albert had been a dear husband, but he never once had apologized to her for anything. Not that he had often had cause. Her brother Paul had suggested more than once that a woman should not expect such words from a man, who must always maintain his pride. Had she been misled, or was Lorenzo Wolfe truly the peculiarity among the *ton* as she had heard in London? Could he be a man who preferred the quiet of country to the pleasures of Town and who had turned over his cousin's title and its prestige without a quibble? Curiosity once again teased her. What other aspects of the new Lord Moorsea would surprise her?

Again she silenced the enticing thought. She owed Lord Moorsea the duty of an explanation of her arrival here, although she wondered how he would react when he understood the total of her predicament.

"I came to Moorsea Manor for the first time," Valeria said, as her fingers found a loose thread on the chair, "not more than an hour before you, Lorenzo. It was while I was speaking with the household staff that I realized David had vanished. You saw the results."

"May I ask the reason for your call?"

She wished he would not be so polite. He had every reason to be furious with her. The red spot left on his cheek by her hand was fading, but her offensive words suggesting his intentions were scurrilous must have been even more wounding. She wished she could apologize, too, but she feared that would make matters more uncomfortable.

"The late Lord Moorsea was my guardian until my marriage to my late husband. But surely you must have known that if you are his heir."

"I know very little about the previous earl." He smiled wryly as his gaze went back to the bookshelves and the niche behind them. "And I know even less about this house and estate. I look forward to exploring it, so I understand your nephew's eagerness that has apparently led him to misadventure."

She could not help smiling back, for his expression invited

one to put aside all cares and trust him without question. "I have learned in the past three months that David has a gift for making himself scarce at the worst possible moment."

"The past three months?"

"I—"

"Get your blasted hands off me!" came a shout from somewhere out in the hall.

Valeria leapt to her feet as David appeared in the door, the collar of his coat firmly in the hand of one of Lorenzo's men. "David!"

"Tell this blackguard to get his blasted hands off me!" he cried.

She did not scold David for his language as she stared at him. His coat was ingrained with dirt, and she wondered how he could have ripped both knees of his pantaloons in such a short time. His boots were scraped, and she hoped the Jack boots here would be able to get them to shine again. If the manor even had a lad to handle that job . . .

The man holding onto David tipped his cap to her. "Told you I would retrieve the boy for you, my lady."

"Thank you. Thank you so much . . ."

"Kirby, my lady." He grinned. "I am Lord Moorsea's valet."

She gave Kirby a sympathetic glance. Working for this earl must not be an easy task. Pushing Lorenzo's idiosyncratic ways from her mind, she put her hands on David's shoulders. She ignored the dust and dirt as she said, "David, you must tell someone where you intend to go before you run off like that."

"How can I tell you where I'm going when I don't know where I am going myself?" He gave her a ragged-tooth grin as Kirby released him. "I never know where I might be going when I start exploring." His voice dropped to a conspiratorial whisper as his eyes glittered with anticipation. "You should see the amazing things in this house."

"Later you may tell me all about it. We shall have plenty of time to explore this house together."

"How is that?" Lorenzo asked as he came to stand beside

her and David. "Are you planning an extended call here at Moorsea Manor?"

Again she was tempted to laugh, this time at his dismal expression. Again the circumstances were so bleak she could not.

"No, we are not calling at Moorsea Manor, Lorenzo. We have come here to live. As you are now Lord Moorsea, I fear that you have become responsible for us exactly as you have for Miss Urquhart."

Looking from her to the boy who appeared to have gathered every mote of dust in the manor house to Kirby's wide-eyed amazement, Lorenzo wondered what he had done to deserve this fate. This was supposed to be his quiet home, far from everything and everyone, where he could enjoy working on his poetry. He had not expected to be overseeing the lives of his late uncle's dotty, old high-flyer and his ex-ward and her wayward nephew. He would find more tranquillity along the docks of the Pool.

"Thank you, Kirby," he said quietly as he tried to organize his thoughts. A dozen questions demanded to be asked all at the same time. "While I speak with Lady Fanning, would you and young David go to see if there is any supper ready for us?"

"Just as far as the kitchen, David," Valeria added in a strained voice. "You would not want to miss your supper, would you?"

David scowled at Kirby. "Tell him not to put his hands on me!"

"He shan't," Lorenzo replied, "as long as you give him no reason to put you on a leash."

The boy continued to frown as he stamped out of the room with every bit of his youthful dignity. Kirby gave Lorenzo another sympathetic smile and followed.

Turning back to Valeria, Lorenzo was amazed to see her regarding him with her chin high and her hands clenched at her sides. He resisted the temptation to take her hands and ease the strain from her fingers.

Before he could speak, she said, "I should have told you

as soon as you arrived, but, with David and all, my mind was on other matters."

"He is safe now."

She sat again in the chair and raised her gaze to meet his. Although he had expected her to wear a pleading expression, pride filled her eyes. "I came here because I had no other place to go."

"If Albert Fanning was your husband, you should be well off. He was renowned for his skill in managing his estate."

"He was, but my brother Paul was not."

"David's father?"

She nodded as a smile flitted across her lips. "Yes. My brother was ill-equipped to handle his finances."

"A gamester?"

Valeria nodded once more. "Of the worst sort, for he could not allow a chance to wager to pass him by. His forlorn hope was the bequest my late husband left me." She lowered her eyes before she could see the pity that had been her constant companion since she had been informed of Paul's want for sense and how he had signed his three vowels with the understanding that his sister's estate would pay for his gambling debts once his own money was long lost. "I had no idea until his unexpected death several months ago."

"But how could he do that? Your estate should have been protected."

"It should have been, but apparently Paul had some friends who knew the law well. They helped him circumvent the provisions of Albert's will. In a moment, I went from a life of comfort to dependence. I did not wish to burden my friends in London, so I came here to my former guardian's estate, not knowing he too had died until I arrived upon the doorstep." She meet his gaze evenly. "Tell me, my lord, what else would you have me do?"

"There must be—"

"There is nothing. In addition, David is now my responsibility." She smiled coldly. "Or more truthfully, we both are your responsibility, my lord."

Lorenzo fought back a surge of sympathy when her proud

façade shattered into sorrow. Her heart-shaped face seemed too delicate for such pain. He took a step toward her, but she put up her hands.

"I have no appetite for pity," she said in the same cool tone. "I wish only to know if you will honor your obligations as your uncle's heir to my nephew and me."

"As you should know, a guardian's duties come to an end when his ward comes of age."

"Does that mean—?" Her eyes filled with luminous tears.

He sat facing her. Taking her quivering hand in his, he thought she might tug away and storm out of the room. Then he comprehended what she so clearly knew. She had no place else to go. Her pride, which he admired, would not allow her to rely on charity. Nor would she beg him to help her. She hoped to persuade him to assume the duty his uncle had, even though she was an ace of spades with a young nephew to oversee.

"Valeria," he said, "I believe there is a way we can work this out to our mutual satisfaction."

She looked at him, and his breath caught, smothering his next comment. In her amethyst eyes swirled emotions only a brave man or a widgeon would dare explore. He was not sure which he was as he slanted toward her, drawing her hand to him. When she closed her eyes with a soft sigh, then opened them to divulge a dull acceptance, he pulled back as if she had struck him again. Where the devil! Did she believe he was trying to seduce her and she had no choice but to capitulate if she wished to provide her nephew with shelter and food?

With a curse, he stood and turned his back on her. He stared at the fire. "I think we both shall find this discussion easier after a good night's sleep in whatever quarters this house can offer. If possible, I shall endeavor to choose rooms in the wing farthest from yours."

"Lorenzo, I am sorry. I did not intend to suggest . . ."

He faced her and smiled sadly when she came to her feet. "Nor should I have retorted so with such force. We both have gotten off to an ill start."

"You have been the epitome of kindness in the wake of this upheaval." She moved closer, then halted and held onto the back of the chair. "If I have insulted you, I apologize. It is just that after . . . I mean . . ." Color slapped her cheeks before they became icy gray. "I am sorry."

"Let us begin this discussion anew on the morrow. I shall have a tray sent to your rooms tonight so that you and the boy might retire early."

"Thank you." Did he see tears glowing in her eyes or simply relief?

Lorenzo said nothing as Valeria rushed out of the room. Dropping back into the chair, he rested his chin on his fist. Dash it! He would have understood if she had been frightened of being turned out with nothing. Of course, she had no reason to fear that, for she would find shelter among her bosom-bows, because, in spite of her pride, she would not allow the child to starve.

She treated him with the contempt due a rake. He could not perceive why. He had done himself no damage in her eyes, but she acted as if his name were on the despairing lips of every matron in London who feared for a young miss's reputation. Every motion, every kindness he tried to show her was misinterpreted. Yes, she was a lovely woman, but he had, as he had thought so many times in the past hour, no interest in a flirtation. Did she? Did she hope to secure her home here by marrying the new earl?

Egad, he hoped not. She was charming and beguiling, but he had no place in his life for a wife now. Later, when he had had a chance to savor this old house and its tranquillity, he would think about getting himself an heir as was now his duty. Egad! He had gotten rid of this onerous mantle of responsibility once. He had not thought he would be smothered by it again. Yet, if her intentions were to become his wife, she should be more eager to please him instead of denouncing him at every turn.

What was he thinking of? This was all utter nonsense. Guessing why Valeria acted as she did was futile, because he would never learn the truth without asking her.

At the sound of footfalls, Lorenzo smiled and motioned for his valet to come closer. The sight of Kirby holding a tray with a glass of brandy that glowed in the firelight was the exact one he had imagined while on his way here. It was a shame he could not enjoy it, for Valeria Fanning and her problems plagued him.

Kirby handed him the brandy. "Your cellars should meet with your approval, my lord." He grinned. "I found them with the help of the boy, who seems to have explored them extensively already."

"It appears he shall have as much time as he wants to become acquainted with this house." Lorenzo took an appreciative sip. Kirby was right. The brandy was excellent. "Lady Fanning and young David shall be staying here longer than I had planned."

When Lorenzo had explained the situation, Kirby's face grew somber. "What will you do, my lord?"

Lorenzo took another deep drink of his brandy. "There is a singular, simple solution if I wish to have peace and quiet in my own home without any disruptions from Lady Fanning and her nephew. A solution that should be in her best interests, as well. I must not delay at beginning the task of finding Lady Valeria Fanning a more convenient arrangement." He smiled at Kirby. "She is still young—"

"And quite fetching, if I may say so."

Lorenzo smiled. "You always are honest, Kirby. She is quite fetching, and a proper marriage with one of my new neighbors should not be difficult to arrange." He glanced toward the hall as he heard the lad whoop as he raced down the stairs with his aunt in pursuit. "I hope."

Three

The rain threw itself against the windows like a child having a tantrum, incessant, loud, and keeping Valeria from sleeping. Not that she would have been able to find sleep even if thunder did not rumble beneath the clatter of the rain. The hour was too early and the house too unfamiliar.

Why had she come here? There had been other places she could go, for her friends were many in London. Her dearest bosom-bow Emily would have made her welcome to stay as long as she wished.

Pride. That was all she had left, and she was not willing to compromise it by begging to have doors opened for her that once had been swung wide with enthusiasm. Pride and pain, for she had not believed that her brother would satisfy his lust for the card table by squandering her inheritance before dying when his phaeton crashed on a slick bridge. Now she had left only pride and pain . . . and David.

Valeria glanced toward the connecting door between her rooms and David's, a smile uncurling gently across her lips. Lord Moorsea was proving to be kinder to her and her nephew than she had any reason to expect. These adjoining rooms were perfect, because she could keep a watchful eye on the boy who had too much curiosity for his own good.

She pushed the window open a finger's breadth and took a deep breath of the rain-freshened air. These rooms might be convenient and spacious with glorious furniture that recalled the best of the last three centuries, but they stank of a lack of use and too many years of being left to molder in silence.

She went back to where her trunk waited at the foot of the tester bed that was comfortably large, but yet far less grand than the bed in the library. Heat slapped her face. How could she have accused Lorenzo Wolfe of ulterior motives when he had been the epitome of kindness to her? She could blame fatigue, but the truth was that she no longer trusted anyone, either friend or family or stranger. She knew that was wrong, but she could not keep from expecting the worst from everyone around her.

Sitting by the trunk, she blinked back tired tears. She had spent the past few days of traveling down from London telling David how wondrous it would be once they reached Moorsea Manor. She had lied.

A knock was set upon her door, and Valeria dashed away any tears that might have been so brash as to try to escape her eyes. No one must see her distress. A lady always made those around her feel at ease. That had been one of her earliest lessons, and how often Albert had told her that her success as a hostess was a result of the welcome guests received at their home?

A round face, that was brightened with a smile that seemed more sincere than Valeria's, peeked around the door as it came slowly open. "Thought you might still be awake," said the woman, whose hair was a lighter gray than her gown. "Can I come in?"

"Of course." She wanted to add a name, because she knew she had been introduced to this woman just a short while ago. No name could be tugged out of her mind's mire. So many new faces, and the only familiar ones were David's and hers which she avoided catching a glance of in the cheval glass by the window.

The woman came in. "Guessed you would be thirsty after chasing the lad about the house. Thought I would bring it myself." She set the tray with the bottle on a table. "When I saw your light still on, my lady, I thought you might want something to ease your disquiet."

"Thank you, Mrs.—"

"Mrs. Ditwiller," the gray-haired woman supplied with a smile. "His Lordship brought me here to be the housekeeper, so if you need anything, I'm here to help."

Valeria was too tired to be diplomatic. "I need answers."

"To what?"

"I am curious about Lord Moorsea. I have heard some poker-talk about him."

"My lady, it is not my place to discuss the earl."

She sighed. She could not mistake the sudden wariness in Mrs. Ditwiller's voice. Of course, the housekeeper was loyal first and foremost to Lorenzo Wolfe. Valeria knew that, and she would not think to ask anything that would put the housekeeper into an uncomfortable situation.

"I understand that, Mrs. Ditwiller. I would not ask you to do anything that makes you uncomfortable." *Again the gracious hostess, but this time to get what you want instead of what your guest wants,* chided the voice within her, but she ignored it. "Will you sit down? You must be tired from your long trip here."

"Thank you, my lady."

Valeria silenced her sigh when Mrs. Ditwiller picked a chair close to the door and sat on its very edge. The housekeeper wanted to put an end to this as soon as politely possible.

"I simply wish," Valeria said, "to make David's and my intrusion into Lord Moorsea's life as unobtrusive as possible."

The housekeeper smiled. "My lady, do not misunderstand when I say that your good intentions are for naught. Lord Moorsea likes a very quiet life. He enjoys his books and his writing and his studies. When he inherited his uncle's title, he decided this place in Exmoor would be perfect for his pursuits."

"And for entertaining."

"Lord Moorsea prefers quiet."

"A small group of—"

"The quiet of his own company."

Valeria wrinkled her nose. "That is all well and good if he wishes to live in a morgue. This is a wondrous house that was built to include many guests. It would be a shame to shut its doors forever."

"My lady—"

"I have an obligation to my nephew. He needs an education and a chance to explore his imagination. I shan't have him spend the rest of his childhood tiptoeing around this house, making no more noise than a mouse."

Mrs. Ditwiller's smile grew wider. "I believe we all have seen how difficult that would be for the boy. I would suggest, my lady, that, once you and the boy feel more at home here, we arrange for rooms for Gil near young Mr. David's. The two of them should enjoy each other's company greatly, in my opinion."

Letting her shoulders relax from their stiff stance, Valeria returned that smile. Mrs. Ditwiller understood what a trial a young boy could be. And, belatedly, Valeria was beginning to see what a trial her new "guardian" might prove to be.

Lorenzo spoke his prayers backwards as his foot struck something and sent it skittering along the hall. Picking it up, he frowned. A child's shoe. No doubt, it belonged to Valeria's nephew. Glancing both ways, he wondered where the boy was. With any luck, he was fast asleep in his bed where he would spend the rest of the night.

He heard voices from the other side of the hall. Hurrying a pair of steps farther along it, he reached the door that was his. He closed it behind him and sighed as silence surrounded him. By all that's blue, he needed to speak to Mrs. Ditwiller about how she had arranged this household. He had suggested that it would be simpler for the staff if Valeria's rooms and the boy's were not too distant from his, but he had not guessed she would put them directly across the hall. A rambunctious lad and a most exasperating woman would not be conducive to the quiet work he had intended to delve into here.

He frowned when he realized the antechamber was as dark as the night outside the windows. Kirby had assured him, not more than a hour past, that his rooms were being readied. So why had his valet left no lamp lit to welcome him? Stretching out a hand, he edged around a large table in the middle of the room. But which way now?

A light flashed to his right. Candlelight he guessed, for it had too warm a glow for moonlight sifting past an open drape. Realizing it was coming through an arched doorway, he turned in that direction.

In spite of himself and in spite of the grandeur that had filled every corner of Wolfe Abbey, he could not keep from gasping as he stared at the inner chamber. Not at the large bed that must be a twin of the one in the library below or at the floor-to-ceiling window that had been added centuries later to the old fortress or even at the writing table that was set in front of it with his small bag placed in the middle of it. He stared at what appeared to be a giant man leaning back against the wall, its arms folded over its chest, its piercing eyes catching blue fire from the candle's glow.

"Startling, isn't it?" asked a voice.

Lorenzo flinched, but realized the voice was not coming from the motionless giant. He glanced to his left and saw a bent man crouched by the hearth that was almost as broad as the giant was tall. A candle burned on the floor next to the man, washing him in its soft glow.

"What is it?" Lorenzo's words struggled past the shock clogging his throat.

"Mummy case." The bent man chuckled. "Brought from some tomb along the Nile by one of Napoleon's soldiers. Somehow, it ended up in a shop in London, and then it came here."

"Mummy?" Now this was interesting. Maybe this was why Mrs. Ditwiller had arranged for these rooms for him even though Valeria and her nephew were lodged directly across the hall. She would have known he would be fascinated by anything this old.

He edged around a stack of boxes that were not his and another stack that he had brought from Wolfe Abbey and stretched out to touch the smooth wood of the mummy case. Too many boxes were between him and the case, that was a foot taller than he was. On closer examination as he stepped around more wooden cases, he could see where some of the paint had vanished since a nameless artisan applied it to the surface. Only the eyes remained untouched by time. He put out a hand to examine them.

"You shouldn't do that," chided the man by the hearth. "Old things like that don't need fingers poking at them."

"But the eyes—"

"They are made of lapis lazuli."

Lorenzo looked over his shoulder at the man who was still squatting by the hearth. "Is that so?"

"You'll find, my lord," replied the man, a hint of amusement in his voice, "that most of us in this house are familiar with the best pieces of the collection. That way, no one would be careless around them."

"An excellent idea."

"Always thought so." More humor filled the bent man's voice. "And there's no need to try to open the case, my lord. It's empty."

Sorry to hear that, because it would have been interesting to examine the mummified body within, Lorenzo asked as he shrugged off his wrinkled coat and tossed it on the back of a chair, "Who are you?"

"Folks call me Earl." The old man chuckled again as he stood and put his fingers to his forehead and dipped his head toward Lorenzo. "You are *the* earl now, my lord, but I'm just Earl." He bent again and rearranged the logs on the hearth. "Here to help with whatever you need."

Walking over to where Earl was tending the laying of the fire with as much attention and concern as if it were a child, he asked, "How long have you been working here?"

"Been with the last Lord Moorsea all his years on this

earth." Earl smiled and picked up the candle, spreading its glow completely around him. It outlined every wrinkle in his face. "Glad you are here now, my lord. This house needs a young man with some imagination to take care of it. Saw all the books you brought with you. Like reading, do you?"

"Yes."

"Good for you." He crossed the room where Kirby must have unpacked Lorenzo's small bag, because there were pages spread across the top of the writing table.

Lorenzo rushed to follow, but the old man was already picking up the sheet of paper. "That is private work," Lorenzo said.

"Work?" Earl tilted the page toward his candle. "Your work, my lord?"

"Yes," he said, even more reluctantly than he had before. He shivered and glanced toward the window. Odd. It was too chilly here, although the rest of the room had been warm. Mayhap one of the windows had been left open or a pane of glass was missing high in this window where it was hidden in the shadows.

"Most interesting. You write poetry."

"Yes."

He set the page back on the table. "It is good work, although I would have expected a man of your youthful years to be interested more in pursuits of the heart than of the vagaries of nature. Surely you must be familiar with the work of Byron and Scott and the Marquis de la Cour."

"I have read them all." Taking the sheet, he folded it carefully. "I admire their work, but what I write is my business alone."

"Quite true. If I have said something to offend—"

"No, you haven't." Lorenzo set the page back on the table. The staff at Wolfe Abbey had known not to disturb his writing desk, even if it was fuzzy with dust when his muse left him. He would speak to Mrs. Ditwiller about training the staff here as well. As they had respected his uncle's eccentricities, surely they would respect his as well.

"Glad to hear that. If—"

"My lord, are you within?" Kirby's anxious voice resonated off the high roof.

Lorenzo swallowed his groan. Kirby seldom lost his composure, so any time he did, it signaled a crisis. How many more would he suffer before his stay at Moorsea Manor was even a day old? "In here, Kirby."

The valet had changed from his dusty clothes to a simple frock coat that suited him better, for it made him look taller and more dignified. Tonight there was no need for sober livery to counteract his smile, for it had fled from his lips. Lorenzo suspected he had never seen his valet so grim. Not at all a good sign.

"Forgive me for disturbing you when you're alone with your work, my lord." He was almost panting, and Lorenzo wondered if he had been running down the hall.

"No need to apologize. I wasn't working. I was speaking with Earl."

"Earl? You are the earl, my lord."

"No, *Earl*. This chap over here by the . . ." He turned and discovered the bedroom was empty, save for him and his valet. The old man must have left the candle on the table and taken his leave just as Kirby was rushing in. At least, one of the servants in this household had been trained well to be polite and hushed-footed. "Never mind. What has you all agog?"

"The boy."

"He's vanished again?"

"Yes."

"People seem to make a habit of that around here." He wondered if a door lurked in the shadows beyond the hearth. Earl must have taken his leave in that direction.

"My lord, what did you say?"

"Nothing of import. So the boy has disappeared again?"

Kirby's lips twitched. "Apparently out the window and down the side of the house."

"A brave lad."

"Mayhap."

"A foolish one, most definitely." He glanced wistfully toward the bed. It was clear he would not be enjoying a full night's sleep tonight. "Very well. Alert the household and anyone who might be in the stables."

"Done that, my lord. We found his trail, and it seems to have led back to the house, although we have seen neither ears nor tail of the lad."

"Get Gil and do what you must to retrieve the boy from his hiding place. Lady Fanning is, no doubt, quite distressed."

Kirby nodded and hurried back out of the room.

Touching the pages of his poetry lightly and with regret, Lorenzo grabbed his coat from the chair and shrugged it on. Every wrinkle was so sharply ingrained in the coat that it cut into his arms and shoulders. Striding across the outer chamber, he had almost reached the door when it came flying open. It crashed against the inner wall. He jumped back with a swallowed curse.

"Oh, I didn't realize this was your room, my lord."

Lorenzo resisted the temptation to laugh at young David. He had worn that expression himself often as a child when he and his cousins' plans had been foiled by an adult. Then they had been cornered and caught in the act so completely that no inspired half-truths would keep them from punishment for the misdeed.

"Do come in, David," he said, motioning to the inner chamber.

The boy hesitated, and Lorenzo knew he was weighing the decision of whether to obey or take flight. Lorenzo was glad to see the boy had had some training in heeding his elders, because David nodded and walked with the shuffling step of a convicted felon toward the chair where Lorenzo's coat had been hanging. Pausing only long enough to tell a passing maid to let Lady Fanning and Kirby know that the boy had been found, Lorenzo followed.

He smiled when he saw David staring at the mummy case. "What do you think?"

"It's Egyptian, isn't it?"

"Yes. Have you been taught about the ancient Egyptians?"

"My last tutor thought it was interesting. He spoke of the kings and pyramids often." He grimaced. "When he wasn't talking about Aunt Valeria."

Lorenzo quirked an eyebrow, but said only, "Please sit, David."

"I would just as soon—"

"Please sit."

Again Lorenzo could see that the boy was unsure whether to obey or not. And again, David took the wise course and did as he was told.

Folding his hands behind his back, Lorenzo searched his mind for the proper words. He had not guessed he would be taking on the responsibility of a recalcitrant child upon his arrival at Moorsea Manor. If David's aunt had tended to his discipline, this would be unnecessary. He tried to recall what his uncle, the late Lord Wulfric, would have said in these circumstances.

"David," he began, "you must cease these escapades immediately."

"Why?"

"Because they are upsetting the whole household."

"I don't care a rap about that."

Lorenzo frowned. The boy was quite insolent. "Your feelings in this are of less importance than the household's. They have enough to do without chasing you hither and yon while you explore the house."

"But I wish to see what's here."

"And you shall. On the morrow, when we both are rested, I shall arrange for you to begin a tour of each section of the house." He bit back his inclination to offer to take the boy about himself while he investigated Moorsea Manor. The boy would be a constant intrusion on his own explorations.

"Arranged tour?" David set himself on his feet, crossed his slender arms across his chest, and glowered. "That's no fun!"

"It will be interesting, I am certain." He glanced at the mummy case. "I have seen only a few rooms of this house so far, and all of them have contained surprises."

"You haven't seen my room," he grumbled.

"No, I haven't. Is something wrong with it?"

David crossed his arms in front of him again. "I'm not an infant! I don't need a room connected to Aunt Valeria's. In London, I had my own rooms."

"Which allowed you to come and go as you pleased."

"I'm eight years old!"

"So I understand. What you must understand is that the arrangements for you and your aunt are only temporary. One of the reasons I had hoped to arrange a tour is for you to select other, more convenient arrangements." *Far from my private space.*

"Isn't that kind of Lorenzo, David?" asked a strained voice from behind him.

Seeing Valeria walking toward him, Lorenzo almost choked when he tried to keep a groan from reaching his lips. Was there no end to the disruptions tonight?

"David?" prompted his aunt again as she emerged from the shadows into the dim light of the single candle.

That light was enough, for even its dim glow danced in her lustrous hair as if each strand were on fire. Although she was frowning at her nephew, relief was easing the lines on her brow. A tingle cut through his fingers as he imagined smoothing away the last of her worry. Then that wondrous hair would brush him with its flame that might burn right to the quick.

Why was he acting like a complete chucklehead? He stepped back as Valeria walked past him to where David stood with his head hanging. Instead of admiring her glorious hair, he should be chiding her for not keeping her nephew in his bed where he belonged.

"I would appreciate," Lorenzo said, "if you would, in the future, maintain some control over this child."

Her hands curled into fists at her sides as she replied, "I'm sorry that you've been disturbed, Lorenzo. Apologize please, David."

"For what?"

"For disturbing Lord Moorsea." She scowled not at the boy, Lorenzo noted, but at him.

"I was just looking about."

"You shouldn't look about in here without permission."

David gave a longing look at the mummy case, then squared his narrow shoulders. "You don't have to fret about that, Aunt Valeria. I shan't again."

Lorenzo was astonished when Valeria took the boy at his word. He suspected David intended to return to pry open the mummy case and peek inside at the first opportunity. Dash it! That would mean the lad might snoop into Lorenzo's private writings as well. Carrying the whole of them about with him all the time was not a pleasing prospect.

"Will you accept his apology, Lorenzo?" Valeria asked.

"I believe I have not heard one as yet."

"He has said he will not bother you again."

Lorenzo met the boy's eyes and was surprised when David did not look away. Then he noted how the boy's chin jutted out like a bruiser looking to be knocked down in the boxing ring.

"I believe, Valeria, he said he would not enter my rooms again without permission. Quite the different matter."

She lowered her voice. "This is not the time to discuss this. He needs his sleep."

"As we all do. As we all could be doing, if he had stayed in his bed where he belonged."

"Lorenzo, please. Let you and I discuss this on the morrow." She glanced over her shoulder at David who was wearing his defiance openly. "Please."

His answer slipped out of his head as her hand slipped onto his arm. The motion was meant to be no more than companionable. Of that, he was certain, but the glorious fire sweeping through her hair flowed within him. His fingers covered hers before he realized what he was doing. At that instant, the flames converged in her wide eyes. Her lips parted with a soft breath of astonishment, and it was as if they were alone again in the library. Alone in the world, for even the sound of the crackling fire was diminished by the throb of his heartbeat that matched her pulse beneath his touch.

The lush color of her eyes was unquestionably violet, for the shade was too rich to be called an ordinary blue. Hotter than the center of a fire, they possessed the ethereal purple at the very edge of a perfect rainbow. And what treasure would be waiting for him if he dared to follow that arc to its very end?

"Can I leave now?" asked David in a vexed tone.

Lorenzo hastily released Valeria's hand. This woman infected his mind with hey-go-mad humors in an effort to bend him to her will. As she hurried to stand next to her nephew, he took a deep breath and let it go more slowly than he had her hand.

"I believe," she said, "we are all of one mind."

"Do you?" Lorenzo asked, wondering if her mind were as betwattled as his.

"We shall meet at breakfast, and you can share with David and me your plans to take a tour of the house with us."

"Us?" David asked, wide-eyed.

"Us," she replied in a tone that brooked no argument, and Lorenzo was amazed when she received none from the boy who looked at his feet.

"I said nothing of the sort." Lorenzo would not be bullied in his own house by either an eight-year-old boy's misbehavior or by his aunt's beguiling touch. He wanted to find a haven for doing his work, not to entertain them. This was *his* house, not Valeria Fanning's, and most certainly not young David Blair's.

"Of course you did, Lorenzo. I heard it quite clearly."

"I believe you are mistaken."

"Am I?" She smiled. "I heard you tell David you would arrange a tour for him. What difference does it make for one more?"

"No difference, of course, but—"

She smiled. "Then it's settled. We shall meet for breakfast, and then we shall spend the day exploring the manor house." Putting her arm around David's shoulders, she added, "You must not think of this as a chance to find more places to scurry off to, giving us another fright."

"I just wanted to see the house." His shoulders sagged, and he yawned. All resistance faded from the boy as he leaned his head against her arm, abruptly looking younger than his few years.

"Of course you did, and now you shall thanks to Lord Moorsea." She steered him to the door. "Good night, Lorenzo. See you at breakfast."

Lorenzo muttered something under his breath which he would have been embarrassed to have her hear. It had not been a good night, and he suspected the morrow would be even worse.

Four

Valeria hummed to herself as she came down the broad staircase. The sun shone through the stained glass windows, banishing the tribulations of last night. She could do this. Somehow, she could make living in this dreary old house less dreary. Her late husband had often told her that no one could make the best of a sorry situation better than she did. After all, she had been able to introduce the Marquis de la Cour to the *ton* and then hold a party to celebrate the man's utter disappearance only a short while later when he left Town to continue his work.

She smiled. The latest of the marquis's books of poetry had been published only a fortnight ago, and her dear bosom-bow Emily had made sure Valeria had one of the first copies available. Emily had been curious why Valeria had sold her London town house and was leaving for the wilds of Exmoor, but she never probed. Emily was like that, good at knowing when one needed to talk and when one needed to keep one's counsel.

Her smile dimmed. It might be a long time before she saw Emily and her sister again. This house was in no condition to host even the most rustic country weekend. However, Mrs. Ditwiller seemed to be a most capable housekeeper. Mayhap she would be able to train the staff in short order to have the house ready for a gathering.

The very thought brought a smile back to her so she could continue humming as she entered the room that was serving as the breakfast-parlor. She doubted if its beginnings had been that grand, for the floor was stone and so uneven that narrow strips of wood had been set beneath three legs of the table. It could have been a stillroom or a dairy that had been connected to the house years ago. A single window let morning sunshine surge into the room, but that only made the cobwebs clinging to the corners and the simple lamp overhead even more obvious. She hoped nothing with lots of legs would fall into her breakfast.

One of the first tasks should be to have the walls of all the rooms they intended to use regularly repainted or decorated with wall coverings. She would speak with Mrs. Ditwiller about it this very day. Then she would . . . Again her smile wavered. This was not her house. She was welcome here only as a petitioner, dependent on a stranger's goodwill for her food and the roof over her head. If she had had any idea that her erstwhile guardian had been put to bed with a shovel, she would have remained in London. Emily or one of her other friends would have helped her find a way to make a new life.

No! She would not beg for a home among her bosombows. Yet, she reminded herself, would that have been worse than living in this musty, dirty stack of stone with a man as odd as Lorenzo Wolfe? She had made her decision. Now she must live with it.

"Good morning," she called, trying to sound cheerful. She need not have bothered, for the room was overflowing with an obvious silence. Lorenzo and David were sitting as far apart as possible at the round oak table.

Lorenzo looked over the top of his newspaper and nodded. "Good morning," he replied before ducking back to read.

She gave David a kiss on the cheek and was pleased that he no longer shied away as he had when he first came to live with her. Now he just wiped his cheek with the back of his hand. Her grin widened as she took a seat exactly between David and Lorenzo.

"David, I'm glad to see you have chosen old clothes to wear. I'm sure the seldom used rooms of this house will be very dusty." She spooned eggs from a bowl in the middle of the table onto the plate in front of her. Dear me, she was going to have to inform Mrs. Ditwiller that this was something else to change. Breakfast should be served from a sideboard, not the table.

A door opened, and the housekeeper rushed in. "Is everything as good as can be expected?"

Lorenzo drew down the newspaper far enough so he could ask, "Are you having problems with the staff, Mrs. Ditwiller?"

"Nothing I cannot put to rights in no time at all, my lord."

"I'm glad to hear that." He returned to his reading again.

Valeria gave Mrs. Ditwiller a sympathetic smile. "I would be glad to speak with the cook and the butler with you later, Mrs. Ditwiller."

"Thank you, my lady." Relief lightened her face as she went back through the door, and Valeria knew that the staff of Moorsea Manor had not taken well to having a new housekeeper put in charge of them.

She glanced at Lorenzo, or, more truthfully, at the back pages of the newspaper. She could not believe he was so oblivious to what took place below stairs. Then she recalled that he never had been in a position to oversee a household. She would have to speak to him of these matters posthaste as well.

David asked, "Where are we going first?"

"You have seen more of the house than I have," she replied. "What do you suggest?"

"There's an old section of wall that I saw from my room. If we climbed up it and—"

Lorenzo said without lowering the paper, "Let us confine our explorations today to the interior of the house."

"But this looks so interesting!"

"Mayhap."

"And I saw what looked like a door. The wall might have rooms in it." David forgot his manners enough to lean both elbows on the table. "Who knows what we might find!"

"Exactly."

"So we'll go there first?"

Lorenzo still did not look at David. "We shall go there last. I don't fancy the idea of having something falling down on my head today."

"But—"

"It will have to wait."

Valeria put her hand on David's arm as he sank back against his chair, a pout on his lips and bright tears of disappointment in his eyes. He shook off her hand and, crossing his arms in front of him, scowled across the table.

She wanted to scold both of them. If Lorenzo chose to hide behind his paper and David brooded all day, it would not be a good beginning for their time here. They needed to learn, if nothing more, to tolerate one another.

"Lorenzo? David?"

"Yes?" asked Lorenzo.

David just grunted.

Before she could respond to either of them, the clatter of wooden heels came toward the breakfast room. She put down her fork. All of her appetite had fled, and she doubted if it would return now as Nina Urquhart appeared in the doorway.

Valeria had no idea why anyone would consider the turquoise gown the old woman wore as anything but a horrible fashion mistake. Rolls of lace dropped at every possible angle over the skirt that was nearly wide enough for being presented at court. Beads had been sewn on in some pattern that she could not discern. As Miss Urquhart entered the breakfast-parlor, two fell off and rolled into a corner to mingle with the dust. She leaned on her gold-topped cane as she walked with careful steps in shoes whose heels must be more than four inches high.

"Good morning!" chirped Miss Urquhart as she sat right next to Lorenzo and reached for the bowl in the middle of the table. "How studious you are this morning, my boy! In every way, you remind me of your dear, departed uncle Francis. It is too bad he could not be here to see this." She chuckled. "Of course, if he were still here, you would have no reason to be at Moorsea Manor, would you?"

"I suppose not," he said from behind his newspaper which he raised even higher.

Valeria wished she could say something to let Lorenzo know how she sympathized with him for having to deal with his uncle's eccentric ex-mistress. She said nothing, for she did not want to irritate the old woman more.

"Your uncle used to read the paper at breakfast and lunch," Miss Urquhart continued. She reached up with her cane and pressed the pages down toward the table. As Lorenzo stared at her, shocked, she said, "I warned him that it was an intolerable habit, and I shall say the same to you."

"Miss Urquhart, I—"

"Bother! Do not ply me with your excuses. I have heard them all from Francis." She plucked the paper away. "Say now!"

Valeria could not keep from staring. Lorenzo had not been reading the newspaper but a book. A novel, she noted. One of Jane Austen's. Her eyes narrowed as she read the title. *Mansfield Park.* She had not read that one yet.

"Lorenzo," she began.

She did not have a chance to ask him if she might read it once he was finished, because Miss Urquhart scolded, "Shame on you! 'Tis bad enough that you are reading at the table, but you need not lay claim to the newspaper and not read it when others of us might wish to enjoy it during breakfast." She snatched up the newspaper and snapped it open so sharply that it tore halfway down in the middle. Ignoring that, she held up the paper and began reading aloud an article about road construction in Exmoor.

Valeria put a hand on David's arm before he could protest. She did not blame the boy for being distressed. Either this old woman had been on the wrong side of the hedge when heaven handed out brains or else she had taken a knock in her cradle. Whichever it was, her mind must be quite addled to be acting this way.

"Forgive me, Miss Urquhart," Lorenzo said, startling Valeria. "You are correct. I was being rude. My sole excuse was that I could not wait to finish this chapter."

Miss Urquhart lowered the paper only far enough so she could peer over it. "That doesn't explain why you had the newspaper as well."

"I thought it would appear less ill-mannered if I did not prop a book between me and young David."

"A waste of a perfectly good newspaper, because it was clear from the unhappy expression on his face when I came in that young David was just as glad not to have to look at you." Miss Urquhart laughed when Valeria gasped. "Never be afraid of the truth, young lady. It will serve you well. That is a lesson your family should learn."

"Pardon me?" she asked, again astonished. "What do you mean?"

Miss Urquhart raised the newspaper again instead of answering.

Valeria looked at Lorenzo, who shrugged, then at David who was staring at all of them, obviously growing bored by the adult conversation because he was shifting in his seat.

"Can we go?" he asked. "The day's nearly half over."

"It is early still," she said with a smile.

It was no use. He would not be placated. Slumping in his seat, he frowned. His face contorted, and she realized he was trying to hide a yawn. She wondered how much he had managed to sleep last night.

No one spoke again during breakfast. Valeria began to comprehend why David was so anxious to begin exploring the house. He had been sitting here in this quiet since before she arrived. Her few attempts to initiate a conversation were drowned out by the silence.

Finally, having tolerated all the hush she could, she pushed back her chair and motioned to David to do the same. When Lorenzo looked up from his book, he wore a startled expression.

"Done with breakfast already?" he asked.

Miss Urquhart tapped one corner of his plate with the newspaper. "Look there, my boy. You have but a bite or two left yourself."

"So I do."

Valeria saw David roll his eyes, and she almost laughed. The situation, however comical, was exasperating as well. If this was the pattern every morning meal would take, she might ask Mrs. Ditwiller if she could have her breakfast in her room. That would work for breakfast, but for luncheon and the evening meal . . . She did not want to think about it. She would go deaf in this silence.

She stepped aside to let David scurry on his way out of the room, because he was rocking from one foot to the other, growing more impatient with every passing second to explore the house. He frowned when Miss Urquhart put out her hand and halted him.

"You should know that a gentleman waits for the ladies to rise before he takes his leave, young man," she said. "Or ask if one would like your assistance with her chair." She tweaked his cheek and smiled. "Especially when that lady is beyond the first blush of her youth."

"Pardon me?" he asked.

Valeria bent to whisper in his ear.

"Oh," he said, smiling, "you mean old."

"David!" Valeria gasped, then frowned when she heard a muffled laugh. Lorenzo Wolfe's manners were no better than her nephew's if he found this amusing. Her eyes widened as she realized Lorenzo was as aghast as she at David's unthinking words. Then who was laughing?

Miss Urquhart tapped David on the arm and freed her gusty laugh. "Ah, the honesty of the young is always refreshing to those of us who once held it dear." When David started to ask another question, she waved him to silence. "Pull out my chair, young man, and help your old auntie Nina to her feet."

"Yes, yes," he said, clearly nonplused by her mercurial moods.

"Yes, yes what?" she prompted.

"Yes, yes, Auntie Nina."

She came to her feet as he helped her draw back her chair. "You are a good lad. I shall have to remember that when next I remake out my will."

"Are you planning to do that soon?" asked Lorenzo as he put his book on the table and started to set himself on his feet.

"Finish your breakfast, my boy," she ordered. "I just poured you another cup of coffee. And, for your information, I redo my will whenever necessary. Seven times so far this year."

This time, Valeria found herself trying to keep from laughing. The old woman could not be serious, but she was, for Miss Urquhart prattled on about how the solicitor from Bath had refused to come out to Moorsea Manor the last time so she had the coachman and the cook witness the latest changes.

"Left them a pretty penny for helping," Miss Urquhart said. "They'll appreciate it." Resting her hand on David's shoulder, she added, "Let us get going. Half the day is over."

David grinned and led the way toward the door. As he passed Lorenzo, he put out his hand and yelped as if he had tripped. He struck the coffee cup.

"Look out!" Valeria cried, trying to reach the cup.

It tipped, splashing coffee all over Lorenzo. He looked from his speckled waistcoat and breeches to David, who was fighting not to smile and losing.

"Sorry, Lord Moorsea," he said, his lips twitching.

"How could you be so clumsy?" Lorenzo stared at the spots dripping down his waistcoat. "The cup was halfway across the table."

Miss Urquhart tossed a napkin at Lorenzo. "Dab yourself off, my boy, and change so we may be on our way."

"Our way?"

Valeria was glad that Lorenzo had asked that first, because he was the one whom Miss Urquhart's frown was aimed at.

"Of course I am going with you, my boy. Who among you knows the manor as well as I?" She patted Valeria's hand. "I don't want you to jump to the wrong conclusions again as you did in Francis's book-room last night. This poor boy cannot endure too many more facers such as you gave him then."

"You hit him, Aunt Valeria?" David asked as he grinned. Valeria said, "David, you need to understand—"

Miss Urquhart slipped her arm through David's. "I'll tell you all about it while we wait for these two in the front foyer. Ten minutes, my boy. That should give you a chance to change, and you, Valeria, the opportunity to select another shawl." She ran her fingers along the fringe on Valeria's shawl. "This is boring. I liked the one you were wearing last night much better."

Lorenzo pushed back his chair and stood as Miss Urquhart and David went out of the room, chattering like two squirrels with a single nut. When Valeria turned to him, she said, "I'm sorry for this, Lorenzo."

"Other than the fact that you brought the boy here, this is hardly your fault."

"Where would you have had me leave him?"

He held up his hands and surprised her with a tired smile. "You are misunderstanding me. I don't blame you for this. I suspect, if David were not here, Miss Urquhart would find different ways to make our lives interesting."

"What are you going to do with her?"

"With her?" His eyes grew as wide with boyish bafflement as David's had.

"It isn't a good practice to promise the household something in a will, when the will is worthless."

"I'm sure the staff here knows that."

"David doesn't."

"Then you should explain that to him." He threw the brown-spotted napkin on the table and stared down at his speckled waistcoat. "Mayhap he will explain to you why he felt compelled to begin the day this way."

"I need not ask him, for I know exactly how he feels about being compelled to start the day this way." She tapped the cover of the book. "If children are ignored, they find ways to make sure you must pay attention to them."

"I was not ignoring the boy. I was reading a book with my breakfast as is my habit."

"And it's David's habit, if he believes he is being ignored

or if he is suffused with *ennui,* to do something that will bring him attention."

"An inexcusable habit."

"More inexcusable than being a poor host to your guests?"

"Is that how you see yourself? As my guests whom I must entertain endlessly?"

She frowned. "Of course not! However, we have not been here long enough to be comfortable so that we can find ways to entertain ourselves."

"If you will recall, Valeria, I have been here a shorter time than you." He picked up his book, being careful to hold it away from his damp waistcoat. "I shall change and meet you in the foyer as Miss Urquhart ordered. I trust you can manage, during our wanderings around the manor house, to find something to entertain you and the boy, that does not require me to fear again for my clothes."

When he dipped his head toward her and walked toward the door, she called to his back, "David had the right idea."

"Excuse me?" he asked, turning.

"Dumping that coffee on you. It was, without question, the wrong thing to do, but it was the right idea. It's most unfortunate that it failed, however."

"What failed?"

"That the sugar in your coffee could not sweeten your disposition. Mayhap next time, I shall suggest to him that he simply tip the sugar bowl over your head instead." She pushed past him, leaving him gaping after her in amazement.

Oh, how she had hoped it would be different this morning. She had hoped *he* would be different this morning, but Lorenzo Wolfe was as irritating as he had been last night. Somehow, she must find a way to provide for her and David without Lorenzo's help, but how? She needed to ascertain an answer to that question . . . and soon before she dumped something over Lorenzo herself!

Five

Lorenzo wiped the back of his neck and wondered how much farther this corridor ran along the hillside. The air was close, and the walls bedecked with cobwebs. He doubted if anyone, other than Miss Urquhart who seemed quite at home even here, had been along this passage for years.

When Miss Urquhart did not pause as they passed yet another door, Lorenzo lingered and opened it. He sneezed.

"Dusty?" Valeria asked as she walked past.

He did not reply to the obvious. Looking in and trying not to breathe in too much of the dust clumped in every corner, he saw the room was empty except for a wooden bed frame and what looked like a small table. Now this was interesting! He had not guessed until now that Moorsea Manor might have once been a monastery. Although the title was as ancient as modern England, he had no idea when this house had come into the family.

His hand fisted on the dirty door frame. So many questions, and the only person who could answer them was an old woman who was half-crazy. He smiled. Mayhap Earl could shed some light on this. The old man seemed in full control of his brain, and he had owned that he had lived here for as long as Lorenzo's uncle.

Closing the door, he nearly bumped into David who was trying to peer past him. He gave the lad a chance to look in.

"Just like all the rest," David grumbled. "I thought there would be something interesting out here."

"I find this interesting."

"That's no surprise."

Trying to disregard the youngster's petulant tone, Lorenzo said, "You may not be surprised, but I am."

"At what?"

"That you don't find this interesting."

"Dirt and dust and broken furniture?"

"But it's more."

"How is it more?"

He continued with the boy along the corridor. He had piqued David's curiosity, so now might be the time to win over the lad enough so that Lorenzo need not worry about coffee in his lap or a missing boot that somehow—and with David's help, he suspected—had found its way out onto a window ledge where it had collected an inch of rain last night. The leather was already hard and threatening to crack.

"This is the oldest part of the house, David. Who knows who might have stopped here? Mayhap Vikings who terrorized the coasts so many centuries ago, or Henry Tudor on his way to battle the forces of Richard III at Bosworth Field. It appears that this building caught the attention of Henry's son, for I believe these doors we are passing once led to the cells of monks."

"Cells? Like dungeon cells?"

He shook his head and watched as David's enthusiasm drained away. "Cells were what the monks called their private chambers. This might have been a monastery before it was taken over by Henry VIII and sold to my ancestors."

"Do you think there's a dungeon in here?" Obviously the boy had a single thought in his mind, and he would not be budged from it.

"I believe you found it last night."

David scowled. "I did not!"

"From what Gil told me while he was searching for you the *first* time, the wine cellar might once have held prison cells."

"I didn't see them." He grinned. "But I can show you the way there now, and—"

"Whoa! We need to take the ladies into consideration. Miss Urquhart may not be able to manage those twisting stairs."

"She's doing pretty well over there on those stones."

Lorenzo looked past David and groaned. Miss Urquhart was trying, despite Valeria's pleas not to, to climb a pile of rocks to peer into a hole near the ceiling. Why was she interested in this when she had not stopped at a single door along this corridor? Mayhap she had dragged them all through here just for this. He could not allow her to break a limb or her neck, so he rushed up to her and took her arm.

"Leave off, my boy," she ordered. "I want to see what is beyond."

"It is too dangerous."

"Don't treat me like a child."

"I'm not." He turned. "David, come here!"

"Lorenzo," Valeria said, drawing more closely around her shoulders that garish shawl Miss Urquhart had persuaded her to wear, "you can't be thinking of having David crawl up there."

"Why not? He's already crawled about the house elsewhere and escaped unscathed."

"But he could get hurt here."

He handed Miss Urquhart back to the floor, then stepped in front of the scree to keep her from climbing it again. Only then did he look at Valeria. Dismay furrowed her forehead beneath her hair that, even here in the dusty shadows, was a lustrous shade.

He folded her hand in his before the warning went off in his head. Too late, because the soft caress of her fingers trembling ever so lightly in his hand, sent that powerful pulse through him again. Why was he reacting so to her, a woman who vexed him beyond belief and considered him just as aggravating? He had offered other women his arm or a consoling hand, but never had experienced this delicious surge of sensation that strengthened and weakened him at the same time.

"Lorenzo?"

His name sounded like music as she spoke in a breathy whisper that warned he was not the only one aware of this confusing connection that seemed to have no rationale. Clasping her hand with his other one, he stepped nearer to her so he could gaze into her exquisite eyes. Her lips parted as if she were about to speak. He waited for her words, longing for the sweet melody of her voice to weave them into a cocoon where this sense he could not name might metamorphose into something even more incredible.

Suddenly she tensed and cried, "Lorenzo!"

He recoiled as if she had struck him. When she pointed past him, alarm erasing the softness from her eyes, he spun.

With a curse he knew he should not speak in the women's hearing, he plucked a too plucky Miss Urquhart from the rubble and set her firmly on her feet on the floor. He did not lower his eyes from her frightful glower.

"Scowl as you wish," he said as he folded his arms in front of him, "but you shall not sway me from my opinion on this. *You* shall remain where you are. David will be our climber."

"Now see here, my boy, I was climbing rocks before you were born. I may be climbing them after you have dropped off your perch."

"That may be so, but you are not doing so today."

Miss Urquhart muttered something which Lorenzo thought best that he did not hear. Turning to David, he offered the boy help by locking his fingers together and letting David put his foot on them. He lifted David easily most of the way to the ceiling. Even when the youngster had a good grip on the stones, Lorenzo stood close, his hands outstretched to catch him if the stack gave way.

"What do you see?" Valeria called as David pulled himself up to the hole by the ceiling.

"Just more piles of stone beyond here." With disappointment on his face, David scrambled back down to the floor.

Miss Urquhart tapped him with the tip of her cane. "You are too young to take things for granted. Just because it looks like nothing more than jumbled rock, you should not assume—"

"That it's safe," Lorenzo finished, earning a frown from both Miss Urquhart and David.

Valeria smiled and gripped his arm, squeezing gently. Lorenzo Wolfe might want to be a recluse, but he was no air-dreamer. He could see the inherent danger if David took it into his head to explore the ruined sections of the manor. As they turned to go back the way they had come, she whispered, "Thank you."

"I shall have that hole sealed up without delay," he replied as lowly. "I may not know your nephew well, but I recognize that eager expression of his. My cousin Corey usually wore it before he attempted to scale the highest tree or swing out of the hay mow and risk both life and limb. Fortunately, he only damaged the latter on his adventures."

"He sounds like David. Even if you cut down every tree in Exmoor, he would find something to climb. He tried to go down the trellis at the back of my town house in London. He was lucky that he was close to the ground when it gave way. A sprained wrist was all he suffered."

"If you wish, I can have Gil oversee him."

"Gil? I believe Mrs. Ditwiller mentioned giving him a room near David's."

He smiled. "I should have guessed she would have seen the commonsensical solution to this problem already. Gil has only a few more years behind him than young David, but he possesses good sense."

Which David doesn't. Valeria could not be angry at Lorenzo when her own mind had supplied the words he purposely had chosen not to say. Or had he? As he strode away to offer his arm to Miss Urquhart, Valeria sighed. Lorenzo was being princely with them, offering them a home and treating them with respect. Even if his main concern was with having someone keep an eye on David simply so his reading went undisturbed, Lorenzo's offer was generous and kind. She was an ungrateful wretch to see it as anything else.

But she did not want to be here. Everything that was familiar, everything that was comfortable had been lost when she was forced to sell her home in London. Here the quiet was too quiet. Her ears strained to hear wagon wheels like those that had rung along London's streets and voices other than the ones belonging to this household.

As she hurried to catch up with the others, she heard Miss Urquhart saying, "I don't know of a man named Earl who brings in wood for the hearths."

"Mrs. Ditwiller is making a few changes," Valeria said. "Mayhap that is a change she made."

"Not a good idea." Miss Urquhart aimed another of her scowls at Lorenzo. "You shouldn't let her change things that have been fine for years."

"She is the housekeeper," he replied, glancing at Valeria with a tired expression.

She wondered how else Miss Urquhart had been lambasting him before she rejoined the conversation. A surge of sympathy flooded her. She should not be lamenting her own situation when she should consider how Lorenzo's hopes for his inheritance had been dashed by all the obligations that came with it.

"And she shall be a fine housekeeper," Valeria said with a smile. "You must give her a chance to do what she deems right, Miss Urquhart."

"You are a lamb," the older woman answered, "but you know nothing of Moorsea Manor. We have traditions that should not be disturbed." She stopped in front of a set of double oak doors. "Traditions that are as old as this." With a muttered groan, she threw the doors open.

Valeria heard Lorenzo gasp, but she could not manage even that as she stared at the room beyond the doors. Nothing in the simplicity of the corridor had suggested such grandeur would be waiting here. Stained glass glittered in the windows that were set about ten feet apart along the wall. There must be a dozen on each side, marking the enormity of what might have been the original manor house.

The gasp clogging her throat escaped when she realized what she had thought were just reflections of the colored glass on the opposite wall were elegant murals that encircled the room. A battle, as grand and glorious as the one embroidered in the Bayeux Tapestry, was being fought around the room. She guessed the painting must be over five centuries old, because its style had been disdained for many years.

An octagonal hearth was set in the center of the otherwise empty room. As she looked up, she saw smoke stains on the rafters over it. This room once had been much in use.

"What a perfect place for an assembly," she whispered, not sure if she should speak more loudly here. Even so, her voice echoed oddly through the chamber. "You could fit half the Polite World in here. It must be larger than the Assembly Rooms in Bath."

"Having an assembly here would be a mistake." Lorenzo walked past her and gazed up at the roof.

"Oh, no!" She whirled around, wishing she could hear the lyrical notes of the first dance even now. "It's spacious and exotic and—"

"There are spiders in every corner and mice have taken up housekeeping in the walls." He pointed to a small hole, then toward a broken window half-hidden by the rafters. "And if you look up, Valeria, you may notice they are not the only vermin who have made this their home."

"Bats!" she gasped. "Where?"

"Right there."

"I don't see them."

He pointed. "Third rafter from the back wall."

"I still don't see them."

Wondering if she could not or would not, Lorenzo said, "Come with me. I'll show you."

"But if there are bats—"

"They are asleep at this hour."

"Are you certain?"

He gestured again at the windows high under the rafters. "As long as the sunshine comes through there, they will be dormant. They prefer the night."

Lorenzo noted that Valeria kept a wary eye at the rafters overhead as they crossed the room. He had, he must own, the temptation to put his hand over his nape and draw up his collar to keep any of the creatures at bay. Glancing up at the broken windowpanes, he knew that the bats would not be banished from here until every possible entrance they might use was closed up. Another task to add to the long list he was making today.

"This is lovely."

He glanced toward where Valeria was running her fingers just an inch from the wall. Standing behind her, he squinted to make out the figures that had been painted on there. The paint had dimmed or chipped away in several places, but most of the scene of the moors that rose beyond the house remained intact.

"This section is new."

"It doesn't appear to be part of the rest."

"I suspect it was painted over this section of the battle scene more than fifty years ago," she said.

"How do you know that?"

"The clothing." She bent toward him and whispered, "The women's clothes look just like what Miss Urquhart wears."

He chuckled, then he laughed out loud, as he had not in a long time. When she put her fingers over her lips to halt her laugh, she was no more able to control it than he had been.

"We must hush," he said softly, "or she will come to see what we find so amusing. It would not be easy to explain."

"No—no, it wouldn't." Her efforts to keep from grinning tempted him to laugh even more.

Lorenzo turned as he heard a clatter behind him. A pebble or a bit of mortar that had come loose bounced across the floor. Blast it! This whole house was falling down around them.

"Mayhap," he said, raising his voice to reach David and Miss Urquhart on the far side of the room, "we should continue on without delay. This ceiling might not be—"

Something clunked against the rafter above him. He looked up, then put his hands over his head as dust and other debris rained down on him. Motioning toward the door, he called, "Get out now!"

David shouted, "Look out!" The boy was bouncing from one foot to the other in excitement.

"For what?"

Lorenzo got his answer when something whizzed past his head. He heard Valeria cry out in horror. As frightened bats flew down out of the rafters, he grabbed her hand and pulled her toward the door.

She shrieked as the bats flung themselves outward from the rafters in a frightened pinwheel. He threw his arms around her and pulled her beneath him as he crouched. Her face was pressed against his legs as one of her arms grabbed him around the waist while she tried to hold her gown off the floor.

"Don't move," he gasped as she shifted.

"More bats?"

"Yes." But that was not the only reason. Pressed against him as she was, any movement was too intimate. The scent of her cologne was making him as dizzy as the circling bats, and her breath sifted, warm and moist, through his breeches to his leg. His fingers itched to pull her back from him before he gave into the craving to bring her closer. He must be as mad as Miss Urquhart.

"Make them go away," she breathed.

His own voice was breathless. "They shall calm themselves in just a moment."

"Are you certain?"

"Yes," he lied. He could be certain of only one thing now—of how he ached to pull her up against him and forget the bats as he delighted in her softness. If he thought of something else . . . There was nothing else he wanted to think about, save for her enticing form draped around him.

Lorenzo had no idea how long they huddled there. Or how long they might have huddled there if Miss Urquhart's cane had not tapped him on the shoulder.

"Are you going to squat there all day?" the old woman asked irritably.

Valeria lifted her head, and Lorenzo wondered if he dared to move. Her lips were just below his. A single motion could have brought them together. Gazing down into her warm eyes, he knew he had seen this color only once before. The sun had disappeared into the night, setting the sea awash with this rich shade at the very point where it met the sky. That night had been lush with warmth . . . just as her eyes were.

"Thank you," she whispered.

"You're welcome."

"I hate bats."

"I thought you might."

When her smile glowed in her eyes, he watched her lips part. Would they be as soft as her curves against him? If he brushed his mouth against hers, what would she do? She had enjoyed at least one Season in London and had been married. Would she sense that he had never—?

"Are you going to squat there all day?" repeated Miss Urquhart, jabbing his shoulder with her cane. "We haven't seen half of the house yet."

Coming to his feet and holding out his hand to assist Valeria to hers, Lorenzo cleared his throat and said, "I believe I speak for both Valeria and myself when I say we have seen enough for today."

"You are spooked by a few bats?" Miss Urquhart laughed. " 'Tis a good thing we didn't start with the attics."

"There are more bats up there?" David asked, grinning.

"More than you can shake a stick at." She gave a sly glance toward Lorenzo. "Or throw a stone at."

Valeria paused in brushing dust from her gown. Her eyes narrowed, no longer soft with gratitude. "What do you mean by that? Did someone throw a stone to wake those bats?"

When Lorenzo stared at the lad, he was not sure if David would own up to his crime, even when he must have been the one to rouse the bats. Blast it! Was there no end to this boy's vexing dog-tricks?

David ground the toe of his shoe into a crack between

two stones in the floor. "It was my fault, Aunt Valeria. I'm sorry."

"Just sorry?" Lorenzo asked. Scaring the bats and them went far beyond the boundaries of mere naughtiness.

David avoided his eyes as he looked up at his aunt. "I didn't think the bats would scare you, Aunt Valeria. I didn't think you were scared of anything."

Lorenzo clenched his teeth to keep from spitting out the angry words battering at his lips. The explanation made it clear that David's apology was only to his aunt. The boy seemed determined to disrupt Lorenzo's life as much as possible with his pranks.

"Step forward, young man," he said, remembering how his cousin's father had confronted them with a punishment when they were caught climbing the trees in the orchard or playing along the strand when the tide was coming in.

David hesitated.

"Do as Lord Moorsea says," Valeria said quietly.

With a grimace, David edged forward a half-step. He was not going to surrender his will to Lorenzo's any more than he must.

Lorenzo bit back his curse. This battle, he feared, was far from over. Although it was one he did not want to fight, he guessed the boy had other ideas. Locking his hands behind his back, he faced the boy and said, "I suggest you go to your room and stay there. Your supper will be brought there to you, and I suggest, as well, that you plan on going to bed early because your lights must be out by an hour after dark." He took a deep breath, then added, "Gil will be there to be certain you do as you've been told."

"Aunt Valeria—" he pleaded.

She put her hand on David's shoulder. "Lorenzo, that is rather harsh. It was just a childish whim."

"Which scared a year off your life." Lorenzo was not sure if he was more irritated at the exasperating boy or his even more exasperating aunt. "It is time the boy considered the consequences of his actions before he embarks upon them. I'm just giving him time for that contemplation."

"I think you are making a mistake."

"Mayhap, but," he went on as David began to grin, "David made a greater one by not thinking before he acted."

The lad's smile evaporated in the heat of his scowl. "Aunt Valeria—"

"Go to your room, dearest." She gave him a kiss on the cheek and a shove toward the door. "I will be there as soon as I have a few words with Lord Moorsea."

Lorenzo did not move as the boy bounced out of the room, abruptly happy. Miss Urquhart followed, mumbling something to herself.

Keeping his hands clasped behind him, Lorenzo faced Valeria. His determination faltered when he saw luminous tears in her violet eyes. He was about to offer compassion for her lingering fear when her voice lashed him.

"How dare you!" She spoke in no more than a whisper, but he recoiled from her fury. "David is not your son."

"No," he said as quietly, "but this is my house, and *you* are my guest. I shall not have my home in an uproar merely to entertain a bored child. Nor shall I have my guests disturbed to give him a laugh."

"He did not mean to cause any harm."

"Of course he did." He laughed without amusement.

The wrong thing to do, he realized, as she turned on her heel and strode out of the room. Dashed woman! If he had half a brain, instead of wandering around Moorsea Manor today, he would have started looking for a husband for her.

Tomorrow, he would begin the search across the moors. Then he would make sure the banns were read in the nearest church with all speed while the household arranged for a grand wedding here that would be the perfect sendoff for her and her naughty nephew. Then, and only then, would he have serenity in his own home.

And then, only then, would he be able to forget how he longed to share more than angry words with Valeria.

Six

Valeria tapped her chin, then asked, "Where is the biggest room in Moorsea Manor?"

Gil's forehead rutted in thought. "Other than the old hall, you mean?"

"Yes."

The footman pondered her question for a moment, then said, "There is a big parlor on the opposite side of the staircase from the library."

"Have you and David been in there?"

"Not me, my lady." He rubbed one foot against the back of his other leg. "Don't know about Mr. David. He'd explored a lot of the house before Mr. Wolfe—I mean, Lord Moorsea asked me to keep an eye on him."

"Where is he now?"

"Lord Moorsea? Don't know, my lady. Reading, most likely. He likes to do that, you know. Reading and writing and writing and reading all the time."

"I meant David."

"He's in the kitchen helping Cook with the cakes."

Valeria smiled. It was comforting to have one aspect of their lives unchanged. David never missed a cake-baking day, glad to offer to clean out the mixing bowl and watch the baking so he might have a piece of warm cake.

"Shall we see this parlor for ourselves then?" She started up the stairs, then paused. "You do have a broom, don't you?"

"A broom?"

"In case there are bats."

"I'll get one from Mrs. Ditwiller."

"Meet me by the parlor door as soon as you have it."

Valeria ran her fingers along the smooth banister as she climbed the steps. How many hands had touched this before hers? She turned to look back at the huge foyer. It would be the perfect place to greet one's guests as they arrived along the long drive and came to fill this mausoleum with life once more. A small orchestra might fit in the corner near the curve of the staircase with more musicians on the landing above. The music would surround the guests as they flowed up the stairs and into the parlor.

Hurrying to the double doors, she looked back over the thick railing. Yes, musicians at both the entrance and up here. The hallway was wide enough for guests and footmen with trays of fine champagne to add conviviality to the evening. With lamps set between on the window ledges and mayhap a few brands burning in the torchières by the library door, the gloom would be banished.

"Along with that blasted bear," she mused aloud. "It will frighten any lady so much that she'll have no interest in dancing and conversation."

"Dancing and conversation?"

With a gasp, she turned to see Lorenzo behind her. "I hope you don't intend to make it a habit to sneak up on one like that!"

"I'm sorry I startled you." He gave her no chance to reply before he went on, "Are you planning a party?"

Valeria smiled. "How better to become acquainted with our new neighbors? And Gil tells me there is a parlor here." Throwing open the doors to a room that was as large as the library, she walked in, giving a cautious glance at the ceiling. No rafters offered a haven for bats. "Isn't this a wonderful room for a gathering?"

"I'm not so sure about that. How can you see anything but these boxes?"

She stepped over a pry bar and eased around a stack of wooden cases that reached higher than her head. Her smile broadened when she discovered a Palladian window on the far side. It must be the most recent renovation to the old house. Squeezing past another pile of crates, she found what could be the edge of a raised platform. Mayhap Gil had been wrong. This might not be a large parlor. It might instead be a small ballroom, which would be the perfect milieu for the first gathering in years at Moorsea Manor.

"Where are you?" Lorenzo called.

She laughed as she pushed through the stacks to where he stood, looking perplexed, by a settee and a pair of tables which might be the only furniture in the expansive room. "Isn't it perfect?"

"How can you say that? All the furniture must have been taken apart and put in these crates, although I cannot fathom why."

"It shan't take long to unpack whatever we need."

"Need?"

"For a gathering." She flung out her hands. "It will give this grand old house a chance to show how it can be glorious once more."

"Valeria—"

"Cook has told me that she can have all preparations for a small *soirée* within a fortnight." She ran her fingers along one of the tables and smiled as she wiped dust from them.

"A fortnight?"

"That will allow Mrs. Ditwiller time to have this room cleaned and the furniture unpacked while you have a footman deliver invitations to our neighbors." She clapped her hands together. The sound echoed wildly along the high ceiling of the room. Turning, she laughed with delight. "This house was built for having country weekends and gatherings for the Polite World."

"I believe you are mistaken. My uncle—"

"Should have shared this with everyone." She threw aside the drapes on the nearest window. Dust assailed her, and she sneezed. Shaking her head in dismay, she wondered if she was being optimistic. Two weeks might not be long enough to clean up this jumble. Sneezing again, she said, "Lorenzo,

your uncle was only the latest master of Moorsea Manor.
This house is grand and old and must have welcomed many
people over the centuries."

"No one will feel welcome here if stones tumble down
on them or bats dive at them from the rafters."

"Both the roof and the windows are already being fixed
in the old hall, as you know since you hired the artisans.
We need only use the rooms that are not in bad repair. This
one would be perfect."

He shook his head. "I have no interest in further interfer-
ence in my life by having to entertain people I have not met
before."

"How else will you meet them?" She smiled. "Lorenzo,
you are no longer the younger cousin. You are an earl, and
you must own that there is much curiosity about you and
this house."

"Is there?"

She laughed. "Don't be a goose! Of course there is."

"How do you know that? You didn't know I had inherited
the estate and title from my uncle until you had left London
and arrived here, and you haven't wandered farther than the
gardens since your arrival."

Hitting the back of the settee and jumping back as another
cloud of dust rose, she said, "I lived among the Polite World
long enough to know that such an inheritance always is the
cause of poker-talk. This one should be more than any other,
because you once held your cousin's title briefly."

"Egad! The *ton* needs to find something to do other than
blither about me."

"Exactly, which is why we should hold a gathering here
and let them have a chance to gossip about the members of
the Polite World who choose not to attend. Now you understand why you should host a gathering, don't you?"

He rolled his eyes and walked toward another stack of
boxes.

Valeria stared after him. Why hadn't he given her the cour-
tesy of an answer? She was no closer to understanding how
Lorenzo Wolfe thought than she had been upon his arrival.

When he picked up the pry bar that she had stepped over, he slipped it under the top of the nearest case and tried to lift the top. She almost clapped her hands with joy. If he was willing to take out the furniture that had been packed away, surely he would be willing to agree to host a small party. Mayhap she had persuaded him to see sense.

"What the—?" He tore off the top of the box and tossed it aside. When he ignored its crash on stone floor as he peered into the box, his grin was as boyish as David's. "Utterly fascinating."

"What is utterly fascinating?"

He took her arm and drew her closer. "Look in here."

Standing on tiptoe, she tried to see over the top of the box. Whatever was in it must not reach high inside the box because she could see nothing but the slats on the other side. "I can't see what's in it."

"Allow me." He put his hands on her waist and lifted her with an ease that suggested he did not spend all his time at his quiet pursuits.

She stared at what looked like cracked pottery, but her mind could not focus on what was before her when she could think only of the man standing behind her, his hands on her waist.

"What do you think of that?" he asked.

"Of what?"

"The pots in the box." He set her back on the floor and reached past her to poke his fingers at the shards in the box.

She knew she should step away, but she could not without ducking under one of his arms. "I think—" Her voice trembled on the two words, and she frowned. Was this his way of changing the subject? "Dusty and broken, if you want my opinion."

"I prefer my own, thank you."

"Is that a kind way of telling me to mind my bread-and-butter?"

He wiped his dusty hands on his breeches, turning them a sorry shade of brown. "Of course not, Valeria. I wouldn't do that."

"You're interested in my opinions?" My, she was endlessly amazed at how tall he was. When they stood this close, she had to tilt her head back to meet his gaze.

Mayhap she should look away, because a gentle smile slipped along his lips as his icy blue eyes warmed to the clear color of a cloudless sky. A shock of something sharp and heated raced through her when she thought of how he had held her and protected her from the bats. Then his large hands, which often were spotted with ink from his writing, cupped her, keeping her safe, making her sure that, as long as she was with him, nothing could harm her.

"Of course, Valeria," he said, chuckling. "I find that the opinions that are most in contrast with my own are often the most interesting."

"I don't." Drat this man! He thought of nothing save his studies.

"Another way we differ." He reached past her to the box.

She was as amazed as he when she grabbed his arm and drew it back. When he stared at her, she knew she could not be subtle now. "Lorenzo, are you going to ignore my comments about a gathering here?"

"I had hoped to, but it appears that you wish to continue this fruitless discussion."

"Fruitless? Why do you say that?"

He lifted the box off the stack, his muscles straining as he gritted his teeth. When threads snapped in the seam on his shoulder, he cursed as he set the box carefully on the floor. "Now I shall have to have this coat repaired." As he knelt by the box, he slipped the coat off and held it out to her. "Will you ask Mrs. Ditwiller to tend to this while I see what we have here?"

"I am not your servant, Lorenzo!"

Looking up at her, he said, "I should think not. I simply asked you as a favor. I had no thought that you would wish to stay to help me sort what was in these boxes."

"Sort?" She stared at the scores of boxes in the room. "All of this?"

"I thought you wanted to host a party here."

"I do, but—"

"We cannot have a gathering here until this is sorted and cataloged. It appears that my uncle had more interest in collecting antiquities than taking care of them. Some of these appear to belong in a museum, but I shan't know which until the pieces are properly catalogued."

"It could take weeks to go through all of this."

"Months, I would suspect." A smile played across his lips. "If this box is reflective of what is stored here, this room alone must contain more than a thousand different items."

"You cannot be serious."

"I am always serious."

She rolled her eyes. "As I can see. Too serious. You cannot think that I will sit quietly in this big house and do nothing while you check each item in this room."

"Of course not." He drew out a chair she had not seen before and lifted a box from it. Dusting the seat off with a handkerchief, he said, "If you wish to do something, you are welcome to sit here and join me in investigating what my uncle stored in this room."

"That was not what I meant."

"Mayhap not, but I was offering you the invitation if you wish to accept it."

"Do not be absurd! I have no interest in these dusty things."

He picked his coat up from the floor where he had dropped it. "Then will you take this to Mrs. Ditwiller?"

"Take it to her yourself." She turned toward the door, then paused as good sense reminded her that his lack of manners was no excuse for her to be the same way. Coming back to where he was pawing through what was in the box, she said, "I'll take your coat, if you wish."

"It's over there." He pointed to the chair without looking in her direction. "Ask her to check all the seams so the threads don't break again."

With a curse, she grasped the coat and dropped it over his head. Its sleeves struck the broken pottery, spraying dust everywhere. When he came to his feet, sneezing, she did not expect him to seize her by the shoulders.

She stared up at him. In the dusty sunshine, his hair glowed with the same fire as in his narrowed eyes as he spat, "Be careful! These pieces must be older than this house."

"I didn't mean to do them any damage."

"Only me?"

Her lips were suddenly as dry as the dust settling around them. "You were acting disagreeably high in the instep."

"You are right." His hands softened on her, becoming a caress. His voice became hushed as she was caught by his potent gaze. "I get that way when I find something new I want to investigate and learn everything about."

She fought not to quiver as his fingers glided down her arms to cup her elbows. When they drew her even closer, she whispered, "Really?"

"Yes," he murmured as his hand brushed her hair back from her cheek. "I become so intent on satisfying my curiosity that nothing else matters. I want to study every inch and impress what I learn into my memory so I may savor those textures and beauty whenever I wish to bring the sensations from the recesses of my memory to enjoy anew. With such intimacy come the phrases that will give my poetry life and create even more curiosity that must be satisfied once more."

"I understand."

"You do, don't you?" His husky voice freed the quivers she had struggled so unsuccessfully to hide. "It is an endless cycle, seeking to learn more and to find gratification in the learning. It is an exquisite pleasure. I am so glad you understand."

"Yes, yes." She stepped back and was torn between regret and relief when he released her.

She watched as he bent over the box again, pulling out a potsherd and examining it. She backed one step, then another toward the door and hoped that he would not guess she had been lying.

She had not understood what he meant. She had thought

he was speaking of the broken pottery, but was he? Was she? She had no idea any longer, and that alarmed her as nothing else had.

"I think that makes excellent sense, Mrs. Ditwiller." Valeria handed the list back to the housekeeper.

"This household has been lax about their duties for far too long." Mrs. Ditwiller smiled and slipped the page into a pocket.

"I suspected much the same." She shuddered. "The bats were bad enough, but, at least, they are confined to unused rooms. However, I found a spider in my room today that, I vow, had legs as long as my finger."

The housekeeper nodded. "I shall send a lad to sweep out the corners again, my lady."

Coming to her feet, she smiled. "Thank you." She rubbed her hands together as she went to look at the stack of books on the shelves. In spite of Mrs. Ditwiller's efforts, the library still was the only room on this floor that was comfortable. The rest either needed cleaning or were so filled with the late earl's collections that they were still a jumble.

Lorenzo had been insistent that each item must be checked before it was moved. He had invited both her and David to join him in the task, but both of them had declined. David, she guessed, considered it a way for him and Lorenzo to get to know each other better, something he had resisted vehemently. Her own reasons were not so different, because she had been careful to avoid being alone again with Lorenzo. The man irritated her beyond reason, but there was something about him that drew her toward him with the madness of a moth flirting with a flame.

"My lady?"

"Yes?" She faced Mrs. Ditwiller.

The housekeeper wore a strained expression. "It may not be my place to speak so, my lady, but . . ."

"Say what you feel you must."

"I'm . . ." She hesitated, dampened her lips nervously, then said in a burst, "I'm sorry you are so unhappy here."

Valeria blinked at the housekeeper's forthright words. In the past few days, she had come to respect Mrs. Ditwiller's huge task of trying to bring the house back to a level of respectable cleanliness and to oversee a staff that resented having a new housekeeper. Not that Mrs. Ditwiller had whispered a single word of complaint, but Valeria had sensed the tension in every word the housekeeper spoke, as well as the ones Mrs. Ditwiller carefully did not say. Yet, not once had Valeria considered that Mrs. Ditwiller might be as aware of Valeria's growing distress as each day unfolded too much like the one before.

When she did not answer, Mrs. Ditwiller continued, "I've never been to London, my lady, but I've heard that it is right wondrous during the Season and endlessly busy. You must miss it dearly."

"I do."

"Words you'll be repeating again soon," Miss Urquhart announced as she came into the library. Setting a book back on one of the shelves, she frowned. "You might want to keep that in mind, young lady."

Valeria shared a puzzled glance with Mrs. Ditwiller, who quickly and quietly took her leave. One thing that she had not grown accustomed to in the past week was Miss Urquhart's baffling comments that were interjected into the middle of too many otherwise sane conversations.

"Pardon me?" she asked as she had twice before already today when the old woman spoke her mind.

Miss Urquhart shook her head. "How can you have had the benefit of that fine education that Francis arranged for you and a London Season and a marriage to a good and decent man and still be so unbelievably naïve?"

"About what?"

"For what else do you need the words *I do?* Marriage, young lady!"

Valeria bit her lower lip to keep from smiling before saying, "You are mistaken, Miss Urquhart. I have no intention of remarrying any time soon."

"I realize that." She hit her cane against the floor and frowned. "But the boy has plans for you."

"David?" This was amazing. She had not thought he had his mind on anything but mischief aimed at irritating Lorenzo. Every effort she had made to persuade him to try to treat Lorenzo with respect had come to naught and to naughtiness. David found a way to circumvent every promise he made.

Miss Urquhart's frown deepened, adding even more lines to her face. "Do not be want-witted, young lady. I don't mean young David. I mean *the boy.*"

"Lorenzo?"

"Who else?"

Valeria could have given her a dozen replies, but knew the futility of arguing with the old woman. Quietly as she adjusted two books that, after Miss Urquhart set her book back in place, were ready to fall off a shelf, she said, "I think Lorenzo is wise to consider his obligations here as the earl and the need to marry and produce an heir."

"Not his marriage. Yours."

"Mine?" Her voice squeaked on the single word.

Miss Urquhart grinned, obviously pleased at having garnered all of Valeria's attention now. She went to the closest window and tapped the top of her cane against the time-stained mullions. "There he goes again."

"Yes, Lorenzo rides out to enjoy the view on the moors every day at this hour," Valeria said as she looked past the old woman to see Lorenzo on the road leading to the outer wall of the house. He rode with the ease and grace of a man who was comfortable in the saddle and with his own solitary thoughts.

"Is that why you think he goes for a daily ride across the hills?"

"Yes, of course." *I would not have said so otherwise.* She could not speak those harsh words. The old woman might be a bit touched, so it would be better to let her enjoy her delusions of . . . Valeria had no idea what delusions Miss Urquhart might be delighting in today.

"Then you are utterly jobbernowl." Miss Urquhart whirled in a swish of satin from her unfashionably full skirt. Poking Valeria with the cane, she said, "I thought you had realized by this time that he rides out in pursuit of a husband for you."

"A husband for me?" A laugh burst from her. "You are—" She bit back the words she should not speak.

Miss Urquhart was not so reticent. "I am what? Mad? Mayhap, but I know what I know, and I hear what I hear. Chap in the stables was telling me that the boy was asking about other country houses of the gentry that are within a day's ride. Other houses with young men who might be seeking a wife."

She stared at the old woman, then turned away. She clasped her hands in front of her and swallowed the mixture of anger and disbelief clogging her throat. It all made sense, for, once she had remarried, Lorenzo would not be bothered by her company or by David's. It seemed like an excellent solution—for him—even though she did not want to accept that Lorenzo would do such a thing without consulting with her first.

She had not thought of remarrying. All she had thought of was sanctuary, far from her brother's creditors and the shame that had spread from Paul to her. Worrying about a home for David and her nephew's future had kept her from thinking of her own. Only now did she realize that each of those problems would be resolved if she made a wise second marriage.

"I had no idea," she whispered.

"You do now." Miss Urquhart walked toward the door, but paused to add, "I suppose I should check how the lads are doing on clearing out the last of the bats. Weddings at Moorsea Manor always take place in the old hall, I understand."

"There is no need to hurry."

"You may think so, but I suspect the boy thinks differently.

He has said more than once he wants tranquillity around here so he can concentrate on his studies and his writing." Miss Urquhart's smile grew calculating. "He can solve part of his problem with a husband for you, but I wonder how he'll deal with me?" She glanced at the ceiling. "I do hope he doesn't intend to lock me away in some attic like in one of those novels Francis had an odd predilection for." Coming back to the bookshelves, she took down a pair of books and shoved them into Valeria's hands. "I trust you will call here at Moorsea Manor once in a while after your marriage to check upon me to see that I am not a reluctant prisoner in a tower."

Valeria nodded, not sure what to say. As Miss Urquhart walked out of the library, still chattering about how she would fight anyone who tried to imprison her on the upper floors, Valeria glanced down at the books the old woman had given her. Their titles were the same, for they were two volumes of the same tale, and the titles made Miss Urquhart's message clear.

The Idiot Heiress

She pushed the books back onto the shelf. If Lorenzo thought he was going to try to trip her the double by arranging a marriage for her without her knowledge, he would learn his mistake without delay. David was not the only one who could make his life uncomfortable.

Slowly she sat as she shook her head. Doing that would only guarantee that he would not be waylaid from his determination to get her married and out of his house. She must act in just the opposite way, not disturbing him and convincing him that she was necessary at Moorsea Manor until such time as she decided to leave.

She shuddered. That would mean giving up all plans to brighten this house with guests and entertainments. If she did that, she feared she would grow as quoz as Nina Urquhart, lost in the past with little idea of what was going on in the present beyond the walls of this house.

There must be a compromise that would save her sanity even as it kept her from an unwanted marriage, but what?

How could she persuade Lorenzo that letting her stay here at Moorsea Manor was a better idea than arranging a marriage for her? He must think he was acting out of kindness for her and David, as well as in his own best interests. She could not imagine that he would not force her to marry . . . or would he? He had never made it a secret that he had no place in his life for anyone or anything else but his studies, so this might seem, to him, a very convenient arrangement.

For him, it would be.

For her, it could be a disaster. She must find answers to the questions tormenting her before she found herself standing in front of a parson with a man she did not even know now.

Seven

Lorenzo woke to a scream. Sitting up in his bed, he looked around, bewildered. How had the windows in Wolfe Abbey been moved and changed shape while he was sleeping? The big window should be on his left as lief his right, and the hearth should be . . .

Another scream rang through the room. It whisked the remnants of sleep from his head. A woman's scream! Egad, he hoped David had not found another colony of bats and set it to prey on someone else tonight. No, that wouldn't be possible at this hour. The bats would be hunting in the darkness.

Or had the boy set some other prank in motion? During the past week, Lorenzo had found sour milk in his tea, pepper on his facecloth, and a trio of frightened frogs hidden beneath the blanket on his bed. David was, he knew, the creator of each prank, although Lorenzo had yet to catch him in the act of sneaking into his room.

So what was he up to now?

Grabbing his cream satin robe, Lorenzo pulled it around his shoulders as he rushed out into the corridor and right into something soft and silky and wondrously fragrant. Something a man could enjoy being next to for days on end and during nights without number.

"Look out, Lorenzo!" Valeria's prosaic words were the antithesis of his momentary lapse into fantasy.

And that was all for the good. What was he doing thinking about her like this when he had spent the past two days riding until his bones were sore in an effort to meet what eligible bachelors might be living near Moorsea Manor and arrange for them to call on Valeria? Their number was small, and most of them were either in London or calling on friends elsewhere in England. Lorenzo had ignored the questioning glances in his direction that suggested he was an odd volume for preferring the quiet of the moors to other places.

"Pardon me," he said when he recalled that Valeria was waiting for an answer, "but I thought to see who might be screeching at this hour."

"As I did."

"Is David—?"

"He's asleep in his room." Her voice was cool, as it had been since his return to Moorsea Manor this afternoon. He had been curious about that, but she had given him no time to ask a question then, and this was not the time now.

"Are you sure of that?"

Her frown was visible even in the dim light. "He was the first thing I checked, Lorenzo."

The scream sounded again. Not pausing to see if Valeria followed, Lorenzo sprinted along the hall toward the tall window at the far end. In the light of the half moon, he could see a form clinging to the drapes and staring out at the night.

He seized the young woman by the shoulders and spun her about. "What is wrong? Have you seen bats flying in at this window?"

"Bats, my lord?" She cowered as she looked toward the ceiling. "Here?"

"You tell me."

"Lorenzo," scolded Valeria, drawing even with them, "don't chide the girl when she obviously is distressed almost beyond words."

"I wish only to discover what has set her screaming."

The maid gasped, " 'Twas a ghost, my lord."

"A ghost?" He shook his head. "Impossible."

"I saw it with my own two good eyes."

"Don't you know that ghosts are only the offspring of a fertile imagination and reading the wrong sort of novels?"

"I don't read much, my lord."

"But you have an imagination, I trust."

She stared at him as if she feared for the state of his sanity. "I saw a ghost, my lord. 'Tis not my imagination that brought it forth. 'Tis the moonlight and shadows that have given birth to this ghost, my lord." She raised a quaking finger toward the window. "Look for yourself and see."

Before Lorenzo could remonstrate, Valeria drew aside the drapes and peered out. "There's nothing there."

"But there was, my lady." The girl twisted her apron in her hands. "I swear 'tis so. I would not lie."

Valeria smiled gently. "I'm sure you thought you saw—"

"I know what I saw!" Her voice rose on every word. "I was born and raised in this house, and I've never seen its like. Taller than a man and with limbs that glowed with a demon's light."

Putting her arm around the quivering girl, Valeria said, "You are shaking too hard. Why don't we sit and calm ourselves? I trust we can use your rooms, Lorenzo."

"My rooms?"

"Yes, I don't want to disturb David. He's become so exhausted lately after his long days of his tramping about the moors with young Gil, so he needs his sleep."

"As we all do."

"And which we all shall get once this matter—and its ghost—are put to rest." She steered the maid along the hall.

When she opened the door to his rooms, Lorenzo sighed. Had any man ever gotten Valeria Fanning to heed his words and halt her headstrong ways? If so, he wished to meet that man straightaway and learn how he had persuaded Valeria to think sensibly.

His bare feet were cold as he went back into his rooms. When he saw Valeria had seated the maid at his writing table and was lighting the lamp there, he rushed forward to collect his papers before they were read.

"I'm sorry to intrude, my lord," the maid whispered.

"It isn't your fault." He dropped the pages onto the messed bed and drew up the covers, not wanting anyone to see the phrases he had been working on tonight. Had he been out of his mind to put pen to words like *deep sea-purple gaze and hair the color of a sunrise of expectation?* He reached to pull the pages back out and toss them on the hearth, then realized that could call more attention to them.

Valeria poured some of his best brandy into a glass and handed it to the maid. Wide-eyed, the girl looked from her to Lorenzo.

"Drink up," he said quietly. "It will fortify you and help you sleep."

"At the same time?" the maid asked.

When Valeria smiled, Lorenzo sighed. Mayhap his cousin Corey had been right when he warned Lorenzo that he needed more experience with women in order to begin to comprehend their ways. Reading about the fairer sex in a book would not serve him in good stead when he was in their company, Corey had told him on so many occasions. Tonight, Lorenzo wished he had heeded his cousin. He did not begin to understand why Valeria scowled at him one minute and wore a lighthearted expression the next.

"Tell us about what you saw," he said.

" 'Twas a ghost, and he—it—I'm not sure if it was a man or a woman or what."

"It was nothing but moonlight, I assure you. There's no such thing as a ghost."

"I know what I saw."

Lorenzo was startled by the maid's back-answer. The lass must have been deeply frightened to speak to him with such vehemence. "I know what you *think* you saw. Drink up the brandy and take yourself off to your bed. You should find that morning light will clear your eyes and your mind."

"But, my lord—"

"Drink up."

She nodded and sipped the brandy. As soon as she was finished, he took the glass while Valeria helped the lass to her feet.

"I can't!" the maid gasped when Valeria bid her to hurry

to her bed. "If I see that thing again—" She hid her face in her hands, then hiccuped.

Lorenzo went to the door and threw it open. He was amazed to see Gil coming toward him. The footman should be asleep at this hour. Was the whole house taking after the bats in the old hall and wandering the night?

"My lord!" he cried. "I didn't—that is—"

Lorenzo waved him to silence. "I'm glad to see you, Gil. I need you to help this young lady back to her room in the attics." He stepped aside as Valeria led the frightened maid to the door.

Gil grinned as he looked at the maid, who gave him a shy smile in return. "Glad to do that, my lord." He held out his hand to the maid.

She took it as her smile widened. "Thank you, my lord, my lady." She fluttered her eyelashes at Gil as he led her along the hall. "And thank you, Gil."

Lorenzo stifled a groan as Valeria tugged on his sleeve and whispered, "I do believe those two should have someone watching over them."

"Valeria—"

As always, she paid him no mind. She crossed the outer chamber and knocked on a door.

Kirby groggily came to the door and mumbled, "Yes, my lord." His eyes bulged in his face. "My lady!" Looking past her to Lorenzo, he gulped.

Lorenzo fought a yawn and said, "Lady Fanning is concerned that young Gil might need a *duenna*."

"My lord?"

"Just go and keep an eye on him so we might all get some rest tonight."

"Yes, my lord." He pulled on a robe and lurched out of the room.

"Thank you, Lorenzo," Valeria said with a smile.

How could she look so lovely at this hour when he was sure he resembled something dragged back and forth through a knot-hole? Her luxurious hair was pinned primly up for sleep, and her eyes were soft and hooded with not enough sleep. The lace on her wrapper flowed around her face like the petals of a flower.

"I did nothing." His exasperation at her turned inward, for he should not be admiring her at the same time he was vexed with her.

"Thank you anyway." She wrapped her arms around herself as she sat on the chair by the desk. "I wonder what she really saw."

"Mayhap we can get some sense out of her when she is not so frightened."

"I doubt that. She honestly believes that what she saw was a ghost."

"And she is wrong."

"Mayhap, but she saw something. It should be looked into before the rest of the house is scared by tales of a haunting."

"There's no such thing as a ghost," he repeated for what seemed like the twentieth time.

Hearing a laugh behind him, he turned to see Earl standing by the hearth. The old man held a candle high, its light stronger than the weak glow of the lamp on Lorenzo's desk.

"I would not be so certain of that when you're standing in a house this old," Earl said. Without waiting for an invitation, he sat on the raised hearth. "There have always been sounds and sights here that folks couldn't explain."

"But ghosts?" Lorenzo shook his head with a grimace. "Fear will make folks believe they have seen things they can't explain."

"True, true." He chuckled again as he balanced the candle on the knee of his worn breeches.

"Valeria, this is Earl," he said when the old man looked past him and smiled.

"I know Earl. He has been kind enough to arrange for my hearth always to be well-lit. Good evening." She gave him a warm smile before scowling at Lorenzo again. "However, Lorenzo, you are ignoring my point completely."

Egad, she intended to continue this bangle in front of the old man. "I will have someone go out and see what might be on the lawn." When she began to smile, he added, "In the morning."

"It might be gone by then."

"Any self-respecting ghost would be," Earl said with a chuckle. "Ghosts don't like sunshine."

Valeria smiled again. "You know a lot about this house, Earl. Have there been other reports of ghosts?"

"Of course. Headless monks, lovers who cast themselves from the walls, all of the customary sorts. Mayhap the lass saw one of them."

"One of them?" Lorenzo shook his head. This discussion was leading nowhere. "Please do not burden us with more than a single ghost at a time."

"So you believe it might have been a ghost?" Earl asked, surprising him.

"Of course not. In spite of all you have said, I believe in what's right before my eyes, and that is not a ghost."

Earl came to his feet and laughed. "I bid you good night, my lord. I hope your dreams are less mundane than your words."

Rising, Valeria said, "I should return to my bed as well." She went to the door and opened it. "Good night, Lorenzo."

He put his hand on the open door. "I hope the rest of it is a quiet one."

"I'm sure it will be. One ghost a night is sufficient."

"More than sufficient."

A dimple he had never noticed in her left cheek teased his fingers to touch it, but he clenched his hand at his side and the other around the door. "Good night, Valeria." He smiled. "That is, if you don't need someone to walk you to your rooms in case you encounter a ghost."

"No, I don't think that would be such a good idea."

"The ghost?"

She raised her hand toward his face, then lowered it quickly to her side. "No, not the ghost." She whirled and, in a cloud of white, vanished into her rooms.

Lorenzo closed the door and looked across the rooms to where Earl had added wood to the fire. He sat in the closest chair as he stared into the flames. For once, he had understood Valeria completely. Gil and the lass had needed a watchdog to keep them, but Valeria suspected the same could be said for her and Lorenzo, so she wisely had demurred when he offered to escort her.

Dash it! He needed to step up the search to find her a husband before one of them did something that could make this complicated situation even more complicated.

Like surrendering to his overwhelming urge to kiss her.

Valeria sighed as she closed the magazine and set it on the table beside her in the sitting room that was now free of spiders. How much she had taken her years in London for granted! She had delighted in the chance to visit her favorite *modiste,* to chat with her friends during an at home, to enjoy an occasional evening at Almacks's, and especially being a hostess for parties that drew the *élite de l'élite* and luminaries like politicians and poets. It had been such a short time ago that she had introduced the French poet Marquis de la Cour to the Polite World. Now she was on the far side of England, lost in this desolate place where nothing ever happened—no gossip, no fashion, no anything.

She went to look out the window, then turned away. If Lorenzo went for his ride, as he did every day at this hour, and chanced to see her peering out at him, he would think her even more of a problem. She had tried to remain quiet so he could work uninterrupted, and she was thankful that Gil was keeping David amused by taking him through every field and bog on the moors. The two were becoming good friends, because almost every sentence David spoke began with "Gil did" or "Gil said."

At a knock, Valeria turned. "Come in." The door opened, and she gasped, "Lorenzo!"

He held the brim of his tall hat in his hands. The well-tailored lines of his riding coat emphasized his lean height.

His pantaloons looped beneath boots which wore a recent polish.

"I thought you'd left," she said before she could halt the words.

"Excuse me?"

She ran her hand along the back of a chair and struggled to smile. "I know you ride each day. Please don't think that I'm keeping tabs on you."

"No need." He smiled and tapped his hat onto his head. "I know I am a creature of habit. However, today I am delayed because I was receiving Mr. Pettit from Bristol."

"We had a caller, and you did not tell me?" She looked away as heat soared up her face. "Forgive me, Lorenzo. This is your house, and your callers are none of my business."

He laughed, but gently. "If I had thought you might be intrigued with the discussion I was having with Mr. Pettit, I would have sent for you to join us. I did not think you would enjoy our mutual interest in my uncle's odd collections."

"Mr. Pettit came from Bath to see the jumble in this house?"

"Apparently he and my uncle were in correspondence about some items that Mr. Pettit has long been intrigued with the idea of purchasing from him. I told him I would give the matter some thought, although I am loath to allow anything to leave this house yet." He smiled. "But that is not why I came to your rooms. I thought you might want to join me today. Would you like to join me for a ride across the moor?"

"Join you?" She stared at him. "You want me to go for a ride with you?"

"If you prefer not to . . ."

"No, no!"

When that teasing smile curved along his lips, she wondered why she was acting like a witless child. Mayhap because she never could guess how *he* would act. One moment, he was making it clear that she was a burden he could not wait to rid himself of. The next, he was the most gracious, genial host she could ever imagine. And on the rare occasions when he touched her . . . No, she did not want to think of that, of how all thoughts of the contemptible turns her life had taken, all thoughts of how she longed to be back amid the whirl in London, even all thoughts of her anger at her brother who had betrayed her and David—everything vanished beneath the craving for him to touch her again.

So why was she agreeing to go with him *alone* as soon as she could change into her dark green riding habit? She did not want to think of that either.

Lorenzo drew back on the reins and looked out across the rolling hills. To the north, waves curved around a headland and crawled up onto the shore, leaving white foam. That foam seemed to be splashed upon the hills as sheep dotted the fields. Taking a deep breath, he could almost believe he was back at Wolfe Abbey, for that house, too, overlooked the sea. Now he understood why his mother had loved her husband's family's home and had not missed her own.

Or had she? He had no idea, because this part of her life had been denied to him. Curiosity taunted him anew. What had driven his mother and her brother so far apart that they had not been able to reconcile years later?

"My uncle never spoke to you of his sister?" he asked.

Valeria glanced at him, and he could see she was startled by the sudden question. With a sympathetic smile, she shook her head. "The few times I saw him, I was very young. As I recall, he spoke to me of things that one would speak of to a child. Not knowing what drove him and your mother apart bothers you, doesn't it?"

"The questions prey on my mind. I knew my mother well, and she was a good, kindhearted woman. Until now, I would have sworn that she would be able to forgive anyone for any crime against her. Yet she could not find it in her heart to forgive her only brother."

"Mayhap she tried, but he would not allow that."

"Do you know of some quirk of his that would have prevented a reconciliation?"

Again she shook her head and put up her hand to keep her hat from being carried away by the breeze that was growing more powerful as they followed the curve of the stone wall up the hill and away from the trees clinging to the road. She steered her horse around a prickly bush. "Your uncle offered only the greatest benevolence to me. If not for him, I would never have married Albert."

"He arranged your first meeting?"

"He arranged our marriage." She smiled sadly. "Albert had lost his first wife several years before, and he did not enjoy the life of a widower. When he let that fact be known to his tie-mates, your uncle suggested a match between him and me."

"And you agreed to this?"

"Why are you so astonished? Many marriages are arranged."

"True, but you are not like other women."

Her eyes narrowed. "Please explain what you mean by that comment."

Lorenzo would have been glad to explain his words, if he had an explanation. Or, more honestly, if he had an explanation he could speak. He had been acquainted with many of the ladies who lived near Wolfe Abbey because his cousin and his wife had insisted that Lorenzo steal some time from his writing to attend various functions about the shire. He had had many conversations with them, albeit often stilted ones. He had joined in outings on the beach or near a stream, which he always had considered a worthy use of time because it allowed him to collect ideas for his poetry. He even had danced on occasion, although no woman had been interested in standing up with him again after her toes endured a pummeling by his awkward steps.

None of those women had been like Valeria. He could talk with her, even though much of what she had to say infuriated him. Today he was enjoying this ride, in spite of the fact not a single phrase had found its way out of his mind to be jotted down on the paper stored in the purse hooked to his saddle, so he might use it later in a poem. And, as he looked at her sitting so gracefully on her horse, he could imagine her helping even a heavy-footed chap like him move about the dance floor smoothly.

But how could he say any of that to her? She would think him insane, and he could not fault her. Instead he mumbled something that must have appeased her because she turned again to look down at the pearl gray sea.

"Mayhap," she said so softly her words were almost swept away by the wind, "your mother and your uncle simply could not own to a mutual mistake. Pride leaves people with nothing else, but they will cling to it at the price of everything else, even their happiness."

"Were you happy?"

She faced him. "In my marriage? Is that what you mean?"

"If it is not too personal."

"Too personal?" Her laugh lilted across the hills as they continued along the curve of the moor and through a meadow where sheep grazed. "Lorenzo, you really should come to London at least once for the Season. Then you will learn that nothing is too personal. Yes, many were astonished when I chose to marry Albert, not one of the other suitors who were vying for my hand, but he was a good man and cared deeply for me. We were very happy."

"Until he died?"

She took a deep breath and released it slowly, and he tried to keep his gaze on her face instead of the enticing motion. "We had three wonderful years together. So many things we had in common. A love of the theater, delight in the company of good friends, the invigorating quality of a fine wine. He introduced me to poetry and contemporary artists and the waltz. I taught him it was all right to be young at heart."

"I'm glad."

"So am I." A smile played across her lips, and he guessed she was savoring memories that would always bring her pleasure. When she reached over and grasped his hand, he stared at her, startled. "Thank you."

"For what?"

"For reminding me how much I have to be thankful for."
She squeezed his hand. "I believe it is possible you and I,
despite our vast differences, might come to consider each
other a friend."

"Anything is possible."

"Exactly." With a laugh, she slapped her horse and rode
neck-or-nothing up the hill.

Lorenzo followed, eager to see where this path they were
taking might lead. Of one thing he was certain. Wherever it
was, it would be more interesting because Valeria was with
him. Nothing could alter his determination to make her a
match with all possible speed, but he might as well enjoy
her company today.

While he could.

Eight

Valeria was not surprised when Lorenzo slowed his horse by another section of old wall along the moor. In the hour they had been riding, he had paused and poked at stones with his boot a half dozen times.

He must have sensed her smile because he said rather sheepishly, "I know this is not the ride you thought we'd take. It's simply that I find ancient construction so interesting."

"Do you believe these walls are as old as the Roman expansion? I understand the Roman legionnaires reached this part of England."

"You know about the Roman Empire?" He half-turned in the saddle.

She smiled at him. Good! She had startled him for once. Mayhap, after this, he would not take such delight in befuddling her on every opportunity.

"Simply because I have enjoyed a life in Town doesn't mean I am without any education. Your uncle insisted that I study many subjects that other girls had no opportunity to pursue."

"You never speak of books."

"I have tried." She regarded him steadily, and, for once, he met her gaze without looking away. "I have wished to speak of poetry with you, but any time I have introduced the subject, you have treated my comments with disdain."

"I never—"

"Last night, I was telling Miss Urquhart about meeting the Marquis de la Cour in London."

"You spoke of introducing that French poet of love sonnets to the *ton,* not of poetry."

Letting her smile become sly, she said, "I would have if you had not cut me off in mid-word, complaining that I never speak of anything of interest." She tapped her chin with her gloved finger. "Shall we talk of the unchangeable pattern of sonnets, or would you prefer a dissertation on the rhythms that enhance words? Shakespeare might have preferred iambic pentameter for his plays, but I find it repetitious, don't you?"

He stared at her as if he had never seen her before. And mayhap he had not, but she was determined he would never treat her so again.

"I am amazed," he said.

"You shouldn't be. Among those entertainments that I loved to host and you seem to find the very idea of deplorable, I often held poetry readings and evenings where we read from our favorite passages of both fiction and nonfiction."

"I have apparently underestimated you."

"You aren't the first, and neither are you the first to discover that your initial assumptions were a mistake." She looked back at Moorsea Manor that was a dark blot on the green of the moors. "As I said, your uncle arranged for me to have an excellent education, for he held education dear as you should have guessed after seeing his collection of books and antiquities."

Lorenzo shifted uneasily. "I assumed—that is—"

"You assumed because I'm a female that I would have been taught nothing more than to oversee a household, play hostess at a *soirée,* and to be an ornament to be obtained by some man with marital intentions during a Season in London."

"That is the usual state of a young girl's schoolroom."

"True, but I had thought you would have guessed that

your late uncle holds with the canons of propriety no more than you do."

"I know nothing of him."

"Then you should sit with Miss Urquhart this very afternoon. She loves to bibble-babble about your uncle."

His nose wrinkled. "Mayhap I am not that curious."

Valeria laughed. As much as she irritated Lorenzo with her desire for a gathering at Moorsea Manor, as much as David vexed him with pranks, Nina Urquhart utterly confounded him. He seemed unsure how to deal with his uncle's mistress who had an opinion, valid or not, on every subject and treated him like the boy she called him. Of course, he was not the only one Miss Urquhart baffled.

"What is wrong?" Lorenzo asked, warning that her thoughts had stolen her smile.

"I'm not sure. Miss Urquhart has been the epitome of kindness to me, but she never fails to mention how different I must be from the rest of my family."

"You need only ask. I'm sure she would be glad to enlighten you." He grimaced again. "She seems unable to wait for every opportunity to enlighten me on every facet, no matter how insignificant, of Moorsea Manor. If you were to ask, she would be as forthcoming."

"But she isn't. Odd, isn't it?"

"Why are you acting astonished? Everything about her is quite jiggumbob."

"I—"

Lorenzo peered past the wall and smiled. "Look, there is another rider!"

When he waved, the man turned his mount from amid the trees and rode *ventre-à-terre* toward them. His horse cleared the chest-high wall as if it were nothing more than a bump in the road. Pulling in beside them, he tipped his hat.

Valeria stared. She could not keep from staring. Others had used the word Adonis to describe a handsome man, but, as she stared at him, wide-eyed, she could think of no better term. From his golden hair that fell in glorious abandon across his forehead and into his eyes that were the same rich brown as his horse's windblown mane, her gaze swept over the strong line of his jaw that could not be hidden beneath the stylish cut of his collar. His brawny hands matched the muscular strength of his arms as he held his horse still.

"You must be Lady Valeria Fanning. I had heard of a beautiful woman who was hiding away in Moorsea Manor, and I own to being pleased that, for once, one of the rumors about Moorsea Manor is true," he said in a voice that was a resonant bass. Tipping his hat again, he added, "I am Sir Tilden Oates. This is my sister, Mary."

Valeria's answer vanished unspoken when the dashing man turned and smiled at a woman on a horse beside him. She had not noticed the woman until he mentioned her. Mary Oates was a lovely woman, but her beauty was dimmed by her brother's exceptional looks. Her hair was a pleasant blond, unlike his that challenged the sunlight within each strand. Her features were well-made instead of striking, and even the color of her habit was eclipsed by his.

"Good day, Miss Oates." Lorenzo spoke before she could find any words. "Allow me to present myself and Lady Fanning properly. I am Lorenzo Wolfe, Lord Moorsea, and this is Lady Valeria Fanning."

"So you are Moorsea." Sir Tilden Oates eyed him up and down. "I see nothing of your uncle in you."

"Did you know his uncle and his household well?" Valeria asked. Mayhap here, at last, would be the answers Lorenzo sought as well as the one that clarified why Nina Urquhart seemed to have such disdain for Valeria's family, yet treated her with the kindness of an elderly auntie.

"No." Sir Tilden seemed reluctant to make that admission. "But there is a picture of the old man down in the tavern in Winlock-on-Sea."

"A picture of my uncle in a tavern?" Lorenzo asked.

"Why not? It was his." Sir Tilden chuckled, once again wearing a smile that would threaten the heart of any maiden. "Or, to be more honest, it's yours. Didn't you realize your holdings reached into the village down on the shore?"

"I have barely had a chance to explore the manor house

itself. Valeria and I were riding about to see the lands connected to the estate today, but it appears I have much more exploration ahead of me."

"I hope you won't spend all your time in such serious pursuits." Sir Tilden's words may have been for Lorenzo, but he smiled at Valeria. "My mother has been hoping that you and my sister might exchange calls and become good friends. Isn't that right, Mary?"

Mary nodded.

"You should feel free to call on any Tuesday," Sir Tilden continued. "Mary and our mother always keep an at home on that day. Our mother believes that the ways of Town are the only method of keeping us from surrendering to the uncivilized ways of our untamed ancestors out here on the moors."

Valeria smiled. At last! Some vestige of the life she had left behind in London. She was tempted to throw her arms around Sir Tilden and tell him how much she appreciated his invitation. When he saw how he was candidly admiring her, she doubted if he would object to such untoward behavior. The very thought stiffened her in the saddle. How could she be having such hoydenish thoughts when they were speaking of the ways of the *ton?*

"I am sure Valeria would be delighted to give you and your mother a look-in, Miss Oates," Lorenzo said, again saving her from her own want for sense.

"Yes, yes," she hurried to say. "If I may, I would like to call Tuesday next."

"Of course you may," Miss Oates replied in a voice so hushed the wind almost swept it away. "And will you be calling, too, Lord Moorsea? You know we would be so delighted to have you and Lady Fanning join us at Oates's Hall."

Valeria flinched at the warmth in the young woman's voice. With only a few words, Miss Oates had suggested that she would be happy to set her cap on the new earl.

Lorenzo said, "We shall see if that is convenient. I

mean . . . We would be delighted to call when—as soon as we can."

"You cannot let your life be only duty, you know," Sir Tilden replied with a chuckle.

"I have many concerns . . . My uncle left things in a somewhat unfinished state."

"You mean Miss Urquhart?"

When Lorenzo squared his shoulders, Sir Tilden hastened to apologize. Valeria hid her smile when Lorenzo graciously brushed aside the matter as if the baronet had not over-stepped himself with the crude comment. For a man who insisted he wanted nothing to do with the ways of the Polite World, Lorenzo Wolfe had, when he chose, manners as fine as any gentleman she had met in Town. Better than many, she had to own.

Miss Oates smiled. "Forgive Tilden, my lord. He forgets himself here in grassville."

"I believe I already intimated that it is forgotten." Lorenzo's glance in Valeria's direction warned that he was as confused by Miss Oates's words as by any his late uncle's mistress had spoken.

"Thank you, my lord." Miss Oates put her hand on his arm. "You are very kind."

Valeria was not confused by Miss Oates. The young woman made her intentions very clear. If Lorenzo did not watch his step, he soon would find himself with a wife who had succeeded in advancing herself and her family with the single phrase, "I do."

The echo of Miss Urquhart's warning rang through Valeria's head. Lorenzo was not interested in a wife, but in finding someone else who was seeking one, so he might marry Valeria off with all due speed. It would serve him right if his plan ended up with him standing at the altar.

"You must forgive Mary, Moorsea," Sir Tilden said with a laugh. He edged his horse between his sister's and Lorenzo's. And between Lorenzo's and Valeria's, she noted with a hint of disquiet. Again, as he went on, his words might have been for Lorenzo, but he was looking directly at her, "You have to realize how seldom we have anyone to call upon here on the edge of Exmoor. Our delight at meeting you today goes beyond mere words."

Valeria backed her horse away from Sir Tilden's, but not before he caught her hand and raised it to his lips. The smile he gave her suggested that the matter of their future was already decided.

When she looked past him, she saw both Lorenzo and Mary Oates watching intently. Had this been a chance encounter? With the vast emptiness of the moor, they easily could have ridden past each other without ever taking note of one another. Was this the reason Lorenzo had dawdled along the wall, pretending an interest in Roman ruins that he could have satisfied quite readily amid the collection of broken debris that his uncle had boxed with such care at the manor house? If he had been waiting for Sir Tilden and his sister to arrive, that would explain why he seemed to have a sudden interest in what she had studied and her opinions on an intellectual subject.

She withdrew her hand with some difficulty from Sir Tilden's possessive grip. As she held the reins, making it clear that she would not allow him such an intimacy again, he turned to Lorenzo, his smile still triumphant, and began to speak of matters of the farms across the moor. She could not keep from noting while Miss Oates listened in rapt silence, how the two men spoke as if they had begun this conversation previously. Yet, Lorenzo had introduced both of them to Sir Tilden and his sister, suggesting they never had met.

This was too confusing, but she intended to get answers.

Valeria tried to pose the questions that would ease her curiosity as soon as Sir Tilden and Miss Oates were out of earshot on their way back to their home closer to the sea. "You and Sir Tilden share common opinions about the tenant farms here, don't you?"

"Yes." Lorenzo held out his hand and glanced skyward. "Those clouds have grown too heavy. I believe it's beginning to rain."

"Was that a surprise?"

"Was what a surprise? I think that was thunder, don't you?"

"No."

Another peal, closer this time, contradicted her.

"We need to hurry back to the manor house." Lorenzo raised his hand to slap his horse just as the cloud released its burden.

Cold rain coursed down Valeria's collar before she could turn it up. Steering her horse at the best possible pace down the hillside, she gave it the command, as soon as they reached the narrow path, to go at top speed toward Moorsea Manor. The rain turned the road to mire, but the horse seemed as eager as she to get out of the storm. She did not look back or slow until she reached the stable.

Slipping from the saddle, she handed the reins to a stableboy who started to greet her, then looked past her and gasped, "My lord, what happened to you?"

Valeria spun to see Lorenzo dismounting. He was covered from forehead to foot with splattered mud that was woven with the rain washing over him. Shaking his hands, he shoved his reins in the stableboy's direction.

"Lady Fanning failed to realize how close behind her I was riding." He took a cloth that another boy rushed up with and nodded his thanks. Wiping his face, he motioned for a stableboy to get her a blanket. He draped it over her shoulders. "We might as well continue up to the house, Valeria."

A flash of lightning stilled her answer. One of the horses whinnied nervously, and the stableboys hurried to take them to their stalls and brush them down. When the thunder came slowly, Valeria let Lorenzo draw her hand within his arm and take her to the closest door.

"Lorenzo," she began as soon as they were inside the house and the storm was banished by the thick stone walls.

"Why don't you change and meet me in the library? We can speak there."

"I'm sorry about—"

He looked down at his ruined clothes. "Accidents happen. I am assuming this was an accident."

"Of course!" *At least as accidental as meeting Sir Tilden on the moors.* She could not say that. Not when, beneath the scratchy blanket, her clothes clung to her like an icy caress.

As if he could read her thoughts, and she prayed that he could not, his gaze swept over her. All of a moment, she was aware of how her wet clothes outlined her shamelessly. She wanted to raise her hands to cover her breasts, but she could not move as his gaze rose to her face again. When he brushed her wet hair back from her face, she closed her eyes delighting in the simple touch.

"Go and change and meet me for a glass of something warm to ease the cold," he murmured.

Cold? She was no longer cold. She had needed only his touch to ease the cold.

"I would," he continued, "appreciate your opinions of Sir Tilden and his sister."

The iciness returned doublefold as she put her foot on the first riser. "You really have taken it upon yourself to look for a husband for me, haven't you?"

"That's one of a guardian's responsibilities, you know."

That he did not demur added to her dismay. She did not want to marry Sir Tilden. Once she had agreed to marry a man she barely knew. Albert had been a good husband, but they had been strangers for too long at the beginning of their marriage. She did not want to spend months living in forced intimacy again while she tried to learn about the man whose name and life she shared.

"You aren't my guardian," she said as she clutched the banister.

He looked up her, which was peculiar, for she was accustomed to his eyes being above hers. "I believe you said I had a guardian's responsibility for you when you first presented yourself at my door."

"At your uncle's door."

" 'Tis one and the same."

She shook her head. "It is nothing the same."

"No?" He drew off his muddy coat and folded it over his arm. "I believe you are dependent on me for the roof over your head."

"Yes, but—"

"And the food you and the boy eat."

"Yes, but—"

"And that those responsibilities will be mine until you are married once more."

"Yes, but—"

"Therefore, I—"

"Yes, yes, yes," she said, interrupting him as he had her. "I know you have a guardian's responsibilities for me, but I am a grown woman. I will not be shunted off on the first man you meet."

"That was not my intention."

"No? Then why did you ask me to ride with you? Are you saying that it was a mere coincidence that we encountered Sir Tilden and his sister today?"

"Of course."

"Don't you find it odd that we should chance to meet an eligible bachelor the only time you have deigned to ask me to ride with you?"

"Yes."

"What?" His easy agreement astounded her.

"Yes, I believe it is odd, for I have been riding about for days without meeting anyone I would consider proper to call upon you. Today, when you are along, one pops nearly out of the hedgerow, but, I assure you, 'tis no more than coincidence. With luck, a happy coincidence for you."

"And for you."

"For me?"

She put her hands on her hips and frowned. "Yes, for you. Miss Oates seems to be an intelligent, albeit shy woman. She would make a good and proper wife for you."

He draped his coat over the banister and tried to shake mud from its sleeves. "I have no interest in a wife at the moment."

"You have an obligation to provide an heir." Valeria almost

laughed when color flew up his face, but there was nothing amusing about the whole of this. "Lorenzo, I do hope that you won't continue to blush as red as my hair when you next speak with Miss Oates. She might take it for your customary shade and wonder if you are hale."

"I did not—"

She leaned over the railing and tapped his cheek. "Turn about and look in the glass if you don't believe me, Lorenzo. You are the same shade you were when she dared to inquire if you would be calling soon."

"If *we* would be calling soon."

"She cares little if I call. She was thinking about charming you so that she might obtain the title of Lady Moorsea for herself."

"Nonsense."

"Is it? Then why are you flushing like a schoolgirl at her coming-out?"

She thought he would give her a sharp back-answer and tell her the matter was none of her bread-and-butter, which would be correct. He was playing the rôle of her guardian, not the other way about. But, again, she realized how different Lorenzo was from the men she had met in London, who would never give voice to any suggestion of being less than perfect.

"Mayhap you are correct, Valeria," he said with the quiet dignity that she had come to discover meant he was giving the matter serious thought. "My experience with ladies is somewhat less than my cousin, who, despite his time serving in the king's army, seemed to garner the attention of the fairer sex wherever he went."

"And you were in his shadow?" She arched her brows as she came back down the stairs. She could not rush off when Lorenzo was being so gut-wrenchingly honest with her. "Then you and Miss Oates have something in common. She is outshone by her brother as you were by your cousin. It gives you a starting point to chat about."

"I have no interest in wasting my time in the pursuit of

conversations that are meaningless." He reached for his coat. "Like this one."

"Because it unsettles you?"

"Yes."

There again was that honesty that was so rare in anyone else. When she looked both ways along the corridor and up the stairs, she saw nobody. She did not want anyone overhearing the course of this conversation because she knew how quickly it would be repeated through the servants' hall.

"Because you are shy around women?" she asked softly.

"A fault I cannot rid myself of, as you should have seen, so why are you making that a question?"

"Because you aren't shy around me." She smiled. "You speak your mind openly and berate me when you think my opinions are skimble-skamble."

"As I have said before, Valeria, you are not like other women."

"And you don't consider me a potential wife."

He swallowed roughly, then an ironic smile spread across his face. "Forgive me if I say this wrong, Valeria, but I would be out of my mind to marry you. Not only do you want a hectic life while I seek a quiet one, but you have the responsibility for that lad who seems even more determined than you to make sure I never have a moment of tranquillity in this house." As if on cue, something crashed upstairs, and David's laugh drifted down the staircase. "I trust you see what I mean and take no offense."

"I see what you mean."

When she did not add anything else, he asked, "And take no offense?"

"How can I when you are being honest with me for my own good as well as yours?" She was pleased that her words were as honest as his, because she had to own that he was correct. She and Albert had learned to have a happy marriage primarily because they shared a love of entertaining and being entertained by their mutual friends. The only thing she and Lorenzo had in common was his uncle, and it appeared, with every passing day, that they truly knew nothing of the late Lord Moorsea.

When he folded his coat over his arm and started to turn, she said, "But you know you must marry, Lorenzo. You have no nephew to leave this house to."

"That is true, but it is a matter I do not have to consider today."

"I think you are wrong."

"Valeria, I am soaked to the skin and want to change and enjoy a nice glass of brandy. Can't this conversation wait?"

"No."

He scowled at her. "You are the most unreasonable, irrational woman I have ever met."

"So I believe you have intimated before." She put her hand on his arm. "Lorenzo, we all must start somewhere, you know. As you are trying in your misguided way to help me by trying to leg-shackle me to the first eligible man we meet, the least I can do is return the favor."

"I think not."

"Why? What frightens you?"

"I have not—that is, I—"

She laughed. "A woman is not made of glass or of old clay like those pots you like to examine."

"I never suspected that you would shatter easily."

"I have tried to prove you right." She put her hand on his other arm. "This one goes around a woman's shoulders when you ask her to stand up with you as the orchestra plays a romantic waltz." She looked down and grabbed at the blanket to keep it from falling off her shoulders. "Of course, it may be difficult to imagine that now."

He shook his head and stepped back. "This feels all wrong."

"Of course it does. It only feels right when you are with a person you could fall in love with."

"That's exactly what Corey has long told me."

"And your cousin is correct, but you are going to have to find yourself a wife." She smiled. "Unless you want me to take over that task for you."

"No, it is one I can handle myself." He put his hands on her shoulders and brushed her cheek with his lips. "There."

"There what?" She looked up at him, hoping her smile hid the flush of warmth that surged through her with his unexpected kiss. "If you were to offer that kiss to a woman you are considering as a potential bride, it would make you the laughingstock of the *ton*."

"I would think so. That was a thank-you for proffering to help, but I would rather that you be my friend who leaves such matters in my hands." He pushed back his hair as more water dripped down his face. "I bid you *au revoir* while I change into something a little less damp. I suggest you do the same." The gentle smile returned as he grazed her cheek with another swift kiss. "And thank you, Valeria. You are, although I would not have believed it a fortnight ago, a good friend."

"Yes," she said rather faintly as he strode away, calling for his man Kirby to order a bath for him and one for Valeria. Her breath caught as she imagined relaxing in a steaming bath while his intriguing fingers swept soap through her hair and down her back and . . . She shivered as powerful heat surged through her. Was she mad? Half the time she did not even like Lorenzo Wolfe, who seemed to take pride in annoying her. And hadn't he just said that they were to be friends?

She gripped the newel post. Friends. She wondered if that were still possible when, at his most casual touch, heat ricocheted within her, settling in the most secret crevices of her heart.

She must be mad . . . or falling in love with him.

Nine

Valeria strode across the meadow and almost into a wall before she brought herself to a stop. She slapped her hand against the stones, scowling. The day had begun so well. The sun had been shining, David had been chattering about his plans to spend the day with Gil down by the beach, and even Lorenzo had put aside his newspaper.

Then Miss Urquhart had invited her to share some tea on the terrace near the overgrown water garden. Valeria told herself she should have known the old woman was looking for more than company when Miss Urquhart had poured half of the tea into another cup and reached for a small bottle at the far corner of the tray.

"Was the tea too strong?" Valeria had asked.

The old woman laughed. "My dear, you are so sweet, but the truth is the tea isn't strong enough." Tilting the bottle over her cup, she smiled. "A bit of brandy always adds just the right flavor to a cup of scan-mag." Without a pause, she added, "And I hear the poker-talk is going to be about you."

"Don't assume that rumors have any basis in truth."

"I don't." She smiled. "That's why I asked you to join me for a cup of tea. I wanted to hear from your lips the truth. Are you quite taken with Sir Tilden Oates?"

"I have met the man only once."

"Love at first sight happens. I know. It happened for me."

"With the late lord?"

Miss Urquhart added another dash of brandy to her cup.

"We are talking about the gossip about you, my dear, not me. I have heard—"

"Whatever it is, it is not true," she had argued. "I have met the baronet but once."

But once.

Valeria slowed her pace. She could not out-walk her vexation. By the heavens, she had spoken with the man on a single occasion and already the shire was ready to listen to the banns announced in the church in Winlock-on-Sea. She strode up the hill, following the contortions of the stone wall that was as tall as her shoulder. Behind it, hedgerows blocked any view. That was no problem, because she did not want to see anything—or especially anyone—now.

Her problems kept pace with her. The problem of Miss Urquhart was easily dismissed. The old woman simply loved to enjoy some gossip. Sir Tilden was no more bothersome, although she would have to make it obvious to him, as she had to the late earl's mistress, that she had no intention of considering marriage to him on such short acquaintance.

"Or at any time," she said to the rich pink flowers pointing tall and straight out of the brush.

How easily she could expel those concerns from her mind! What was not simple was banishing thoughts of Lorenzo. She found her thoughts in that direction so uncomfortable that she wanted to be done with them, but it had been to no avail. Could she be developing a *tendre* for this aggravating man? Impossible! She was simply grateful for his kindness in giving her and David a home. Nothing more.

Hearing a bark, Valeria looked down the hill. Then she realized the noise had come from her left where a cottage was hidden amid a clump of trees clinging to the windsculpted hillside. She walked faster. Another bark sounded, and she gathered up her skirt, raising it above her high-lows, and pushed her pace nearly to a run.

A yellow dog bounded out from the trees, cutting her off. She cringed as the dog rushed to her and leapt up. Turning her back on it, she was not quick enough. It jumped again, this time lapping her face. Her eyes widened. It did not wish to bite her, merely to show affection. At this moment, she could use some affection.

She reached down to the pat its head, but froze when she heard another deeper bark. A black dog came darting from the trees straight toward her. It did not lunge, because its girth was too great. When she took a step backward, it shoved its head under her hand.

With a nervous laugh, she realized both dogs were vying for a pat on the head. "Good afternoon," she said with a smile.

The yellow dog lapped her hand, and both looked up at her expectantly.

"I'm walking this way." She pointed along an almost invisible path leading up to the higher reaches of the moor. "You are welcome to join me."

She laughed when they took off up the path, then paused and looked back to see if she was following. They crashed through the bushes and splashed into a rivulet coursing along the hill as she continued along the path that was growing steeper with every step.

By the time she entered a copse near the crest of the hill, her breath was banging against her side. The back of her left leg was aching, and the back of her right was on fire as the path grew more vertical. She glanced back, but could see nothing through the trees. Just a wee bit farther, then she would turn around. Every step was a challenge which kept her from thinking of that blastedly irritating man and his plans to marry her off with lightning speed and of her own uncertainty about him.

"Why can't things ever be simple?" she asked, and the black dog bounced back, dripping and covered with pieces of leaves, to stare up at her with an offer to pet him again. She did and smiled. "I envy your witless enjoyment of this day."

With a bark, the dog ran to catch up with the yellow one that was scampering up a bank that was even steeper than the path.

Valeria shook her head, laughing tersely, because she had

no breath for more. Picking up a long branch, she broke off the twigs attached to its sides. She used it as a walking staff to help propel her up the hill.

A flash caught her eyes as she walked among the trees. Looking to her left, she saw a pool of water gathered on a shelf of earth. It was surrounded by trees and more than fifty feet away. She wondered if she could toss a stone into it.

A proper lady would never do such a thing.

She ignored that irritating thought. What would a proper lady do? Mayhap she would allow the rumors whirling about Exmoor to betroth her to another man she did not know. She had trusted her guardian to arrange her first marriage, but she was a woman grown now. She must depend on her own instincts to decide whom to marry and when.

With a laugh, she picked up a pebble from the path and tossed it through the trees. It struck one tree, then another before crashing to the ground. Gathering up a second, she let it fly. This one became entangled in the branches and dropped only a few feet in front of her. As she reached for another stone, the black dog whined. She smiled. They thought they were part of this game. Patting the dog on the head, she drew back her hand to throw the rock. The dog put its mouth over her hand and looked up at her with eager eyes.

"No, no," she said with a laugh. "This is my stone."

He moved aside and sniffed the ground.

She tossed the rock and laughed when she heard the surprisingly deep, definitely satisfying plop of the stone in the pond. When she wiped dirt from her hands and turned to continue up the hill, she laughed again. The black dog had a stone, twice the size of the ones she had been tossing, in its mouth. It was carrying it as proudly as if it had caught a rabbit in the hedgerow.

The yellow dog was racing about, clearly not wanting to be left out of the game. It pawed at the ground near the wall, then ran after the black dog, nipping at its side playfully.

Valeria followed. The trees thinned, and then she was at
the top. Turning to look in every direction, she knew seeing
the moors from here was worth struggling up the hill. She
should bring someone up here to savor this view, but there
was something wanton about enjoying it alone now. The hills
rolled away like gargantuan green waves in one direction
while the land fell into the gray sea in the other. Along the
hills, sheep dotted the fields, resembling grave markers
bleached in the sun and cast wildly across a churchyard.
Trees, which had survived the battering of the wind, were as
twisted as the path she had climbed.

Running her hand along the moss-covered stones on the
stone wall, she wondered who had first dared to come up
here and try to tame this amazing place. Yes, it was desolate
and often boring and occasionally frightening, but it was glorious on this sun-swept afternoon when the only clouds in
the sky were a brighter white than the sheep.

The black dog came up to her again and leaned its head
against her leg. She smiled and patted it, but said nothing.
Silence seemed too much a part of this land, demanding that
everyone and everything that trespassed on it should respect
that hush. The wind might howl and whistle, but it was a
wondrous music she wanted to enjoy.

"We are well met today."

Valeria whirled and stared up at Sir Tilden. He seemed as
tall as a distant hill when he rode closer to her. With the
wind sweeping through his blond hair, she could believe he
was a direct descendent of some Viking chieftain who had
conquered this moor a thousand years ago. She was about
to ask him how he had managed to ride up the steep hill
when she realized the path leading down the other side was
gradual.

"It is a grand day, isn't it?" she asked as he swung down
from his horse.

"It is now."

She struggled to keep her smile from wavering as his gaze
coursed up and down her like a pack of hounds chasing a
fox across the moors. Turning back to the wall, she leaned

her arms on its uneven top and gazed down at the shore. "The walk up here is worth the view. It is extraordinary."

"Flawless, I would say."

Her hands clenched on the stones, but she forced them to soften from fists. Undoubtedly Sir Tilden had heard the poker-talk that Miss Urquhart had been so pleased to repeat. Mayhap he gave it credence. If so, she would have to disabuse him of his delusions without hurting his feelings.

"Have you lived here all your life?" she asked. The past seemed a safe topic.

"Most of it, save for when I went to school or had the privilege to visit Town." He came to stand behind her.

Even though she waited for him to shift to one side or the other, she realized he had no intention of moving. For her to do so was sure to give him insult, and she could not turn around without being too close to him. Dash him! She never had had any patience for court-promises and come hither smiles, which might have been one of the reasons she had so gladly accepted her guardian's offer to arrange her marriage to Albert.

She could not help thinking of how Lorenzo's breath had created a sensual warmth against her skin when he had protected her from the bats. He was not as handsome as Sir Tilden, and he clearly had no interest in courting her. Then why was she thinking of him now? Dealing with one irritating man at a time was more than enough for her.

"Do you miss London?" Sir Tilden asked, his breath coursing along her nape.

She silenced the shudder, leaving an ache on her tense shoulders. If she had not listened to Miss Urquhart's prattle, she might not be so uncomfortable now. She was being jobbernowl to let an old woman's chatter unnerve her so.

Or was it only Miss Urquhart's gossip? Sir Tilden stood too close for propriety. Mayhap matters were different here on Exmoor, but she was the same, and he stood too near for her comfort.

"This is a big change for me," she said, knowing she must say something.

"Which is difficult in addition to your tragic loss."

She slowly looked over her shoulder and saw sympathy on his handsome face. No man should be this good-looking, and she wondered why some lass had not hauled him to the altar before this. "Thank you, Sir Tilden—"

"I would as lief that you address me as Tilden, if you will."

"I would like that." She faced him, pressing back against the wall as she waited for him to edge away a step. "You must feel free to use my given name as well."

"And I would like that, Valeria." He leaned one hand against the wall, not far from where her own hand rested. "You seem to be recovering very well from your loss."

"Albert's death and then Paul's—"

"Not that, the loss of your home and fortune following your brother's tragic accident."

Her eyes widened. Not even country-put manners were an excuse to discuss the private issue of her finances. This man had met her but once before today, but she could read in his eyes an avid curiosity about the mistakes Paul had made at the card table.

Slipping past him, she said, "I do not wish to speak of that matter."

"I understand."

"I'm glad." Mayhap he was not a complete bumpkin, after all.

"I thought only to ease my mind on what is true and what is nothing more than mumbles on the wind. From what I heard from Lord Caldwell—"

"Do not speak that cur's name in my hearing!"

Valeria hurried back down the steep hillside. When Tilden called after her, she did not look back. She could leave him to stare after her, but she could not escape the horror Austin Caldwell's name conjured out of her memories. The top-lofty man had led her brother into a life of high-stakes gambling and the fast life of Cyprians and blue ruin that may have led to his death. She suspected he had played a part in persuading her brother to use her assets to back his debts until even they were not enough. The pursuit of the game and the chance to win at the price of another's utter ruin were all that mattered to Lord Caldwell. If Tilden was a tie-mate of Lord Caldwell, she wanted nothing to do with him either.

When the dogs whined, she waited for them to catch up with her. She glanced back, but Tilden and his horse were gone. No doubt, he considered her as queer in the attic as Miss Urquhart. She did not care a rush. All she wanted to do was flee, for a few moments, from the problems that haunted her. She would have liked to go back up the hill and linger without Tilden Oates to distress her, but, if she stood still for very long, her uneasy thoughts came back to plague her. If nothing else, she would be as tired as David after a day of meandering across the moors and would be able to lose her cares in sleep tonight.

Valeria followed the dogs at a cautious pace. She reached out to hold onto the wall, so she did not end up skittering down the path like the small stones rolling ahead of her. Blast it! She should not have let Tilden bother her so much. Going down was worse than climbing up.

Her foot slipped into a hole, and she clutched the stone wall. She looked down at the freshly turned earth. This must be where the dogs had been digging. She lifted out her foot and struck something. Whatever it was clunked hollowly against the wall. Her eyes widened.

It was a vase. A cracked vase. Picking it up, she stared in amazement. She could not mistake the figures on the glossy red vase. The design was almost identical to one she had seen at a friend's house in Bath, not far from the Pump Room. Her friend had been one of several people along the street in the shadow of the Bath Abbey, who had been complaining of strong-smelling water seeping into the cellars. When masons worked to stop the leak, they had dug into the floor and found a vase much like this one. She recalled Claudia mentioning that it was very likely from the time of the early Roman empire.

Turning it over in her hands, she noticed a small hole in the back. It still was in remarkably good condition for having been buried more than a millennium. She looked along the wall and saw places where someone had been digging. Was this where the late Lord Moorsea had found his broken pottery that filled so many crates back at the manor house? She peered over the wall and saw, just below, the chimneys of Moorsea Manor sprouting like frozen weeds from the roof of the house.

Lorenzo would be delighted to see this. Excitement pulsed within her as she imagined his smile when she took this to him. Without a doubt, he would spend the rest of the day going through his uncle's library to find information that might help him identify this vase. If she stayed and helped him, she might be able to chase away the ghosts of the rumors that both Miss Urquhart and Tilden Oates seemed to be accepting as the truth.

More quickly than she had guessed, Valeria entered Moorsea Manor. The curve of the moors had suggested she was farther from the house than she had been. She had left her two canine companions at the front gate, noting that both of them now carried a stone as if they thought they were part of a game.

Lorenzo was sitting in the library, as she had expected. When she called his name, he came hastily to his feet. Papers flew across the floor.

"No, no," he said as he gathered up the pages, "I can do this."

"I won't read your poetry if you do not want me to."

He paused as he was reaching for a page that had landed under his chair. Looking up at her, he asked, "You won't?"

"It is *your* poetry, Lorenzo. You should share it only when and with whom you wish."

"You constantly surprise me." He stood and set the paper, upside down she noted, on the table by his chair. Closing the bottle of ink, he smiled. "I had thought the ladies of London were constantly poking their noses into each other's business to know the latest *on dits*."

She chuckled. "Mayhap, but you should realize that when

one leads such a public life, one comes to appreciate small privacies."

"I shall have to rethink my opinions on this."

"Which is not a bad thing."

He motioned for her to sit in the other chair. "Fortunately, for you cause me to rethink my opinions quite often, Valeria."

"Here is something that may cause you to think." She cupped the vase in her hands, holding it out so he could see it.

His mouth grew as round as his eyes. "Where did you find this?"

"By the wall up along the hill that runs parallel to the front wall of the manor. I suspect it supports our assumption that some of these walls were built during the Roman occupation of Britain."

"It's a lovely piece, Valeria. Better than anything I have found among my uncle's collection at the house."

She placed it in his hands. "Enjoy it."

"You are giving it to me?"

"It is yours, Lorenzo. That hill belongs to Moorsea Manor."

"But treasure customarily belongs to whomever finds it."

She smiled. "Then it belongs to two dogs who joined me on my walk. They dug it up. As they have no use for it, it is yours."

"But, Valeria—"

Closing his fingers over the neck of the vase, she said, "It is yours, Lorenzo."

He turned the vase over and over in his hands, examining it from every angle. She smiled as she saw how gentle his fingers were as they outlined the painted design. Mayhap she once had considered him gruff, but she could not now. Yes, he might appear stand-offish or shy. She knew better. He simply kept his tongue between his teeth, evaluating every situation before he spoke.

Again her gaze was drawn to his fingers, and once again her imagination wandered in directions it should not. She looked away before she was caught up in the fantasy of those fingers touching her with that same tenderness.

"This is a wonderful piece," he said, and she knew he had not noticed how she was staring at him. "I'm not sure what to say, Valeria, except thank you."

"If you wish, I can show you where I found it."

"I would like that after I have a chance to study this."

"Mayhap tomorrow if the weather cooperates."

He started to smile, then sighed. "Tomorrow you have other plans."

"I have made no other plans for tomorrow."

"Mayhap not, but I fear I made other plans for you."

Valeria slowly sat. "What do you mean?"

Dropping into his own chair, he said, "While you were enjoying your walk, we had a caller from Oates Hall."

"So that is how Tilden knew where to find me."

"Sir Tilden?" He frowned. "The caller was Miss Oates. She called for you, but when you were not here, came to speak with me. She wished to extend an invitation for you to join her for a gathering at Oates's Hall tomorrow evening. I believe it is to be an evening of music and conversation."

Valeria ignored the warmth along her face. As flushed as she was from her climb and the breeze and the sunshine, she doubted if embarrassment could make her face any redder. At least, she hoped not. "She invited just me?"

"Yes."

"But why didn't she invite you? This is most peculiar."

He shrugged. "You will have to ask her. She seemed very eager to extend the invitation to you."

"Mayhap I was mistaken about Miss Oates's intentions toward you." Coming to her feet, she locked her fingers together and went to look out the window. Storm clouds were rising out of the sea. She hoped they did not herald another tempest in her life. "It seems you have a cohort in your attempt to play the matchmaker, Lorenzo."

"Why are you acting like this?" He set himself on his feet. "First, you state that life here is certain to fill you with endless *ennui* because you have no one to call upon or to receive. When Miss Oates offers you such an invitation, you react with dismay."

"I don't know." That was a lie. She knew all too well. While Miss Oates had been here extending this invitation, Tilden had sought her out on the hill. It was so clear now. Brother and sister must have come to Moorsea Manor together, and, when they were told Valeria was out for a bit of air, Tilden had gone looking for her while Miss Oates delivered the invitation.

"Valeria, if you have no wish to go—"

"No, I would like to spend an evening listening to music and conversation." That, at least, was the truth.

"Do you want me to go with you to the gathering at Oates's Hall?" he asked as he came to stand next to her by the window.

She could not help comparing him to Tilden Oates. Lorenzo did not crowd her, for he left her space to make her own decisions. He saw her as a person, not just a possible wife. No man had ever treated her like this before, and it was confusing and heady at the same time. Without the familiar rules of the Polite World, she had no conventions to use as a crutch. She had to, as he was, rethink her opinions on so many things.

"You would go with me?" she asked.

"Yes." He leaned one shoulder against the wall. "I do profess a fondness for music. It allows for discussion between each performance, so that one might understand the artist's goal in creating the piece."

She suddenly laughed.

"What is so funny?" he asked with a perplexed expression that had become so familiar.

She did not resist the temptation to reach up to smooth the lines furrowing his brow. He caught her wrist between his fingers, but he did not draw her hand away.

"You and I are what's funny," she said, but her voice had dropped to a whisper as his thumb brushed the inside of her wrist.

"What do you mean?"

"Listen to you. You are so intrigued with the idea of an evening of music and conversation that you are willing to make a *faux pas* and present yourself uninvited at Miss Oates's door. She may very well have guessed that you would offer to escort me to Oates's Hall."

"She may have."

"So she need not have asked you, and she could keep from seeming too brazen that way." She gazed up into his blue eyes and saw something flicker within them. It slipped through him to fly along her, leaving a tremor as if she stood too close to a bolt of lightning and its thunder.

"There is nothing brazen about inviting a neighbor to an evening of music."

"There is, if one's intentions have more to do with marriage than music."

"That's an assumption on your part."

"Yes."

"You should be careful of assumptions." He tilted her wrist toward his lips. Her own parted with an eager sigh as his breath glided along her skin, a sweet, moist caress. "You scratched yourself, Valeria."

"I what?" She stared at him. *That* she had not expected him to say.

"You need to be more careful along the old walls."

Jerking her arm out of his hand, she said, "I believe I can take care of myself, Lorenzo. Or are you worried that I might contract some disgusting disease that will keep you from marrying me off to Tilden?"

"What are you talking about?"

She knew she was being outrageous, but she could not halt herself. The daydream, fleeting though it had been, that he might be drawn to her as she was to him was precious. She had not wanted it destroyed by commonplaces and prittle-prattle.

"I need to decide what I shall wear tomorrow evening," she said as she turned away. "And I told David I would spend the rest of the afternoon with him. Enjoy your vase, Lorenzo."

She said nothing more, because she was not sure whether she would have spoken a lie or the truth. Both she feared she would regret.

Ten

Oates Hall seemed modern in comparison with the ancient walls of Moorsea Manor. Made of brick and with windows marching in neat precision across its front, it brought a sense of civilization to the untamed moors. Lights glowed at each of the windows, and torches blazed along the curved drive and on either side of the double doors that had been thrown open to welcome all the guests attending tonight's *conversazione*.

Lorenzo handed Valeria out of the carriage. Her gown tonight was a subdued, for her, shade of blue that made her eyes a deeper purple. The gems in the simple necklace at her throat he guessed were paste, for he knew she had sold everything of value to settle her brother's debts after the carriage accident. No matter, the fake stones glittered in the torchlight as brilliantly as her smile, but he wondered if her smile was any more real than the fake gems. She had been oddly quiet on the trip from Moorsea Manor. He doubted if she had said more than a handful of words during the hour's journey.

When her fingers quivered as he drew them into his arm, he murmured, "I hope that is anticipation, not fear."

"Some of both." She snapped open a surprisingly fashionable fan that Miss Urquhart had found for her. "There will be people here I have not seen since I left London. Once I was their hostess. Now . . ."

"Now they can return the favor."

She glanced up at him, a grateful smile warming her eyes. "Thank you, Lorenzo. That was kind of you to say."

"And it's kind of you not to say how seldom we exchange anything but strong words with each other." He put his other hand over hers as they climbed the steps to the front door in the wake of other guests. "For tonight, at least, shall we pretend that we are the best of friends?"

"I believe I can pretend that." She looked back at the house, and he sensed how she tensed.

He had not thought she would be so anxious about this evening when she had spoken often of spending her time in London attending events much like this. He should be the one anticipating this with dread. His mother had badgered him to go to London for a full Season. His cousin had repeated the same suggestion, but Lorenzo had not gone for more than a fortnight. Everything he had heard of the bustle and the attempts to better one in someone's eyes by belittling another had been true. That single encounter with the Polite World had convinced him to remain at Wolfe Abbey. Mayhap tonight would change his mind, but he doubted it.

As he nodded to the maid who took his hat and cloak, his thoughts were focused on the vase Valeria had brought him yesterday. It was an excellent piece, and he guessed it might have been imported from what was now France, in the early days of the Roman occupation. If he had not agreed to escort Valeria here tonight, he might have put a certain identification on it. He believed he had found the book among his uncle's collection that would provide the information he needed, but had not had time to peruse it. He barely had had time to dress in his seldom-used evening wear.

He longed to snatch his hat and cloak back from the maid, bid Valeria to enjoy her evening, and take his leave to continue his studies. He could send the carriage for her, so it waited when she was ready to return to Moorsea Manor.

Glancing at her face and seeing the strain dimming her smile, he knew he must resist doing as he wished. What he wished right now, he realized with a start, was that he could devise some witty remark to bring a genuine smile back to her. For the first time ever, he regretted his lack of skill in aimless conversation. A chap with Town polish would know what to say to ease her disquiet. He could only pat her fingers as he drew her hand within his arm again.

When she looked up at him, she said, "Don't fret about me. I shall be quite fine, Lorenzo."

"I have no doubts of that."

She gave him an effervescent smile, and he was amazed that he had succeeded in spite of himself. The ways of the *ton* seldom included honesty. Mayhap he did not need a Season in London to soothe her distress. Mayhap honesty was the best cure.

As he led her up the stairs, which seemed cramped in comparison with the ones at Moorsea Manor, he admired the silk wall coverings and the *objets d'art* decorating the cozy space. He had become accustomed to the unrestrained chaos of his uncle's possessions. This serenity where each item was arranged in utmost perfection seemed sterile.

Music and voices coursed down the steps, and Lorenzo turned to his left and an arch where Miss Oates was receiving her guests. Her eyes narrowed as he walked with Valeria toward her, so he could not guess if she was pleased or disturbed at seeing him.

No matter. Valeria needed an ally tonight when she should have been comfortable among friends. He would not abandon her.

Miss Oates's gown was of the palest pink, a shade that made him think of looking at one's fingers through an icicle. However, her smile was warm.

"I am so glad that you joined Lady Fanning in accepting our invitation for this evening," she said as Lorenzo bowed over her hand.

"Where is your brother?" Valeria asked.

He knew she regretted the question as Miss Oates brightened. "How kind of you to be asking for him, my lady. Tilden will be so pleased when he returns from checking the wine for this evening."

"He is checking it only now?"

Miss Oates blushed. "He was dealing with matters of a tenant farmer this afternoon, and the time completely slipped away from him. We are lucky he was able to return in time to be presentable tonight." She reached out and took Valeria's hand. "I know he will be extra glad now."

Valeria's response was only a weak smile.

"This," Miss Oates continued, drawing an older lady forward, "is my mother."

Lorenzo bowed over the gray-haired lady's hand. She was still as handsome as her son and was no bent dowager. In a gown so stylish it must have only just been delivered from London, she outshone her daughter.

"Mother, this is Lord Moorsea."

"Good evening, madam," he said as he raised his head and met her steady gaze.

"So you are the new earl," Mrs. Oates replied. "We are glad you have called tonight. Aren't we, Mary?"

By the elevens! Valeria was correct. Even if Miss Oates had not been smiling as if she had invented him solely for her purposes, her mother's appraisal was a warning that the plumpness of his pockets and his eagerness for a bride would be a topic of intense discussion as soon as he and Valeria stepped aside to let mother and daughter greet their next guest. He did not like being viewed as a prize to be obtained, although he knew that, along with his title, had come the assumption that he was looking for a wife and an heir.

"This is Valeria Fanning," he said when the silence made his nerves sing like an over-taut violin string. "She is my guest at Moorsea Manor and a very dear friend."

The wrong thing to say, he discovered. Both Miss Oates and her mother winced in unison as he had said *very dear friend*. Valeria's hand tightened on his arm as she spoke the proper pleasantries, so he knew she had seen their reaction as well.

Valeria steered Lorenzo away from the two women and tried to hide her smile. He was so innocent of the ways of the Polite World, so he needed someone to look after him. Wishing David could have seen him just now, so that her nephew would not be so irritated with what he called Lorenzo's overbearing ways, she wondered if David and Lorenzo would ever be able to be more than civil to one another.

"Most men would be flattered by such attention," she said as they paused near the empty chairs in the middle of the room. It was a glorious room, reminding her of a friend's house in London, for it was painted the same pale gold and decorated with similar friezes. Three crystal chandeliers hung with huge medallions in the middle of the arched ceiling. A set of doors opened onto a terrace off to the right, and she guessed an identical pair on the opposite wall led to the balcony overlooking the garden to the left of the drive leading up to the house. It was grand, but seemed somehow too familiar. She had been in so many rooms like this while attending so many gatherings like this. It was comfortable, but without the sense of adventure and anticipation she experienced each time she entered a room for the first time at Moorsea Manor.

He shifted uneasily. "I find it uncomfortable to have such private matters openly discussed."

"Marriage and the begetting of heirs?"

"Valeria, didn't I just say I found this an untoward topic for discussion here?"

She laughed. "You need to become accustomed to it, I'm afraid. Or you could simply marry without delay, and then the matter will be settled unless you find yourself in need of another wife in the future."

"One, I suspect, will be enough at any time."

"I didn't mean you should consider marrying more than one woman at a time."

His lips curved in a wiggly line as if he were trying to keep from smiling as she had, and he chuckled. "I shall leave that to the sheikhs with their harems. How is it that I can jest about such unspeakable subjects with you and still not feel comfortable discussing what everyone about us seems to be discussing?"

"Mayhap because you are such a private man," she said,

following his glance around them. He was right. Everyone was looking at them, bending and whispering, and then turning to look at Miss Oates. "I'm sorry, Lorenzo. I should have insisted that you remain at Moorsea Manor."

"You didn't know this would happen."

"I did."

"You did?"

She wished she had not seen the accusatory anger in his eyes in the moment before his face went blank. *Yes,* she wanted to say, *I thought only of myself and how having you here might deflect the poker-talk about me and Tilden.* She could not say that because she must remember how many ears could be taking note of every word she spoke.

"Miss Urquhart warned me of this," she said softly.

"She did?"

"Apparently before she married, Mrs. Oates had hoped your uncle would offer for her and make her Lady Moorsea. As she sees it, if a match could not be made for her and your uncle, then one between you and her daughter would even things out."

He shook his head. "You are making no more sense than Miss Urquhart. I cannot believe that you are heeding her."

"She seems quite lucid in these matters."

"If she is right, then why wasn't I invited to this evening?"

"I explained that to you." She laughed again. "You have to trust me on this. I know of what I speak all too well, for I have seen friend and foe alike use similar tactics in Town. Don't forget. I have suffered through being the target of mindless matchmaking more than once."

"A widow's lot."

"A rich widow's lot I was told in Town, but I was able to deflect any interest by surrounding myself with good friends amid large gatherings. Now that I am no longer wealthy, I had hoped the interest would be gone."

"Then you met Sir Tilden."

"Yes."

"Some men do not think of marriage only with their empty pockets."

She stared at him, puzzled. Would she ever become accustomed to his odd remarks?

"I mean," he went on, "some men think of marriage as a means to happiness, not wealth. You are a lovely woman, certain to catch a man's eye."

"A compliment, Lorenzo?"

"A fact, Valeria." He bowed his head to her and said, "If you will excuse me, I will find us both something cool to drink."

"Beware of Miss Oates in that direction."

When Lorenzo frowned, he asked, "Why should I be wary of a woman who clearly respects me or at least my title? I am aware of her intentions, thanks to you, but she is our hostess, and I owe her the duty of not ignoring her."

Valeria almost gasped. She had thought he would wish to avoid Miss Oates tonight. Hadn't he just been bemoaning the fact that both Miss Oates and her mother were making plans for his future? As she watched him go over to Miss Oates and speak to her pleasantly while he selected a glass of wine from the table, Valeria wondered if she were the naïve one. Lorenzo clearly understood his obligations, and he would be wise to make a match with a lass who was content to remain in daisyville. When he looked back at her, smiling at some jest Miss Oates must have spoken, pain struck her.

"What is amiss, Valeria? You look as if you have lost your best friend." Tilden's laugh was jovial as he handed her a glass of wine.

"I may have." She recovered quickly. "I mean, nothing is amiss. I am so glad you and your sister extended this invitation for tonight."

"It gives me the chance to apologize for distressing you so unwittingly yesterday. I underestimated your grief for your late husband and your despair at the rough straits your brother left you and your nephew in. I apologize if my words brought you more distress."

She took a sip of the wine. Tilden was sincere. That she

was certain. Mayhap she had dismissed him out of hand because his words had reminded her of Austin Caldwell, the bane of her family's future. It was not Tilden's fault that, like Lord Caldwell, his appearance was faultless from his perfectly tied cravat to his sparkling shoes.

"Allow me to apologize as well," she said. "The way I treated you was beneath reproach."

"*Au contraire*. You would have had no need to react if I had had my wits about me." When she opened her mouth to answer, he raised his hands. "Before we spend the rest of the evening in asking pardon, shall we both say we accept each other's apology?"

"Yes." She smiled, astonishing herself. Tilden Oates had more wit than she had guessed.

"Excellent." He tapped his glass against hers. "I would like to reveal a deep wish of mine, if I may."

"Of course." She was unsure what else she could say at this bizarre turn of conversation. Mayhap Lorenzo was not so odd. Mayhap she had not been a part of courting for so long—or ever, she had to own—that she understood men less than Lorenzo insisted he understood women.

"May you always smile upon me as you are right now."

She knew she was blushing and cursed her red hair and pale complexion. "You are too kind, Tilden."

"I hope you will continue to think of me that way."

"I hope so."

"As I do." Miss Oates had her hand on Lorenzo's arm as they entered the conversation. Flashing Valeria a smile, she added, "This is charming. I hope we are not intruding on a *tête-à-tête*."

"You know you are always welcome in any conversation, Mary." Tilden's smile was as broad as his sister's.

Valeria looked at Lorenzo who wore an innocuous expression that was neither smile nor frown. What his thoughts might be she could not guess. As she listened to him and Tilden discuss the weather and the current state of the government, she noted how studied Lorenzo's motions were. Only when Tilden mentioned the plan to widen the road through the moors did Lorenzo gesture emphatically, which, until now, was the only way she had seen him emphasize his words.

As the music began to play beneath the conversation, Miss Oates said, "Enough of politics, you two. Men!" She laughed lightly.

Valeria tried to copy that laugh, but it sounded leaden in her ears.

"I understand you are a poet, Lorenzo," Miss Oates went on like a prattle-box. "Will you share some of your poems with us?"

He shook his head and smiled with regret. "I'm carrying no poems with me tonight, so I must say no. Mayhap next time."

"Mayhap." Miss Oates's dimples deepened before she and her brother were called away to speak with another guest.

Valeria smiled. "You tell out-and-outers with rare skill, Lorenzo."

His eyebrow rose, destroying his attempt to look betwattled by her words.

"I know you have several slips of paper in your waistcoat."

"You do?"

"I heard them crackle when you were punctuating that point about the road with Tilden."

"Those, Valeria, are only nascent parts of poems. Words and phrases that may one day, I am fortunate enough, be incorporated into a stanza."

"May I see them?"

"Here?"

She smiled. "I promise that I will show them to no one else."

When he took her hand and drew her quickly out onto a wide set of steps leading into the garden, she bit back her gasp. Had she become so instilled with the ways of the *ton* that she was astonished to the point of being speechless by every action that would not be expected in Town? She looked back, but no one seemed to have taken note of them. Every head was bowed in conversation, which she hoped was focused on other subjects.

The moonlight washed over the stones which had been swept clean of any leaves. A chill filtered through the air, and Valeria wished she had brought her favorite paisley shawl with her. That coolness vanished when Lorenzo's fingers brushed hers as he handed her several crumpled pages.

"I believe the moon will provide enough light for you to read without someone peering over your shoulder," he said.

She nodded and sat on a bench by the edge of the terrace that led down into a garden that had surrendered to the shadows. Amazement filled her as she read the words in his neat hand. For years, she had been a devotée of the work of the great poets, her favorite being the French Marquis de la Cour. She had not guessed that Lorenzo's work would rival the French poet's.

"I like this one, because it seems so appropriate for tonight. *Silver light dropping from a luminescent moon,"* she whispered, letting the words flow over her tongue. "That is lovely, Lorenzo."

"Thank you. Sometimes the words come so easily, and at other times, not a single one will appear. That's why I write down phrases that might be of use one day."

"Do you always write of nature?" She put the first two pages on her lap and tried to read the third. It was scribbled as if he had been in a great hurry or in a great deal of agitation.

"It is an ever-changing subject. I—" He swallowed so hard that she heard the sound. Reaching out, he said, "Oh, I didn't realize I had that page with me, too. You needn't bother to read it."

She turned away from him and tipped the bottommost page toward the light. Her eyes widened as she read,

Swaying with the gentle rhythm of a woman's secrets

Gentle and fair, fiery and demanding, a dream of femininity

Liquid eyes, a frightened doe ready to protect the one she defends

Sister to one and friend to many, loved by whom

Quickly she folded the page and handed it back to him along with the others. No wonder, he had not wanted to share his poetry with the others. To read even these unconnected phrases together, rough and unrhymed as they might be, had revealed too much of his thoughts. She resisted looking back at the music room where she could hear Miss Oates's lyrical laugh.

It was now so clear. Lorenzo was wise. He knew he needed a wife who would be happy here on the moors, one who did not pine for Town. He was a newcomer to Exmoor, and Miss Oates would offer him *entrée* into the small society that ringed the rough hills.

He hastily hid the pages again beneath his coat. Although the light was dim, she was certain she saw the darkening cast of a blush on his cheeks. She wanted to smile, charmed by this man who had depths even he had not dared to explore.

"Thank you, Valeria," he said quietly.

"Thank you for sharing your nascent poems with me, Lorenzo. I hope you will show me the poem when it is completed."

"Not all phrases are included in a poem." Lorenzo cursed himself. How could he have been so addle-pated to give her that page? Thank goodness, her manners tonight were as impeccable as always. If Miss Oates had chanced to see these, she might not have been so willing to hand them back to him with so little comment.

"But most women would be so thrilled to be the inspiration of a poem," she said.

"Mayhap one of Byron's."

She laughed, the sound brighter than the moon's glow. "I know of many ladies who have claimed to have inspired him, too many even for a man of his tastes. However, I know as many who would be scandalized at the very thought."

"So mayhap I should not continue work in this direction."

"Don't be absurd!" She clasped his hands and smiled up

at him. "Simply share it with her at a time when she can enjoy it in privacy."

"Her?"

"Do not be coy with me, Lorenzo. I have eyes that can see what is right before them. I think you are being very wise to consider this way to win Miss Oates's heart as well as her respect. Write your poems and have them delivered to her instead of bringing them yourself."

"Why?" He could think of nothing else to say. He had not thought Valeria's reaction would be this. Then he recalled how she had agreed to act as his best friend tonight. Mayhap that was what she was trying to do.

"So she might have the opportunity to savor each word and sentiment when no one else can see. That allows her to decide when and how she will share this special honor with the rest of the world."

"You women are a most complicated breed. I would have thought that the presentation of a poem in person, mayhap even reading it aloud, would be preferable."

She came to her feet and squeezed his arm. "Lorenzo, trust me on this. A woman wants to savor what is special for a while until she can contain her happiness no longer and must share it with others."

"All women?"

"All I have met." She gave a delicate shiver. "The night is too chilly for me. Shall we return inside?"

"Go ahead. I want to make sure these nascent poems are secured so that there is no chance of them falling out at an inopportune moment."

Lorenzo sat where she had been sitting and stared up at the moon. He should have listened to his instincts. Then he would have stayed at Moorsea Manor tonight, and his life would not be cascading into this abyss of absurdity.

He glanced over his shoulder and saw Tilden Oates meeting Valeria at the door of the music room. Miss Oates had been eager to tell Lorenzo earlier that his brother was bored with Exmoor and hoped to spend more time in London . . .

exactly as Valeria would want if a match was made between them.

Valeria's suggestions about his poetry tonight had been wonderful, he had to own, save for one small problem. The inspiration of the poems had not been Miss Mary Oates. The inspiration had been Valeria Fanning.

Reaching under his coat, he pulled out the pages. He slowly shredded them before tossing the pieces into the bushes below. The ever-present breeze sent some of them soaring and catching the light like fallen stars ascending once more to the heavens before they dropped back onto the grass.

He rose and walked away without looking back.

Eleven

"He's going to marry you off in ripping time. He just wants to be rid of us."

Valeria regarded her nephew who was slouched in his chair and glowering at her. She wanted to argue that was not true, that Lorenzo was glad to have them at Moorsea Manor, but she would not be false with David. "We do disturb him when he wishes to have serenity."

"But I don't want to leave here."

"You don't want to leave? I thought you despised this place."

He stood and stamped from the hearth to the settee and dropped on it so hard that the wood creaked. "There are so many parts of Moorsea Manor that I haven't been to yet. *He* still refuses to let me go out into the old wall. *He* thinks I'll get hurt, although I wager *he* would be glad if I went out there and broke my neck."

"David! What a horrible thing to say!"

"Didn't you tell me I should always be truthful?"

"But that's not the truth. Lorenzo would be very upset if something happened to you."

"And then *he* would dance a jig, glad I was gone."

"Don't be absurd!" Valeria rose and put her hand on his shoulder. "And don't fret. I have no plans to buckle myself to anyone now."

David hunched down into the settee. "You'll have to marry if *he* decides you will."

"Lorenzo is a reasonable man."

He arched a brow, and Valeria pressed her hand against her chest. Was being able to raise a single brow a masculine skill intended to belittle a woman? She had grown to despise it from Lorenzo, and now David had begun it. Or—and she knew better than to voice this question which would rile David—was it a habit he had obtained from being in Lorenzo's company?

"I'm not going to leave here until I have seen every inch of this house." He folded his arms before him and scowled. "He can't force me to, and neither can you!"

"David, remember your manners."

"Why should I?" He jumped to his feet again, making her dizzy with his ups and downs. "He's going to marry Miss Oates and then bundle us off to Oates's Hall when he insists you leg-shackle yourself to Sir Tilden." His nose wrinkled. "That house is only twenty or thirty years old. It's not fun like this house."

"You could come here to visit any time you wish."

David jammed his fists against his waist. "What will that make Lord Moorsea if you marry Sir Tilden and he marries Miss Oates? My uncle?"

"Not exactly." She rubbed her hands together, but could not ease the cold aching across them. "David, let us speak of something else."

"What else?" he asked with an eight-year-old's logic. "It's all *everyone* is speaking of."

"Everyone? Whom do you mean?"

"Everyone is everyone. Cook and Gil and Miss Urquhart and the upstairs maid with the missing tooth and the blond stableboy and Kirby and—"

He continued to list names, but she did not listen. If Kirby was repeating such *on dits,* there might be some validity to them. She had to own it was a convenient solution to a problem that Lorenzo had not anticipated when he came to claim his inheritance. Tilden had been an excellent host last week, and she had enjoyed going into dinner with him. She had been prejudiced by her disquiet that Lorenzo had arranged their first meeting, an assumption that Tilden had contradicted when he told her, upon their parting at Oates's Hall, how glad he was that his sister had asked him to ride toward Moorsea Manor that day. Yes, her marrying Tilden would be an excellent solution for Lorenzo. And for her, she had to own, for he offered her everything she wanted, save for the pulse of delight she savored when Lorenzo spoke to her.

"What are we going to do?" David's voice came out in a groan of pain.

She held out her hands to him. She must think of the child, not her own unsettled future. He buried his head in her lap and wept. As she stroked his hair, wishing she could soothe his fears of losing yet another home, she whispered, "It shall be all right, David. I promise you that."

"But how—?"

"I don't know, but I promise you that it shall be all right."

The village of Winlock-on-Sea was a throwback to the previous century. Thatched roofs and stone walls had weathered the storms tossed up out of the sea and the sunshine cooking them on this unseasonably warm morning. Villagers sat doing chores on the steps in front of their doors on either side of the narrow road unraveling down the hill from Moorsea Manor.

As Valeria emerged with Lorenzo from a small shop in the very center of Winlock-on-Sea, she said, "Thank you."

"I am pleased I could help you find something for young David for his birthday next week." Lorenzo set his hat on his head and smiled. "Mayhap the toy soldiers will give him something to do but think up pranks to torment me."

"He is just—"

"A boy, I know." He offered his arm as they walked up the twisting street. "A most imaginative boy, which is why I hope this gift will entertain him."

"I have never seen him play with toy soldiers, but mayhap he will enjoy these." She looked in the window at the tin knights mounted on painted horses. The shopkeeper had assured her that they represented the great armies of the War of the Roses. The soldiers would be delivered to Moorsea Manor in time for David's birthday.

"One can only hope so."

At Lorenzo's grim tone, she did not answer. She doubted if David would spend all his time playing with the soldiers, when he was so determined to enjoy every bit of Moorsea Manor before it was no longer his home. Nothing Valeria had said would convince the boy that Lorenzo would not force her into an unwanted marriage. It made no difference to David. Wanted or unwanted, marriage, he knew as she did, was inevitable for her, and then they would be gone from the old manor house. Her suggestion that Lorenzo might be less eager to find her a husband if they caused no problems in the house was something David ignored.

She did not want to be down-pinned today. The sky was a wondrous blue, and the air was sweet with fragrance from the flowers climbing the cottages. Even the breeze off the sea had tempered, and the only clouds were fluffy.

When Lorenzo paused in front of a building with a sign calling it *The Old Master's House,* she asked, "Is this the tavern that belongs to you?"

"It must be." His smile was ironic. "It appears to be the sole building of its ilk in Winlock-on-Sea." Reaching for the door, he asked, "Shall we pay it a call?"

Valeria hesitated. In London, she never would have considered entering a tavern. That was a place reserved for gentlemen or worse. While traveling here, she and David had stayed overnight at inns, but she had avoided going into the taprooms. Such an action would label her no better than a Cyprian.

"If you would prefer not to . . ." Lorenzo started to close the door.

"Yes, why don't we visit your tavern?" she replied before she could halt herself. Lorenzo had been generous to her today, escorting her to Winlock-on-Sea and paying for David's gift. To balk when he was making a not outrageous request was worse than rude.

His smile widening, he held the door for her. She noted that he had to duck his head to enter the low door, which was not a surprise, for the feathers on her bonnet had brushed the top of the door frame when she walked through. The tavern was small and close with the smoke from the pipes of the dozen men crowded around its bar. A single table sat near the window where the stains left by a recent storm ran along the uneven glass as if the rain had tried to create a new route to the sea.

The men stared at her, but came to their feet as Lorenzo edged into the choke-full room. The man, who wore an apron and stood behind the bar, came forward. He was shorter than Valeria, so he had to crane his neck up to meet Lorenzo's gaze.

"You're the new earl, aren't you?" he asked in a broad accent.

"Lorenzo Wolfe." He took off his hat before it bumped into the rafters. "You are?"

"Trenton, my lord." Glancing uneasily at Valeria, he asked, "Can I get you and yer lady somethin' to ease yer thirst?"

"Ale for me, and a sweet cider for Lady Fanning."

The barkeeper's eyes grew big as he looked at Valeria again. She fought not to let her smile waver. If he had assumed that she was Lorenzo's convenient, he was sadly mistaken. There was nothing convenient about anything between her and Lorenzo.

When Lorenzo's hand guided her to the single table, Valeria sat with her back to the taproom. She would prefer to pretend the men were not staring at them.

Lorenzo did not pull out his chair. Instead he peered at a frame set over the hearth. "Is this the painting of my uncle, Trenton?"

"That be the old earl." He set the two mugs on the table and swished a damp cloth across the uneven boards.

"Which one? There are two men standing by their horses here."

Trenton shrugged. "One be him. The other be the older earl. Not sure which is which. Paintin' was here when I came here about thirty years ago. Can I get you somethin' to eat, m'lord?"

"Whatever you have simmering will be fine." Lorenzo pulled out his chair and sat across from Valeria. As soon as the barkeeper had gone into the kitchen behind the tavern, he added, "My uncle might have had a closer relative than me."

"What do you mean?"

"Look at the painting."

She went to it. The painter had not possessed a remarkable talent, and the pose was commonplace. Two men stood stiffly in front of two horses with excellent lines. In the background was a building that was clearly supposed to be Moorsea Manor, although several of the windows were in the wrong place. "What about it?"

"Look at the older man." He chuckled and took a deep drink of his ale, wiping the foam from his lips with the back of his hand. "Does he look a bit familiar?"

Valeria squinted to make out the small faces, then gasped. "He looks much like Earl."

Lorenzo laughed again as she took her seat. "My thoughts exactly. I suspect, although the subject has been oddly unspoken of at the manor, that my grandfather may have more than one son. Could it be that no one else has noticed the resemblance?" He grinned and leaned back in his chair. "I think I would have liked my maternal grandfather who named his by-blow after his own title."

"Lorenzo!"

"Do not act shocked, Valeria. You have to own that it is a grand jest." His smile faded. "I hope this was not the reason that divided my mother and her brother."

"An illegitimate half-brother could not have been the reason. Earl's birth, even if you are right, had nothing to do with them."

"I know, but I would like to discover what caused the schism that they never were able to bridge."

She put her hand over his on the table. "You cannot let this tear at you, Lorenzo. That was their lives. This is yours."

When he put his hand atop hers, he smiled. Not a brilliant smile as he wore when he was enjoying a jest. Not an exultant smile like she saw on his face when he had uncovered some tidbit of information on one piece of his uncle's collection. Not his satisfied smile when the words were coming easily for his poetry. This smile was nothing like any of them. It possessed a warmth that was both a promise and a provocation, daring her to push aside common sense and discover something most uncommon.

She withdrew her hand from between his. Only a sap head would play this dangerous game of hearts knowing its inevitable end. Lorenzo had owned to the fact that he was seeking another man to be a husband for her.

Lifting her glass of cider, she said, "I would like to arrange for a gathering at Moorsea Manor."

"Valeria, we have spoken of this before." The familiar exasperation returned to his voice.

She was glad. Exasperation she could deal with more easily than her own errant thoughts. "Not a large gathering, Lorenzo. I thought to invite the children of the parish to join David for a celebration of his birthday. It would last only an hour or two, and, if the day is fine, the whole of it can be held in the gardens."

"You would risk losing any smaller children in that maze of weeds."

"Mrs. Ditwiller will arrange to have an eye kept on all of them." She put her mug on the table and locked her fingers around it. "A challenging task like this might help make the household run more smoothly."

"There have been problems?"

"Some lingering resentment that Mrs. Ditwiller is now in charge of the household."

He smiled. "She was aware of that problem when I asked her to come to Moorsea Manor. However, if she and you think this party will help, by all means, go ahead. Just include David in the planning. It should keep him occupied."

Before Valeria could say that she found it impossible to imagine David sitting and discussing a guest list, Trenton returned with bowls filled with steaming stew. Thick vegetables and chunks of meat sent out an aroma that reminded her that she had not eaten breakfast this morning.

She reached for a spoon, but a shadow crossed her hand. She looked up to see a large black and white cat perched on the windowsill beside her. The cat's gaze was focused on the spoon in Valeria's hand.

"That be Kitty." Trenton gave them a gap-toothed grin. "You need to be keeping yer eye on Kitty. He's got a fearsome temper, he does."

Valeria drew back. "I was about to pet him."

"That be fine, if'n he wants to be petted." He pointed to her bowl of stew. "I think he's got more of a hankerin' for what's in yer bowl."

"Is it all right to feed him?" asked Lorenzo.

She was shocked anew. She had had no idea that Lorenzo had a fondness for cats. Every day, she realized once again how little she understand this most enigmatic man.

Trenton chortled. "You would be most wise to share a bit of yer sup with him, m'lord. Elsewise, he might take a swipe or two at you. As you can see, he hones his claws on the sides of the sill."

"Oh, my!" She stared at the wood that had been etched with the marks of the cat's claws. "Do give him something, Lorenzo."

With a chuckle, he held a piece of game out to the black and white cat. Kitty accepted the offering with delicate disdain as if he were offended that he had to go through this ploy to get what was so rightfully his.

"The poor thing must be hungry," she said as Kitty swallowed the piece with barely a single chew.

" 'Tis all an act, m'lady," the man said. "He gets fed thrice a day when the maids each come to work. He eats those meals as fast as he can and hunts out back until someone comes in and orders somethin' from the kitchen. Then he comes to beg, don't you, lad?"

The cat gave him a yellow glower and turned his head

back to Lorenzo. A hint of a feline smile suggested that another offering would be most welcome.

"He seems quite at home here," Lorenzo said as he gave another piece of meat to Kitty. "Whose cat is he?"

"The cat's yers, m'lord, unless you decide to sell the tavern. Then he goes to the new owner. Old Kitty's part of the lease here." Trenton turned away, then paused. "Once yer bowls be empty, you'll be wantin' not to stay sittin' here. Kitty gets impatient with folks who sit at his table and don't have any food for him." He chuckled as he walked back to the tap.

Valeria took a bite and saw the cat watching her. She chewed it quickly and swallowed. "That cat could prove to be unnerving, Lorenzo."

"He just knows what he wants and is doing what is necessary to get it." He cleared his throat as he set his spoon on the table. "This may not be the best time to broach this subject, Valeria, but Tilden Oates sent a message to me this morning."

"Did he?" She lowered her own spoon to the table and ignored the cat which made a warning growl deep in its throat.

"He asked if he might call upon you."

"It is something I shall think about. Mayhap after David's party, I can give it some proper consideration."

His eyes widened. "But, Valeria, I already sent him a message saying that he was welcome to."

"You sent him that message without conferring with me?"

"I saw no reason to."

She pushed back her chair and came to her feet. "You saw no reason to confer with me about whom I might consider as a future husband?"

"Valeria," he said, setting himself on his feet, "anyone who saw you and Oates together at his house would have assumed you would have welcomed him to give you a look-in at Moorsea Manor. You were laughing together and obviously very taken with one another."

"But how could you agree to this without telling me

first?" Tears blurred his face in front of her, but she would not let them fall. She was not a child. She would not weep like a child, and she would not be treated like a child. "I know you cannot wait to rid yourself of me, Lorenzo, but I—" Her voice broke.

As she whirled to go out the door, she discovered every eye in the taproom was, once again, focused on her. She looked back at Lorenzo, who was wearing an astonished expression. If he thought so little of her that he handled her future like this, then he was not the man she had believed he was.

She would not be so foolish again.

Twelve

"Women!"

Hearing a laugh behind him, Lorenzo looked over his shoulder. He had not seen Earl. The man walked so quietly, it was almost as if he was not there until he stood right in front of a person.

"You sound exasperated, my lord." Earl walked past him and set another armful of logs by the hearth. Cool air from the back stairwell followed him. "At all of them or at a particular one?"

"Not all of them. Some are not so irritating."

"Which one?"

"Do you know Miss Mary Oates?"

"Sir Tilden's sister?" Earl squatted as he brushed ashes back under the fire. "A fine lady, who has more wit than her brother, if you want my opinion."

"Your opinion agrees with mine, Earl."

"Sir Tilden is not such a bad chap. The problem is that no one likes him as much as he likes himself."

"Valeria seemed quite taken with him."

"Did she now?" Earl set himself on his feet with no sign that his years were slowing him down. "I collect that you do not see Sir Tilden as a proper mate for your ward."

"Quite the contrary. He seemed taken with her right from the beginning, but, when I told her that I had agreed to allow Oates to . . ." Lorenzo dropped into the chair and glowered at the hearth. "Women!"

Earl chuckled. "They do cause problems for a man. I recall my father—"

"Your father!" He looked at the old man. "I wished to ask you about that."

"What of my father, my lord?" A smile teased the corners of his mouth.

Lorenzo guessed Earl knew what he was about to ask, but he was in too deep now to halt. "I saw a painting of my uncle and his father at the tavern in Winlock-on-Sea."

"I've seen it as well." He wiped his hands on his breeches and picked up the candle he never seemed to be without. "And, yes, 'tis true. The older earl was my father, though it's been many, many years since I last saw him."

Coming to his feet, Lorenzo held out his hand to the old man. "Then you are—"

He shook his head and stepped back. "I'm just old Earl. Nothing else now. Don't try to make something of what doesn't really matter any longer."

"But you should not be laying the fires if your father was my grandfather."

"I like what I'm doing now." He smiled. "It's fitting that I'm here now doing this. Don't fret about me, my lord. You have enough to worry about with Lady Fanning and the lad."

Lorenzo grimaced and nodded as Earl took his leave. It was true. How could he have guessed that Valeria would be upset when he had done only what he had thought she would have wanted?

Going to his dressing room door, he opened it. He yelped as water splashed over him. A bucket crashed to the floor, splattering everything nearby. He shook his hands, then his head. Blast! That water was cold. The lad had gone too far this time. A purloined boot or a jumble of papers that left him hours of work to put them in proper order had been bad enough, but this was unconscionable.

"My lord! What did you do to yourself?"

He scowled at Kirby who was coming into the room. Had the man taken a knock in the cradle? He had not done anything to *himself.* That blasted bratchet had done this.

"Send for Lady Fanning!" he ordered.

"Now?"

Lorenzo was about to reply, but caught a glimpse of himself in the glass. His clothes were lathered to him, revealing more than was proper. "Tell her I will speak with her in ten minutes."

"She will wish to know about what."

He raised his hands and spouted a curse as more water dripped off his sleeves. "Tell her that I have suffered my last indignity at the hands of her nephew. It is time we put a stop to this one way or another."

By the time a knock sounded on his door, Lorenzo was decent once more. He did not turn from tying his cravat as he called for Valeria to enter.

"What is wrong?" she asked when she opened the door.

"What makes you think anything is wrong?"

"You do. You are frowning into the glass like a judge at a felon, and your voice nearly pierced through the door's wood to lash me."

He gestured toward the wet clothes. "I believe I have cause to be distressed."

"Wet clothes? I shall have Mrs. Ditwiller speak to whichever maid delivered them here instead of the laundry yard."

"They were delivered here quite dry, Valeria. In fact, I was wearing them only a few minutes ago before I encountered this thanks to your nephew." He poked at the bucket with his toe.

Her face grew pale. "You don't mean that David . . ."

"Exactly."

"This is outrageous!" She picked up one sleeve of his coat, then dropped it as water dribbled down her fingers.

"Exactly."

"This cannot go on."

"Exactly." This was going so much better than he had expected.

"You should never have let it get to this point."

"Exac- What did you say?"

Valeria faced him and folded her arms in front of her.

"You cannot let this continue. Allowing this to go on is teaching the boy all the wrong lessons."

"Me? You think I'm allowing this? I have sent him to his room more times than I wish to count after explaining to him the error of his ways. What more do you expect me to do?"

She laughed, but he heard pain in the sound. "You are so confused. You treat me like a child."

"Valeria—"

"Yet you treat David as an adult, Lorenzo. You cannot do that and think that he will respond as one. He is still not nine years old."

"I thought he would appreciate the guidance of an older man."

She laughed. "Did you?"

He wanted to fire back a sharp retort, but found he had none. Yes, his uncle, Lord Wulfric, had treated him with the same firm hand as his cousins, but always with a sense of humor. His mother had been the gentle voice of discipline, explaining why what he had done was wrong . . . just as Valeria did with David.

"Surely you do not suggest that I give him a thrashing," he gasped.

"Of course not!" Her voice softened to a whisper. "You wouldn't, would you?"

"If I haven't thus far, I believe you can accept that I do not see that as a viable way to persuade him to behave as he should."

"But he is behaving as he should."

"Pardon me?"

Valeria sat on a chair that was not dotted with water. Looking up at him, she said, "He is behaving like an angry, frightened child. For the past few nights, he has wept in his sleep. I have not woken him up, because I hope the night horrors that plague him will disappear before he wakes in the morning. So far that has worked."

"What is he frightened of?" Lorenzo shook his head. "You can't be suggesting he is frightened of me?"

"No, of course not. He is angry at you, but he is frightened of being bustled off to another home without so much as his say so."

"He is a child."

"A child who has lost his father and his home."

"He still has you."

She sighed and looked at the hearth where the fire Earl had rekindled was burning merrily. "Lorenzo, I never spent more than an afternoon with my nephew before he came to live with me."

"I thought—" He sat facing her, then grimaced as he realized this chair had been splattered. Not bothering to move because that might be more embarrassing than remaining here, he added, "I had thought you two were well known to each other. You seem to understand him so well, and he has such affection for you."

"Because I'm his only connection with what was."

"And he's yours."

She bit her lip as she lowered her gaze to her hands in her lap. She looked so desolate that he reached across the space between them and tipped her face up.

"Valeria," he murmured as he gazed into her incredible violet eyes, "let me know what I can do to ease this burden for you and the boy."

"He needs a friend, Lorenzo."

"I thought you were going to solve that problem by giving him a rout and inviting all the children in the parish."

"Since I spoke to you of that this morning, I have been informed by the servants here that the parish is as big as the whole of the moors."

"You are exaggerating. It is much smaller than the complete expanse of Exmoor."

Rising, she said, "The parish is spread out enough that the children would have a long ride to Moorsea Manor. As you have made it clear that you do not wish for me to arrange for a party that lasts longer than an afternoon, the children cannot stay as overnight guests here. Therefore, it is quite impossible to have such a party for David."

"I never meant to cause you to put a halt to the boy's party."

She shook her head. "That is not what's important now. What's important is that you and David learn to live together for as long as we're at Moorsea Manor."

"About Oates and—"

"Lorenzo, David is the only thing that concerns me now."

She was plying him with out-and-outers, he knew, because she again looked back at the hearth. She never would meet his eyes when she was being less than completely honest.

Pulling on a dry coat, he asked, "Where is the boy now?"

"He went riding with Gil. You know they wander all over the moors every afternoon."

He did not want to own that he had had no idea where the two went, because he had been simply grateful that they were not creating trouble in the manor house. Picking up his hat, he said, "I believe I shall go and have a talk with the boy."

"Don't distress him more."

"I have no intention of doing that." He ran his hand along the ruined wool of his drenched coat. "I intend to insist on an end to these gammocks before more is destroyed than a coat. If that bucket had landed on old Earl's head, for example, he could have been greatly hurt."

Again her face became wan. "Lorenzo, don't forget that David is just a little boy."

He put out his hand. He had meant to clasp her shoulder, but somehow his fingers curved along her cheek. The silken warmth of her skin sent a blistering flame through him. Tilting her face toward him, he watched, his breath caught in his chest, as her eyes closed. In anticipation or in resignation? Hastily he stepped away. He must be all about in his head to be acting so.

"Do not worry, Valeria," he said, his voice gruff with the emotions he was trying to suppress. "I shall deal with David in a way that will meet your approval."

As he walked to the door, she said, "Lorenzo, I believe that—"

"Trust me on this."

His hand froze as he reached for the door when he thought he heard her say, "I wish I could." He looked back, but she pushed past him and crossed the hall to her rooms.

Her door closed so softly that he heard the bolt slide into place.

Lorenzo left the house, had his horse saddled, asked a few questions of the stableboy, and then rode in the direction David and Gil had been heading when they left Moorsea Manor an hour before. He doubted if he would find them quickly amid the expanse of the moors, and he was right, but the rough ride where he had to watch the path ahead of him carefully kept him from thinking of Valeria and her peculiar ways.

An hour later, he still had not seen a sign of where the boys might be. He sat on the low stone wall and stared out at the channel. It must be presaging a storm because it was throwing itself against the headland as if the waves intended to try to sweep the beach back into the sea.

Somehow, before Valeria bashed herself as futilely against his unchanging opinions, he was going to have to find a way to explain to her why he thought it was best that she marry someone like Sir Tilden Oates. Then she could enjoy her exciting life in London. He had been awed by how easily she flitted from one conversation to the next at Oates Hall, always finding a welcome and never saying the wrong thing to anyone. Each person she had spoken to seemed delighted that she had sought him or her out. After that evening, he could understand why she pined at Moorsea Manor for the entertainments that had once been commonplace for her.

The very entertainments he despised.

Mayhap he should simply be honest with her, explaining how he preferred the quiet company of a few friends where conversations could continue for hours, rather than moments, where one could speak of matters more important than what color the *haut monde* at Almacks had chosen last week, where he could be comfortable to speak his mind instead of knowing he would make a *faux pas* if he were to open his mouth. Being shy was something Valeria could not comprehend, but it was a facet of himself that he lived with daily.

A shout rippled from the glen above. He stood and, shading his eyes so he could look toward the bright sky, realized at least one of the boys was kneeling by the wall not more than a quarter mile away. Mounting, he rode to where David was digging by the wall. A deep hole had been cut out of the earth, and Gil, a sheepish grin on his face, carried a bucket—the twin of the one that had doused Lorenzo—filled with dirt, and was dumping it over the stone wall.

"What have you there, David?" Lorenzo asked, noting that Gil seemed quick to find something to occupy him on the other side of the wall. He would speak with the footman later. Now he must find a way to ease the tensions between him and Valeria's nephew.

For a moment, he feared the boy would remain intractable and would not reply, but David leapt to his feet and called, "Come and see this!"

"What?"

"This!"

Lorenzo smiled as he dismounted and walked over to the wall. He never had heard such animation in David's voice. Mayhap the lad had found something other than pranks to fill his time.

"I got directions to this spot from Aunt Valeria," David said, staring down at his hands, "and she was right. There was another old thing buried in the dirt along this wall."

"Old thing?" Lorenzo squatted beside the boy who dropped back to his knees.

"This."

He was amazed again when David dropped something onto his hand, and it did not slither or have three pair of legs. The item was not much bigger than the button on the front of his coat, but was caked with earth. He chipped some of the dirt away and ran his fingers over the raised figure on the small circle. "I believe you have found an old coin."

David frowned. "I thought it was something good."

"It is."

"What's so good about an old coin?"

Lorenzo tilted it toward the boy. "A truly old coin, David. I would guess, like the vase your Aunt Valeria brought to the manor, this is Roman."

"From Italy?"

"Mayhap, or mayhap it was minted here in England. Either way, it was most likely brought here over 1500 years ago."

His eyes widened in sudden delight. "So long ago? How did it get here?"

Wondering if Valeria's brother had given the child any attention or education on anything other than perpetrating practical jokes, Lorenzo sat back on his heels. "The Romans came here then and conquered the island."

"Us?" His thin chest puffed out, and he repeated with schoolboy pride, "No one has invaded England successfully since the Norman William the Conqueror came to claim his throne."

"That happened when?"

"In 1066."

"Which was nearly 700 years after the Romans came to this part of England."

David muttered something in surprise under his breath. Lorenzo decided it would be best not to ask him to repeat it more loudly, because he suspected the words were some that Valeria would chide the boy for speaking.

Turning the coin over and over, Lorenzo said quietly, "Long before the Normans, long before the Vikings came to pillage England, even before King Arthur created his round table not far from here at Camelot, the Romans arrived to the island they called Britannia to conquer and to settle and live and die." He reached out to touch the stones protruding in a regular pattern from the earth near the base of the wall. "This may have been a wall of a building or the foundation of a house."

"A house? Is that all?"

"You might find the most interesting artifacts around this

wall. People have been tossing aside their possessions for centuries."

"I have no interest in Roman garbage."

He tossed the coin and caught it. "You've seen the amphorae—"

"The what?"

"The big vases with stoppers on the top. They were used for shipping wine and grain. I know you have seen those about Moorsea Manor."

"Broken for the most part."

"There is that one with the painting of a young man that is still miraculously complete."

David shook his head again. "That's boring."

"True, but one never knows what one might find if one keeps searching." He picked up the shovel and lifted out another layer of dirt. "Remember the Romans were invaders and overlords here. They would have brought many of their best warriors to England to help stave off the threat from the Picts and the Celts."

"Warriors?" His eyes widened, and Lorenzo knew he had the boy's attention now.

"Of course. Exmoor would have been at the edge of the Roman Empire. Beyond the sea awaited the heathen tribes of Ireland, who could have, at any moment, been washed up out of the sea to battle for these lands. Just across the channel to the north is Wales where even more clans hid in the highest valleys, rejecting Roman rule. Those who lived here must have been constantly vigilant."

"Real warriors?"

"The best." He smiled. "And, when they left, they were being recalled to defend Rome from the barbarians laying siege on it, so they could not have taken all their possessions with them. What remained was tossed aside or buried, so their enemies could not use them against the retreating Romans. Years upon years of building on this moor have buried the remnants more deeply, but century upon century of wind and rain have given us the chance to find them again." He poked at another dull glint of tarnished silver with his toe. "I believe that is a match for the coin you found."

David scooped it up and brushed the dirt from it. "It's the same on one side, but the other is different. Mine has a angel on that side. Yours has a lady with a staff."

Lorenzo took both coins and balanced them in his hand. They weighed about the same, and they both had a bust on one side. He squinted to read the letters.

IMP TRAIANO AVG GER DAC PM TR P was on the coin David had found. *M COMMODVS AVG* circled the head on his.

"Yours is from the time of Emperor Trajan," he said as he handed David the coin. "Mine is not quite so old, for it is labeled Commodus, who was emperor of Rome almost a hundred years later."

"So mine is older?" His thin chest puffed with pride.

Lorenzo struggled not to smile. "Quite a bit older. Congratulations. When we return to the manor, we can see what among my uncle's collection is of an age of your coin and of mine. If you will allow me to take this with me, I shall make sure it is put in the glass case in the library."

"Really?"

"It may be the oldest item of all."

David grinned and picked up the shovel. "Take it back with you if you wish. I think I'll spend some more time working here. I want to see what else I can find that's older than you."

"Older than me?"

The boy flushed. "I mean—"

"I know what you mean. Older than my coins." Standing, he said, "Good luck with your search, David." He wiped his hands and called, "Gil, David could use your bucket to carry more dirt."

"Aye, my lord," the footman said, popping over the wall. "I've been—"

"I know what you've been doing." He glanced at David who was listening with a guilty expression on his young face. "I know what you both have been doing. After you finish your work here today, please join me in the library. I think I can show you some other items that you might want to keep an eye out for."

"Warrior's things?" David asked.

"Mayhap."

The boy grinned and bent to his digging as Lorenzo walked back to his horse.

That should solve the problem of what to do with the boy. Now if he could devise a way to solve the problem of the boy's aunt with equal ease, he would finally have the quiet life he wanted at Moorsea Manor.

Thirteen

When a knock came at Valeria's door, she hurried to answer it. This was the hour when Lorenzo usually finished his work and once had sought her out for some conversation or maybe a ride along the moors. In the past fortnight, he had not come to ask her to join him for an afternoon outing or even for tea.

She had no cause to lament his manners since their conversation in his room after David had set what she hoped was his last hoax. Lorenzo's demeanor had been as perfectly polite as any member of the Polite World, but she missed his unexpected remarks and unique insights. When he had spoken to her, which was seldom, for he seemed always busy in some other part of the manor house, it was as if they were strangers. She had not guessed that, by denouncing his plans for her with Tilden, she would lose Lorenzo's friendship.

Friendship and trust . . . She could not fault him for being hurt when she had owned, aloud to her immediate regret, that she was not sure if she could trust him. She wanted to, but in the wake of his agreement to allow Tilden to call on her, she could not be sure if he had her best interests or his own in mind. She doubted if her best interests and his were the same.

Mayhap that was changing. Mayhap he was ready to try again at their uneasy friendship. If he came to her door to ask her to ride with him across the moors, she would agree wholeheartedly. A ride and a chance to clear the air between them would be just the cure for her dreary spirits that had preyed on her since she woke this morning.

Not that she should be in dismals. The past week had brought a sense of peace to Moorsea Manor that she never had known here or in London. Even as Lorenzo seemed to be shutting her out of his life, he and David had developed a common interest in all the debris the old earl had carted into the house. After David returned to the house each day, sunburned and covered with dirt and with Gil in tow, Lorenzo and the boy spent every evening pawing through the boxes. She should be glad that they had found something that brought them together instead of driving them apart.

And she was glad.

They had made it clear that she was welcome to join them in their perusal of the dusty potsherds and illegible coins. Mayhap if she did not sneeze the entire time they were pulling dusty things out of the crates, she might have been able to stay in the room. Instead she banished herself to her chambers where she could pretend she was reading or working on correspondence.

She glanced at the pile of unanswered letters on the table by her bed. All of them were from Tilden Oates. Although he had not presented an offer of marriage to her, she knew it was forthcoming. The first letters had been signed *Your Servant, Sir Tilden Oates.* The most recent *With fondest regards, Tilden.*

Marrying him would be the sensible thing, and she had always been sensible. What did it matter that she didn't love the baronet? She had married Albert Fanning, and she had not loved him when she pledged her life to him at the altar of St. George's Church near Hanover Square. Love had come later, an abiding warmth as he introduced her to the exciting world of the *ton* and treated her with a kindness that had been missing from her life. The previous Lord Moorsea had seen something in his friend that suggested the match would be perfect, and he had been right. Mayhap she should trust his nephew to do the same for her. Then Lorenzo could ask Miss Oates to be his wife, and David would have the family he had lost and two men to help guide him as he became a man himself.

It was a reasonable and unquestionably convenient arrangement for everyone.

Then why did she quiver with fear every time this obvious solution filled her head?

Pushing her uneasy thoughts aside, Valeria threw the door open and tried to mask her disappointment when she saw Gil standing there, tugging surreptitiously at his light blue livery which he was apparently already out-growing. The lad would be ten feet tall at the rate he was still sprouting.

"My lady," he said with a half-bow, "a gentleman has arrived and asks to speak with you."

"A gentleman? Sir Tilden?"

"No, not him. This gentleman came in a fancy carriage that looks as if it has traveled a goodly distance." Gil's voice dropped into a conspiratorial whisper. "From the way the gentleman hobbled when he came to the house, I'd say the trip had been long and hard."

She did not scold him for speaking so of a guest to Moorsea Manor, because a wave of exhilaration swept over her, washing away her disquiet. A gentleman who had traveled far could be a friend among the *ton* who had not forgotten her once she had banished herself from London.

"Have the gentleman wait in the library, and I shall be with him posthaste." She turned from the door, then asked, "He did not give a name?"

"Not in my hearing, my lady."

Another thing she must discuss with Mrs. Ditwiller. Instead of being a good influence on the household here, the servants Lorenzo had brought with him to Moorsea Manor were becoming more lackadaisical in their duties. Not that that had eased the tension between the newcomers and the staff. Only Earl seemed more than outwardly accepting of Lorenzo's changes.

With more haste than usual, Valeria changed from her everyday gown to a tea gown of her favorite gold. She had set it aside for a special occasion, and a caller from Town was just that. Curling her hair up around her face, she pinned it in place with some silk flowers. She tossed her beloved paisley shawl over her shoulders, so it caught the vibrant glow of both her gown and her hair.

She was nearly giddy with anticipation as she came down the stairs. Mrs. Ditwiller was waiting for her, a smile on her face.

"I'm having him wait in the library as you instructed, my lady. Shall I send for some refreshments?"

"That would be a good idea." She did not want to loiter to chat.

"And shall I send for Lord Moorsea?"

"I shall when I ascertain who is calling. I don't want to disturb Lorenzo."

Mrs. Ditwiller nodded and smiled. "A good idea, my lady, and, if I may say so, this caller is as handsome as Sir Tilden Oates and has the manners of a real gentleman. Gave his hat and gloves at the door as neat and polite as you please."

"Thank you, Mrs. Ditwiller." She silenced her groan. The housekeeper was becoming as outrageous in her behavior as the rest of the household.

It was something she would handle later. For now . . . Valeria went to the library door, being careful that her gown did not catch on one of the lances still gathered in the hallway. Taking a deep breath, she walked in.

Her smile vanished as she gasped, "Lord Caldwell! What are *you* doing here?" She had never considered that her caller would be Austin Caldwell, who had led her brother into utter ruin.

As he reached for her hand and bowed over it, the tall blond man gave her a smile that was better suited to a snake, for his eyes retained a reptilian chill. "I decided if you weren't going to come back to London any time soon, Valeria, I would call on you in this horrible place." His nose wrinkled as if some foul stench had assaulted him.

"Why?"

"Because there remains business to be dealt with between us, Valeria."

She shook her head as she snatched her hand out of his grasp. "You are quite mistaken, my lord. There never has been and there never will be any business between you and me. I have nothing to say to you other than that you should take your leave now if you wish to reach Minehead and an inn before dark."

As she walked toward the door, he seized her arm. She stared at him in amazement. His manners had never been, in her memory of the few times she had been forced to speak with him, even as poorly polished as a rough diamond's, but this was the first time he had treated her so uncouthly.

"Valeria, there is business between us, and I wish to discuss it now."

"And I do not. Good day, my lord."

His fingers bit into her arm, and she clenched her teeth to keep from crying out in pain. She would not give him that satisfaction. Keeping her chin high and her gaze focused directly on his, she peeled his fingers off her.

"Have a pleasant journey," she said quietly.

He stepped in front of her. When he reached to seize her again, she grabbed a bookend from the table. Books clattered to the floor as she raised the brass pinecone.

"I hope," came a welcome voice from the doorway, "you are going to show off the bookend's excellent craftsmanship, not demonstrate how far you can throw it."

"Lorenzo!" she breathed, lowering the bookend. She set it on the table and pushed past Lord Caldwell to stand beside Lorenzo. When he gave her a quick smile, she wanted to fling her arms around him and thank him for choosing this moment to come to her rescue . . . yet again.

"Mrs. Ditwiller informed me that we had a caller," he said, his tone still even.

She glanced at Lord Caldwell. He still wore that superior smirk, so she guessed he had been bamblusterated by Lorenzo's words and had not noticed how Lorenzo was balanced on the balls of his feet like a boxer about to strike. She almost gasped at the thought. She could not envision

Lorenzo coming to fisticuffs with anyone. His weapons were words, not fists.

"I'm glad she told you, Lorenzo," she said, although she knew she was being as ill-mannered as Lord Caldwell. "I had told her not to bother you."

"She apparently took it upon herself."

When Lorenzo offered his arm, Valeria was grateful to let him draw her hand within it. She forced her feet to match his paces as he led her back into the room and to Lord Caldwell. Wanting to warn Lorenzo not to trust this most untrustworthy man, she remained silent.

"Welcome to Moorsea Manor," he said.

"Thank you." Lord Caldwell shot her a satisfied grin, and she resisted firing back one in return. She knew Lorenzo Wolfe, and he did not.

She glanced again at Lorenzo's face, which suggested every word he had spoken was sincere. Mayhap they had been. Was she the one who was mistaken? After all, she had been so many times before.

"You're quite welcome," Lorenzo answered. "However, I do have a single question."

"Of course. Ask what you wish."

"Who are you?"

"Austin, Lord Caldwell."

Lorenzo smiled. "Ah, the viscount."

"Yes," he replied, his voice abruptly terse.

Valeria dug her nails into her palms to keep from laughing at Lord Caldwell's irritation at having to own that his title was of far less prestige than Lorenzo's. She glanced again from one man to the other. They were of a height, although Lord Caldwell was more muscular. Yet, she did not doubt that Lorenzo would be his match in any battle—of wits or of a bunch of fives.

It must not come to that. All she wanted was for Lord Caldwell to take his leave and never return. The very sight of him reminded her of her brother Paul's despair at having lost everything he owned and everything she possessed as well. She shivered as she pondered, as she tried never to do, if that despair had led directly to Paul's death on that rainy night.

"Sit down, Caldwell," Lorenzo said, motioning toward the chairs by the fireplace. "Valeria, please ring for something to ease our guest's thirst."

"But, Lorenzo—"

He squeezed her hand out of the viscount's view. "I would prefer brandy, and I suspect our guest will as well."

She turned, but not before she saw Lord Caldwell's brows rise at the words *our guest*. The stray, absurd thought that he must be the only man who was unable to raise a single eyebrow shot through her head like the anguish of the headache left in its wake.

"Stay, Valeria," Lord Caldwell ordered.

"Caldwell," Lorenzo said with the same quiet dignity, "I believe you have spoken poorly. Lady Fanning is a lady, not a dog to obey one's orders."

The viscount ran his hand through his blond hair and scowled. "Forgive me. I wish to speak with Valeria alone about some private business."

"Mayhap it would be more appropriate for you to discuss that business with me."

"Why?"

"I am her guardian."

"Guardian?" He laughed. "She is a widow, not a maiden. She has nothing for you to guard."

"I would guard her ears from your crude words to begin with." Lorenzo held out his arm to her. "Valeria, if you will allow me . . ."

Valeria almost put her hand on his arm, then drew it back. Although she knew very little about Lord Caldwell, save for his tarnished reputation, she had heard one rumor she knew was a fact. He was as tenacious as a mud turtle and would not leave until he had accomplished what he came here for.

"Lorenzo, I believe I shall speak with Lord Caldwell for five minutes."

"No more."

She nodded. "It is the least I can do when he has traveled

so far and he has so far to go before he can find a place to shelter him and his horse and men tonight."

Lorenzo's eyes twinkled in amusement with sparks as gold as her gown. Why had she never noticed them before? When they looked past her, she faced Lord Caldwell, who was scowling.

"Very well," Lorenzo said, "you may speak with him for five minutes. That will give time for the carriage to be turned around and pointed back toward the road." He put his hand on her arm. "I shall be across the stairwell in the parlor if you should want me to join the discussion at any point."

"You need not fear for her safety in my company," Lord Caldwell snapped. "I wish only to discuss mutual business with her."

Lorenzo nodded and walked out of the room.

Valeria had to force her feet not to flee after him. Motioning for the viscount to sit, she took the other chair. "I have no idea what business you wish to discuss with me, my lord."

"Your brother's unpaid debts to me, of course."

"There is nothing of value left. Paul lost it all." She clenched her hands in her lap. "With your help."

"But there is something of value left."

Her laugh was cold. "If you came all the way down from London in hopes of finding some trinket that I was able to hide from Paul's creditors, you have wasted your time. You should know, better than anyone else, how cleanly the bones of my family's heritage were picked clean by you and your fellow ravens."

"You give yourself little credit, Valeria."

"I give myself no credit since you offered my brother too much, knowing that he had a weakness for cards and horses and games of chance."

"You still have your adder's tongue, I see."

She came to her feet. "You should not be surprised when it was aimed most often at you and your cohort Lord Lichton. I own to being shortsighted, for I thought the target of your attempt to lure someone to ruin was Charles Talcott.

I saw how my dear bosom-bow Emily worried about the debts her father was amassing. After her sister's successful Season and her marriage, that fear seemed to dissipate. At the time, I should have been more curious why. Now I see the truth. Charles Talcott was no longer your victim of choice. My dear, witless brother Paul was."

"Valeria," he said, setting himself on his feet, "you paint me with evil intentions when I sought no more than a gentleman's entertainments in Town. Can you blame me for having good fortune simply because your brother did not? After all, how many routs did you hold at your town house during which the gentlemen retired from the ladies' company to enjoy a few hours of cards and conversation and some of the excellent vintages you once served?"

"None that you were invited to, as I recall."

"But your brother welcomed me in your house."

"Which he was bacon-brained to do."

He reached under his sedate coat and drew out a slip of paper. "We are wasting time discussing what is in the past when I wish to know your future intentions in dealing with this."

Valeria did not want to take the page, but she did. She stared at it in disbelief. Above her brother's signature was a single number. *£8000!* "I cannot pay this!"

"It is a debt due to me by your brother and his heirs. You are his heir, Valeria. I shall have what is due me. The law is quite clearly on my side in this matter."

"Whether the law is on your side or not matters little, because I cannot pay £8000."

Lord Caldwell stretched a hand out toward her, and she cringed away. When he smiled and tugged on the bellpull, she wanted to claw that superior expression from his face. She started to ask him what he intended, but turned as a maid appeared in the doorway.

"Send for Lord Moorsea," the viscount ordered.

"Are you mad?" Valeria cried. "Lorenzo is not responsible for my family's debts. You cannot intend to dun him for this money."

"I will speak to him of this matter, Valeria. As you have owned that you do not have the means to even this debt, the matter is no longer in your hands."

Footsteps rushed toward the room. Turning expectantly, Valeria gasped when David ran in, something cradled in his hands. "Look at this, Aunt Valeria!"

She wanted to tell David that she had no time to pick through his dirty treasures now, but she stared at what he was carrying. As big as his palm, the almost closed circle with a straight pin across the back was undoubtedly gold, for it glowed like sunshine through its centuries of tarnish. A pair of red stones glittered at the base of the circle, and what appeared to be birds were carved at the top. She guessed it might be a pin to close a lady's gown, for the ornate etching still visible along the circle seemed feminine.

"What do you have there, boy?" asked Lord Caldwell, greed dripping into his voice. "Something of your aunt's, mayhap?"

"It's mine." David stuck the pin in his pocket as he added, "I know you."

"Do you?"

David eyed him up and down and sniffed with disdain. Valeria stared at him. When had he taken up Miss Urquhart's bad habit?

"Yes, I know you," the boy said, clasping his hands behind his back. "You are the man my father said was a dead set cheat at cards like a tuppenny diddler."

"Your father was mistaken about many things."

The wrong tack to take with David, Valeria knew. She bit her lip to keep from telling David to act civilly. Lord Caldwell might as well hear the truth, and it would allow the boy to express some of the anger that tainted his dreams.

"He wasn't wrong about you," her nephew said, jutting his chin at the viscount. "I heard his tie-mates say the same thing."

"Who?" demanded Lord Caldwell.

"Sir—"

"No need to go into that now," Valeria said before David's

forthrightness could get others in trouble with this horrible man. "Why don't you get that pin cleaned up, David, so it might be displayed?"

"Displayed?" Every bit of the viscount's avarice sprang back into the question. "So it is valuable?"

Valeria put out her hand to try to keep him from grabbing it out of David's pocket. The viscount yelped and pulled back, shaking his hand. A pinprick of blood bubbled out of his palm.

She put her hand on David's arm and was not surprised that it was trembling. With just outrage or with fear? "David," she murmured, "go and clean your find."

"Aunt Valeria—"

Kissing him on the cheek, she urged, "Go, so I may complete my discussion with Lord Caldwell."

"All right." He walked toward the door, but glanced back twice.

Only when she was certain David could not hear her did Valeria say, "You are low, my lord, to try to steal from a child."

"If the item has value, I should know. After all, he, too, is an heir to his father's debts."

She sat and folded her hands in her lap, giving him her coolest smile, the one that Lorenzo had learned was a warning that she was no longer willing to be trifled with. "Even if the pin has a value other than reminding you of your manners, my lord, it was found on the property of Moorsea Manor. It belongs to Lorenzo Wolfe, not in any way to you."

"That is correct."

Valeria looked toward the door as she heard a woman's voice. Coming to her feet, she struggled not to groan when Miss Urquhart followed Lorenzo into the book-room. Lorenzo gave her a wry smile, warning that he was not pleased either with his uncle's mistress joining them.

"Miss Urquhart," he said graciously, "this is Lord Caldwell."

"The viscount?" she asked, crinkling her nose.

"Yes." Lorenzo looked at Valeria with the twinkle still in his eyes, but this time she had no inclination to laugh.

The sense of impending doom that had haunted her since she woke this morning had congealed into this moment. What did the viscount intend to say to Lorenzo? She did not like the way he wore that cool, superior smile.

"Caldwell," Lorenzo continued as if they were all the best of friends, "this is Nina Urquhart, a dear friend of the family."

"Miss Urquhart," the viscount said, clearly trying to curb his impatience. His bow toward Miss Urquhart was curt and dismissive.

Which, Valeria knew, was the worst thing he could do. Miss Urquhart refused to be dismissed as unimportant. Biting her lower lip once more to keep from—She was not sure if she might laugh or cry because her emotions were so raw— she watched Miss Urquhart cross the room to the viscount, her cane hitting the floor to emphasize her outrage.

"I knew your father," Miss Urquhart announced and thrust her nose only an inch from Lord Caldwell's. "I trust you aren't as loathsome as he was."

Color rose in the viscount's face, and his words were forced past his tight lips. "He never mentioned meeting you, Miss Urquhart."

"I should think he would not." She chuckled as she sat and spread her unfashionably wide skirt about her. Gripping the top of her cane, she smiled up at him. "He was on the losing side of that duel. 'Twas his good fortune that the man he challenged—Now what was his name?—was as much in his cups as your father customarily was. The shot only nicked your father." She laughed again. "Your father's shot killed one of the horses standing off to the left, as I recall. Apparently he could not tell one horse's rear—"

"What did you wish to discuss with me, Caldwell?" Lorenzo asked, earning a scowl from Miss Urquhart, who was enjoying telling the tale much to the viscount's discomfort.

Caldwell glowered at Miss Urquhart, then raised his chin

and faced Lorenzo. "I believe you stated that you are Valeria's guardian, did you not? Are you still going to abide by that nonsense?"

"To own the truth, you were quite correct before, Caldwell." Lorenzo paid no mind to Valeria's gasp. When Caldwell was about to explain the true reason he had driven across England to intrude on Moorsea Manor and bring that horrible expression of dismay to Valeria's face, Lorenzo could not tease her about the many times they had had a similar conversation in both humor and anger. "She has no need for a guardian. Although my uncle was her guardian, I am her host."

"You are playing with words, Wolfe."

"You are not the first to accuse me of that sport which intrigues me so very much." He smiled and put his foot on a low stool. Crossing his arms in front of him, he waited. Caldwell could barely contain himself. His demands must spew forth any moment, or he would burst.

"I came here to offer Valeria a way to repay the debts her family owes me."

He resisted glancing at Valeria. No wonder her face was the color of unbaked bread dough. Caldwell had the manners of a conveyancer to come here to prey on Valeria who had already lost everything. Keeping his thoughts from his voice, he asked, "And what is this offer?"

Miss Urquhart piped up, "Don't ask for what you don't want to hear, my boy. The Caldwells are a vile lot who have bought their prominence among the Polite World with other folks' money. Some of it stolen outright, the rest just snuck away when they weren't guarding their purses."

The viscount's face became as pasty as Valeria's, then turned a crimson hue that might foretell apoplexy. "Wolfe, I wished to speak to you, not everyone who chooses to wander into this room."

"Then say what you will."

"I wish to speak to *you.*"

Lorenzo glanced at Miss Urquhart, who had put her arm around Valeria. The old woman would help Valeria out of here if he asked. Mayhap. No! He was not going to let Caldwell act as if he were the master of this house. Tapping his foot impatiently on the small stool, so it rocked against the floor, he said, "Then say what you wish. I believe I saw that your carriage was nearly turned about when I passed the window over the stairs."

Caldwell's scowl became even tighter, if possible, at the reminder that his welcome at Moorsea Manor was nearing its end. "I wish to even the debts between Valeria's family and mine."

"So you have said. More than once, I believe."

"What I haven't said is that she can even her family's debts to me by becoming my wife."

"Your wife?" Valeria gasped. Shaking her head, she gave a brittle laugh. "You must have been taken queer in the attic, my lord, to think I would consider such an offer."

"I do not ask you to consider it. I ask you to accept it in lieu of complete ruin."

"I fear you are too late for that, my lord. Ruin arrived for my nephew and me at your hands months ago."

"You have a choice. You may marry me, so that the debt becomes one to myself, or find a way to pay me what your late brother owes me."

"You know I don't have that amount of money."

"What amount?" Lorenzo asked calmly.

"£8000." Caldwell folded his arms in a copy of Lorenzo's pose and tilted his chin again at an angle that just begged for Lorenzo to punch him.

Lorenzo resisted the temptation. "How long will you allow Valeria to consider your offer?"

"Lorenzo!" she cried. "You can't think that I would consider it, do you?"

"I think you have the choice of providing the viscount with his winnings or of marriage." Turning back to Caldwell, he repeated, "How long?"

"I have business in Bath that will require my attention for a fortnight. When I return here, I will accept her acceptance of my offer."

"That seems long enough for her to decide."

"Lorenzo!" Valeria rushed to him and dug her nails into his sleeve so deeply that they pressed against his arm. "Have you gone mad as well?"

"I am being logical about the whole of this." He added to Caldwell, "We will see you in a fortnight."

The viscount gave her a triumphant smile as he walked out of the room.

Miss Urquhart waved her finger at Lorenzo. "How dare you force—"

"You are excused as well, Miss Urquhart, while I speak with Valeria."

Valeria knew Miss Urquhart's appalled expression must be on her own face as well. For the past week, Lorenzo had acted like a stranger. Now he *was* a stranger, giving orders like a medieval lord of the manor, arranging for her to sell herself to settle a debt of cash and honor. When Miss Urquhart left the room, closing the double doors that were always left open, silence claimed the room.

Lorenzo took her by the arm and seated her in the chair where he had seated her the first night they both arrived at Moorsea Manor. She almost laughed as she thought back to that night and what she had thought he might demand in exchange for a roof over her and David's head. She need not have worried. He had no interest in her sharing his bed. All he wished was to be rid of her.

When he placed a glass in her hand and curled her fingers around the stem, she stared at the brandy. She had not even realized he had walked away to pour it.

"Drink up," he ordered. "You need to have your wits about you while we discuss this."

"What is there to discuss? You arranged—again without conferring with me—my future. What have I done to cause you to despise me so much?"

"I don't despise you." He motioned. "Take a drink and calm yourself."

"Why should I when—"

"I have given you an opportunity to put Caldwell out of your life once and for all."

Valeria closed her mouth that must be gaping. When he gestured toward the glass again as he sat, she took a small sip, then a bigger one. The brandy warmed the icy terror in her center.

Lorenzo took a deep breath and released it slowly through his taut lips. "You will not like what I have to say, but I see it as a solution to your problem."

"You want me to persuade Tilden to marry me."

He nodded. "It seems an obvious solution."

"And a convenient one."

"Exactly. It is very convenient that Oates approached me earlier this week to ask permission to ask you to become his wife."

"And you told him?"

A diffident smile eased the strain on his face. "I told him I would speak with you of the matter. I try not to make the same mistake twice, Valeria. I think you should consider this option. If you are married to Oates, you will be protected from Caldwell's machinations."

"True." Yes, that was her own voice speaking as dispassionately as his.

"In addition, David could continue his excavations on the site near the bog which seems to interest him so."

"You wouldn't mind if he came back here?"

"No. Believe it or not, I suspect I shall rather miss the lad."

And me? Will you miss me?

She did not dare to ask him that at that moment or through the rest of the day that followed as she waited for Tilden to respond to the message Lorenzo had sent to him to call at Moorsea Manor. If he told her that he would not miss her, her heart would shatter. Yet, if he told her that he would miss her even a tenth as much as she would miss him, she doubted if she could receive Tilden.

None of them had meant for things to take this turn, but she knew she had spoken honestly. This was the most convenient arrangement for both her and David. Tilden would see that David was given a proper education, and he would see that she had the Seasons in London that she had loved. In return, she would introduce him to the *élite de l'élite* and try to be a good wife.

And Lorenzo would have the serenity that he craved. It was the best solution for all of them.

But, if that were so, why did she fight back tears when Tilden called at Moorsea Manor the next day and got down on one knee to ask her to be his wife?

"Yes," she whispered as he gazed up at her, as handsome as a Greek statue and leaving her heart as lifeless as marble, "I will marry you, Tilden."

Fourteen

"Tell me it isn't true!"

Valeria put down the letter she had been writing to her best friend Emily and looked at David who was wearing what seemed to be a habitual scowl. "If you mean that I'm marrying Tilden, then I cannot tell you it is not true, because it is."

"Why?"

"It is the time for me to marry again."

David sat on the bed so hard it bounced under him, almost tossing him off. "But you don't love him."

"Love is only one ingredient necessary for a satisfactory marriage."

"That's not true."

She stared at him. When had her nephew become such an expert on the topic of love and marriage? By all that's blue, she was certainly no expert herself. A second arranged marriage was her destiny, and she could only pray that this one would turn out as well as her first one. Her eyes were caught by the words she had penned.

> *He is a fine man, Emily, the very sort of man you have long pestered me to leg-shackle myself to instead of a quiet man like Lorenzo. He is agreeable in temperament, not like Lorenzo who can be so moody. His family is welcoming me with open arms, so I need not feel I am a bother as I have been here for Lorenzo. He shares my interest in the Polite World and seems to be highly*

anxious to start breeding racehorses. You know how I enjoy taking a horse for a run, and a ride with Lorenzo has been a leisurely event while we stop to admire the incredible scenery of Exmoor.

Almost every line mentioned Lorenzo by name, and— She scanned the page in astonishment. She had not written Tilden's name once. She balled up the page and tossed it in the basket.

"Aunt Valeria!" David cried impatiently. "How can you marry him if you don't love him? Sleeping Beauty loved the prince who woke her with a kiss. Snow White was the same way. Cinderella wouldn't have married Prince Charming, even if the shoe fit, if she hadn't loved him. How can you?"

"Those are fairy tales." She stood and put the stopper back in the ink bottle. "Real life is different."

"It shouldn't be." He crossed his arms over his chest and glowered at her.

Her breath caught as she caught a glimpse of Lorenzo's stubborn expression on David's face. Even though they were not related by blood, the two had the same recalcitrant nature.

"Mayhap not, but that changes nothing. I'm going to marry Tilden in three weeks."

He threw himself off the bed. "I won't go to that ugly house to live."

"You haven't seen it."

"Gil took me by there last week. It's a boring house, just like all the ones in London. This house is—" He flung out his hands, unable to find a word to describe the manor.

"I thought you hated it here."

"I did, but I don't anymore."

"You'll get accustomed to Oates's Hall, too." She knew she should have more sympathy for the boy, but she could not lower the wall around her heart or all her grief would come spilling out.

He stormed out almost running into Earl who was bringing wood into the room. The old man watched the boy cross the room, then jumped aside as David came back and slammed the door.

"I'm sorry you had to see that," Valeria said as he set the wood by the hearth. "He didn't strike you with the door, did he?"

"If he did, it didn't hurt." Earl's smile disappeared for the first time since she had met him. "My lady, you are looking very sad. Did the boy say something to you?"

"Only the truth."

"And that hurts you so?"

"Yes." She sat at her table again and looked up at him. He was once again carrying his candle, although the hour was not late. She wondered how he managed to tote that and an armload of wood. "Forgive me, Earl. I should not burden you with this."

"These shoulders have carried plenty of burdens over the years. Some were real. Some were ones that I built for myself out of fretting. It did not matter which, because they both ached when I carried them with me." He sat on the edge of the raised hearth. "I hear you are to be congratulated, my lady. I must say I shall miss seeing your smile about Moorsea Manor."

"I shall not be far away."

"But it will never be the same. Your life will be with the baronet, not with Lord Moorsea."

She smiled fleetingly. "My life was never *with* Lorenzo. He tolerated me as a burden he had to shoulder. Now he will be relieved of that."

"Relief may not be the word I would have chosen." He came to his feet and walked toward her. Coolness came from his bark-encrusted clothes, surprising her, for the day beyond the walls was warm. "Are you certain this is what you wish to do?"

"I know it is what I must do."

"That is not the same thing."

"In this case, it must be."

She had thought he would add something more, but he simply nodded and went to the hall door. It closed behind him, then opened again almost at once when a maid came to tell her that Tilden was waiting to take her for a ride. As she gathered her bonnet and spencer, she practiced smiling past her pain. She suspected it was a skill she would need for the rest of her life.

"Valeria?"

She put down the guest list she had been making for Mrs. Oates as Lorenzo peeked past her door. "Yes?"

"Can I steal you from your work for a few moments?"

"Of course." She dropped the list to the table. Mrs. Oates was being exacting in how the wedding would be arranged, and Valeria would have gladly left all details in her hands. That, however, would have suggested that Valeria was not the happy bride everyone must believe she was.

Everyone, but Lorenzo, she realized as she walked with him along the corridor toward the older section of the manor house. He knew the truth. With him, she could be honest, as she had wanted to be for so long. Only one small fact must she keep hidden, for to speak of how her heart beat more fiercely at the sound of his voice was certain to cause complications she could not afford—literally, because otherwise she might be obligated to marry Lord Caldwell.

"Where are we going?" she asked.

He laughed and threw aside the doors to the hall where the bats had attacked them. "What do you think?"

Valeria could only stare, open-mouthed. What had been half ruins was now completely restored. Lost in her concerns about Lord Caldwell and David before that, she had not followed the progress of the workmen here. The change was incredible. Not only had the bats and their droppings been banished, but the windows had been repaired and the painted walls redone to their former magnificence. Two bronze chandeliers which must have come from another room in the house, because there had not been time to have them made and shipped to Moorsea Manor, hung from the highest rafters and could be lit with scores of candles. Beneath them, the stone floor glistened as if with a recent rain, but it was not damp. The stones had been polished to glimmer under the colors cast by the stained glass windows.

"So what do you say?" he asked, taking her hands and drawing her into the room. "Will it do for a ball?"

"A ball? You're agreeing to have a ball here?"

He released her hands and clasped his behind his back as he walked to one of the windows where he could watch the rain falling, hiding the distant curve of the moor. "It is the duty of a guardian to hold a betrothal ball for his ward."

"But you are not really my guardian."

"This argument I shan't miss after you are married."

She stood and edged toward him. Wishing he would face her, she asked, "And what will you miss?"

"Your enthusiasm for life." He turned toward her, and she was astonished that he was smiling. "It is unquestionably infectious, Valeria. I may have inherited this old house and the obligation of bringing it back to its onetime grandeur, but you have brought it life. I do hope I can retain a bit of that when you leave to live in Oates's Hall. You are, of course, welcome to call whenever you wish."

"Except when you are doing your reading."

"Yes, there's that."

"And when you are writing your poetry."

"You know I do not like to be disturbed, especially on those days when the flames of inspiration burn brightly."

"I know."

"You do know, don't you?" He closed the distance between them with a single step, then another.

"Yes." She gazed up into his eyes which were afire with emotion. For his poetry, or did she dare to believe it might be for her? Raising her hand, she brushed it against the sharp angles of his narrow face.

With a groan, he captured her face between his hands. She stared up at him, not daring to move, fearing that even a single breath could ruin this moment that had come to life right out of her dreams. When he brought her mouth toward his, she did not close her eyes. She wanted to savor every sensation of this wonder that she had feared was lost to her forever.

He released her and turned and walked out of the hall. She took a step to follow, then stopped. Lorenzo was being, for once, the sensible one. No matter what yearnings might draw them to each other, she had promised to speak her vows of love and fidelity to another man.

Valeria went to the window where Lorenzo had stood. He was being kind, as always, to offer to host a ball for her here when she knew how he loathed such gatherings. From the moment she had arrived at Moorsea Manor, she had been pleading for the chance to entertain their neighbors. *Their neighbors.* When had this dreary lump of a house become home? When had she begun to think of Lorenzo as a part of her life? When had she begun to want him to stay in her life?

She shook her head. She was being a fool. Lorenzo did not want her and David in his life. He had made that obvious in every possible way, although his generosity had been unparalleled. And Tilden had written to her only this morning, vowing that he would love her more every day of his life. He had agreed to pay off her brother's debts and accept David as if he were Valeria's son. Tilden longed for her to acquaint him with the excitement of a London Season and to help him fire-off his sister, a fact that should please Lorenzo who would not feel obligated to call on Mary. That would give her the opportunity to play hostess to the *ton* once more. And, in London, David would have companions of his own age, not have to depend on a footman for company.

This had been the best choice she could have made, considering all that. So why did it seem so wrong?

Lorenzo collected congratulations as he walked about the ballroom that was aglow with light and conversation and music from the orchestra that had reluctantly come here from Bath. Some of the felicitations were for his inheritance of his title, some for the work he had supervised on bringing Moorsea Manor a bit of its former glory, but most were for how quickly and conveniently he managed to deal with the problem of his late uncle's ward. A convenient arrangement had been his plan from the beginning, and he had fulfilled that goal with an efficiency and dedication to detail that deserved congratulations.

Valeria was receiving the same congratulations, he noted as she stood with Tilden and his mother at the entrance to the room. In her elegant, brocaded gauze gown of the palest cream, she was undoubtedly the pink of the *ton*. Its modest bodice was decorated with ruffles that emphasized her gentle curves and matched the flounces on her sleeves. Netting dropped over the skirt to the embroidery on the vandyked hem. She had dispensed with the bright colored paisley shawl, but wore a large hat with a quartet of plumes that flowed over its top and had been dyed the same purple as her eyes.

Her clothing caught the attention of each of the guests she was greeting. They would be coming to Oates's Hall next week for the wedding party after the ceremony in Winlock-on-Sea. Oates's Hall had no chapel, and Mrs. Oates insisted that she would not have her only son married in the dusty ruins of the one here at Moorsea Manor.

"Be wary of that one," Mrs. Oates murmured as Valeria turned to welcome yet another guest. "She is eager to advance herself socially."

Valeria smiled as she had each time her future mother-in-law made a similar disparaging comment. If she were to believe Mrs. Oates, half of the guests were here only to see how they could turn this marriage to their own advantage. She was relieved when the dancing began, and she could go with Tilden out to the middle of the floor and enjoy the music.

"My lady," a maid said as the second set of country

dances began. "Forgive me for intruding, but I have been asked if you might speak in private to one of your guests."

"About what?"

"I believe he wishes to congratulate you in private."

Valeria's heart did a somersault as she scanned the room and did not see Lorenzo. She was quite mad, she knew, but she could only hope he was the one who had sent the maid to her. *But she would have said my lord.* She ignored the voice of common sense. She had been sensible for too long, doing as her guardian had suggested, buckling under when confronted with her brother's moonshine because she did not want David's name ruined along with his father's, trying to change to fit into Lorenzo's life to insure them a home. She wanted to be want-witted tonight, throwing aside caution and her arms around him.

Just one kiss to take with her as a memory into her marriage, one kiss that would warm her when she was on the other side of the moors. She must be addled, but, for once, she did not care.

"Will you excuse me, Tilden?" she asked. "I shan't be long."

He squeezed her hands. "I hope not. I was just telling James here about the new breed of horses I've heard about in America and how we'll be sure to see them when we go there for our honeymoon."

"We are going to America for our honeymoon?"

The other man looked uncomfortable, but Tilden merely smiled. "I had thought I had mentioned it. No matter. You know now, so you can make your plans."

"I had thought there would be a discussion of our plans before a decision was made."

When James slipped away into the crowd, Tilden's smile became a dismayed frown. "There was a discussion. You need only ask Mary or Mother if you choose not to believe me."

"I didn't mean to suggest that I did not believe you. I had thought you would discuss our honeymoon plans with *me.*"

"Mother thought it would be better if it were a surprise."
He sighed. "And I have ruined that surprise, haven't I? Oh,
well, now you can talk to Mother and Mary about where the
three of you want to visit first."

"Your mother and sister are joining us on the trip?"

"Certainly." He grinned, and his handsome face lit up like
one of the chandeliers. "And don't worry about the boy—
Danny?"

"David." She clenched her hands by her side.

"Don't worry about him. I've already arranged for him to
go to school before the term begins."

"School?"

"Mother said it would be for the best as we will be gone
for so long."

"How long?"

"No more than a year, I suspect."

"You want me to leave David alone for a year?"

He smiled. "He shan't be alone at school. In addition,
Mother believes you are spoiling the boy with all your attention to him."

"Does she?" She dared say no more.

"She *is* more experienced in these matters, Valeria, as the
mother of two. You would be wise to heed her as I always
do."

Before she could no longer control her temper, she excused herself to speak with her guest who was waiting for
her. Why had she never seen how Tilden catered to his
mother's wishes? The answer was simple. She had not spent
enough time with him or his family before she agreed to be
his wife. Now it was too late to back out of the marriage.
Even if she could, she would have no choice but to marry
Lord Caldwell. She did not have £8000.

Valeria faltered in midstep when she saw who was standing at the top of the stairs. Lord Caldwell had leapt from
her fears back into her life. But why was he here? Not to
congratulate her, she was sure, even though she had sent him
a note telling him of her plans to marry Tilden. A quiver
cramped her at the thought of her desperate agreement to

marry Tilden. No, she would not think of that now. She had to discover why Lord Caldwell was here and convince him to take his leave immediately.

Lord Caldwell threw his cape back over his shoulder and glowered at her. "So how did you convince Moorsea to host a party amid this musty pile of stones? I hope it was not by warming his bed when you should be in mine."

Her hand struck his cheek. When he recoiled, she hissed, "Don't ever say something like that to me again! Get out of here!"

"Not without you."

"I'm not going with you." She pointed to the door at the bottom of the stairs. "Begone."

"My money—"

"Has been delivered to your solicitor's office."

He grasped her arm and pulled her into a nearby room. "What do you mean? You have no money."

"But my fiancé does."

"Fiancé? Moorsea? Don't think you can bamboozle me. What money he got with these dirty acres is already committed to fixing up the house."

Valeria wanted to ask how he was privy to such information, but tried to free her arm. When he would not release her, she said, "I see you did not trouble yourself to read my missive to you."

"What missive?"

"The one explaining that I am betrothed to Sir Tilden Oates. His pockets are plump enough to satisfy my brother's debts to you."

"You will regret this decision, Valeria."

"I would have regretted knuckling under to your ludicrous demands far more, my lord." She yanked her arm away from him. "Do not let me delay you from taking your leave."

Lord Caldwell raised his hand, but froze as he stared past her. With a curse, he lowered it again. "This is not over, Valeria." He gave her no chance to retort as he stormed out of the room.

Valeria looked at the door on the other side of the room—

the door the viscount had been facing. She was not surprised to see Lorenzo standing there.

Never had he looked more handsome, although he could not compare with Tilden's perfect looks. He wore his black evening coat over a light blue satin waistcoat and white breeches. Yet, she barely took note that, for once, he was in prime twig. Instead, she found herself caught by his gaze. Shy he might be, but mayhap that was simply because he feared releasing the strong passions that seared her. Tonight, he appeared to deserve his family's name, for, like a wolf, he possessed an aura of power and potential peril for anyone foolish enough to defy him.

The fury that tightened his face resonated through his voice as he said, "I came here as soon as I heard Caldwell had been allowed into Moorsea Manor. Are you all right, Valeria?"

"I think I shall be." She wanted to rush to him and have his arms envelop her. She wanted to tell him that she was so grateful to him for always being here when she needed him, that she did not want to leave Moorsea Manor and him, that her dreams of the future no longer centered on her return to the whirl of the Season and the chatter of the *ton*. Her dreams were of loving him and the life they could have together. No, there was no life for them together, but that did not change the fact that, want-witted as it might be, she had fallen in love with him.

"He shan't bother you again. He knows he has lost this gamble to win your hand in marriage."

"I wish I could believe that."

"He will not linger here long when he has other prey with plump pockets waiting for him in London."

Valeria flinched. Lorenzo's words reminded her of Lord Caldwell's. "He suggested that you were destitute, save for this house. If I had known that, I would not have asked you to take care of David and me."

"Taking care of you and David has been my pleasure." He offered his arm. "And don't fret. Caldwell has his facts essentially correct, but I'm not ready to don a green bonnet and put the key beneath the door yet. My uncle's investments were not always wise. However, I hope my decisions will turn that around."

"I didn't know." She glanced toward the ballroom. "You spent so much to give me this evening. I am even more grateful."

"Then prove it by risking your toes."

"My toes?"

He smiled. "Will you stand up with me?"

"You're asking me to dance? I didn't know you danced, Lorenzo."

"I have tried to avoid dancing as with anything I do poorly." Lorenzo's smile broadened as he looked over her head at the sound of a door slamming below. He would have to be sure that Caldwell did not return to cause more mischief. But first . . . "However, I have been told by several well-meaning matrons that you and I should dance before the official announcement of your betrothal to Oates is made."

"By well-meaning matrons, I assume you mean Miss Urquhart," she said with a smile that reached inside him and sent pinwheels twirling through his stomach.

"She is the most adamant among those kind ladies who have decided it is their place to remind me of mine." He held out his hand. "So will you dance with me, Valeria?"

When she breathed yes, he swept her against him. Her eyes widened, and he laughed.

"I thought you meant in the ballroom," she whispered as a waltz lilted along the hallway.

"Here," he said as quietly, "I chance only stepping on your toes, not everyone's in the room."

Her laugh was as lyrical as the music. Putting her hand in his, she leaned her head on his shoulder, shocking him. Surely propriety did not allow such intimacy. He forgot the canons of society as she had while he let the music guide his feet. The sensation of her so close, matching each step as if they had danced like this a thousand times before, was intoxicating, but his feet were nimble. Could his cousin

Corey have been right when he said that with the right
woman Lorenzo would not feel awkward? With the right
woman in his arms, Corey had told him, dancing would be
easier than breathing. That must be so, because he was dancing and he was finding it difficult to breathe when Valeria's
soft form was in his arms.

"You are an excellent dancer," she murmured. "I think
you are doing yourself and the other ladies a great disfavor
by lingering at the side of the room."

"And you are being too kind. My usual pattern is a trip
and a step on my partner's toes and another stumble."

She smiled up at him, and his heart thundered in his ears,
drowning out the orchestra's music. Yet his feet continued
moving as if the melody was a part of him and of Valeria,
curling around them, molding them together until each motion belonged inseparably to both of them.

"You haven't asked me what I shall miss most about
Moorsea Manor," she whispered.

"What?"

"I believe, I shall miss your sardonic sense of humor most
of all."

"Really?" He was unsure if he could say more than a
single word as she spoke so easily of leaving Moorsea Manor
to go live with Oates as his wife.

"Yes, really. It drove me almost to madness when we first
met. I never was sure when you were hoaxing me and when
you were serious."

"I have told you. I am always serious."

She laughed so brightly that heads in the doorway turned
toward them. "Lorenzo, that is the funniest statement of all.
At first, you convinced me to believe that, but you know as
well as I that is not so."

"No?" Did she have any idea how her eyes glistened with
purple starlight each time she laughed? "Valeria, I may regret
saying this, but—"

A scream rang from the ballroom.

Fifteen

The scream hung amid a discordant note as the orchestra froze along with the guests. Valeria pushed into the ballroom. If Lord Caldwell thought he could ruin tonight, she would show him he was sadly mistaken.

She scanned the room. He was not here. Then what was going on?

Mary Oates shrieked as she rushed across the room. She pointed back at the window, crying out something that Valeria could not understand. Reaching out to halt the terrified woman, Valeria was knocked backward as Mary ran toward Lorenzo and collapsed in a swoon.

He caught her before she could strike the floor and, putting an arm beneath her knees, lifted her up against his chest. "Oates, where are you?"

Valeria stepped aside before the baronet could run her down in the midst of this anxiety for his sister. She stood to one side while she watched Lorenzo hand the senseless Mary to her brother. When Tilden's knees almost buckled, she stared at Lorenzo. His strong heart and unabashed wit were not the only strengths he hid.

Another scream ricocheted through the room, and Valeria turned to see Mrs. Oates falling to the floor. Miss Urquhart rushed to her side and called out, "Burn some feathers! This woman is suffering from the vapors."

"Is this your idea of a jest, Moorsea?"

She spun when she realized the furious words had been

spoken by her betrothed. "Tilden! Lorenzo would not do anything to hurt your sister or mother. Why—"

"Look!" shouted a man near one of the windows. "There it is again!"

"There is what?" Lorenzo's long legs crossed the ballroom floor with ease, and Valeria hurried after him.

The man pointed. "Look! There, by the shrubs."

Behind her, she heard a prayer and a screech and a thud as a maid crumpled to the floor. Valeria motioned for one of the footmen to tend to the girl, then tried to see past the people in front of her. Even her height was no help, because she was sure every man in the room had crowded in front of the window.

Tossing aside her manners, she elbowed her way through them. Her arm was grabbed, and she started to shake the hand off, then realized it was Lorenzo trying to help her through the press of the guests who were unwilling to give way. He tugged her forward around a man who was gasping as if he had run from London.

She pressed her hands to the glass and stared. It *was* a ghost! Just as the serving maids had been babbling about for the past month. No! She did not believe in ghosts. Lorenzo was right. They were just the product of moonlight and moonshine minds.

"It's a ghost," choked a woman beside her.

She wanted to retort with, "Nonsense!" Her voice was clogged in her throat as she stared at what looked to be an ancient warrior. His breastplate gleamed in the moonlight as if it had a life of its own. A grotesque mimicry of a man's face glowed as well, and something came out of its head, shining as if it was lit from beneath.

Another woman swooned against Valeria. She caught the woman and lowered her to the floor, calling for *sal volatile*. She hoped the horrified guests would let a footman through to the woman.

Standing, she asked, "Lorenzo, what do you think—?"

He had vanished. Irrational fear clutched her. A ghost was here, and Lorenzo had disappeared. She shook the terror aside and pushed her way back through the crowd. They did not halt her.

"A ghost! It's a ghost," cried someone else behind her.

Valeria raised her voice. "I assure you it's not another ghost."

Tilden crossed the room to her, his eyes so wide that she thought they would burst from his face. *"Another ghost?* Do you mean there have been others lately here in Moorsea Manor? You let me bring my mother and sister here knowing that?"

"Don't be silly. Someone is enacting a heinous prank tonight."

"But who would do such a thing? My mother has swooned, and Mary . . ." He shook his head in despair.

Valeria did not bother to demur. "I can give you two guesses. Either Lord Caldwell or my nephew."

"Caldwell? He's mixed up in this?" He raced away as his mother moaned his name from the other side of the room.

She stared after him. He had not asked if she was all right. All his thoughts had been concentrated on his mother and sister. If he acted this way tonight, how would he be after they were married?

No, she would not think of that now. She needed to find Lorenzo and discover who was frightening the guests. Gathering up the cream tissue of her gown, she rushed toward the door.

"It's gone!" she heard from by the window.

She left the guests to speculate on what they had seen as she hurried out into the hall. It was empty, because everyone, guest as well as servant, had crowded around the windows to peer out at the so-called ghost.

Not sure which way to go, she went toward the stairs that would lead down to the door closest to the part of the garden beneath the ballroom windows. She paused only long enough to get a candle to light her way. Hearing a door slam and angry voices, she took the stairs as quickly as she dared. She thought the lower corridor was deserted, too, until she saw two forms coming toward her. Fear tempted her, but she refused to heed it.

"Valeria?" she heard.

"Lorenzo!" She set the candle on a nearby table and ran to him. Throwing her arms around him, she cried, "Why didn't you tell me where you were going?"

He stroked her back gently, but fury honed his voice, "Because I wanted to capture this young rapscallion before the rest of our guests dropped senseless on the floor."

She drew back and stared at an amazing sight. The footman Gil was dressed in what appeared to be a shield. A feather was stuck in his hair, and something was painted across his face. Before she could discern what, Lorenzo ran his finger along the lad's face and held it up away from the light. It glowed like the ghost had in the garden.

"Our ghost," he said. "The phosphorescence—"

"The what?"

"The glow comes from the bogs on the moor. You must have seen the lights near the ground some nights."

She shook her head. "I keep my curtains drawn at night."

"I wish we had in the ballroom tonight." His tone became sharp again as he turned to Gil. "You should be ashamed of yourself. I should turn you off right now."

"I understand, my lord. I'm sorry that some of the ladies were so scared. We didn't—"

"We?"

"David was supposed to meet me here to help with the jest." Gil looked everywhere but at Lorenzo.

"So you decided to frighten the ladies nearly to death without his assistance?"

"Didn't mean to hurt anyone. David and me, when he found this stuff from the bogs glows, we just wanted to make folks laugh." His face lengthened as he sighed. "After all, you didn't ever believe we were really ghosts before."

"It was you before?" Valeria asked.

"Yes, my lady."

"Mayhap Lord Moorsea didn't believe you were real

ghosts," she replied, "but a good portion of the household staff did."

His chin rose in defiance. "Serves them right for treating us from Wolfe Abbey like we carried the plague."

She sighed. So many times she had asked Mrs. Ditwiller how tasks and responsibilities were intertwining between the two staffs, and each time Mrs. Ditwiller had assured her that all would come about as it should and not to concern herself.

"We will speak more on this tomorrow." Lorenzo frowned. "Where is the boy?"

"David?" Gil asked. "Like I said, he was supposed to meet me in the garden." He rapped his knuckles against the plate over his chest. "He dug this up and said it was really old, so I should wear it tonight. I waited for him, but he never showed up."

"I'll have the house searched," Lorenzo said before Valeria could speak. He gave her a swift smile. "We'll find him. By now, we have discovered most of his hiding places. Gil, find some men and begin the search. Let Kirby know we need his help. And Gil?"

"Yes, my lord?" The footman turned.

"Keep what you're doing quiet. I don't want Lady Fanning's guests more disturbed by this."

"Yes, my lord." He raced away, pulling off the breastplate as he ran.

Lorenzo smiled again at her. "It will turn up trumps, Valeria. Don't worry."

"I'll try not to." She picked up the candle. "Let me go and tell the guests about our ghost so their minds are put at ease."

He curved his hand along her face. "You are extraordinary in a crisis, Valeria."

"One learns to be, when one is surrounded by all the skimble-skamble of the Season." She wanted to ask him what he had been about to tell her when the screams began, but that must wait. She went back up the stairs to the ballroom. She steeled herself for the anger which was sure to meet her explanation, especially from Tilden.

Valeria found that her trepidation had been valid, save for her betrothed. He sat beside his mother and his sister, who were stretched out on two benches in the ballroom. While the other guests took their leave and Valeria hoped her letters of apology, which she must write the first thing in the morning, would ease the outrage, Tilden did not look in her direction. He held his sister's hand for a moment before taking his mother's and patting it consolingly. Her single attempt to ask how they were doing was met with stiff silence.

By the time the last guests, save for the Oates family had taken their leave, the clock in the hallway was clanging eleven o'clock. It had been over two hours since the ghost had been sighted in the garden.

She left Tilden with his family and the musicians who were milling about the room and sampling the food that had been ignored. Before she had gone a dozen steps along the hall, Lorenzo rushed toward her.

"You've found him?" she asked.

"Not yet."

"Not yet?"

When he gripped her arms, she feared she was going to succumb to vapors as the women had in the ballroom. The world tilted, and she gasped before she realized that Lorenzo was gathering her up in his arms. Again she rested her head on his shoulder, wishing she could delight in this closeness as she had when they danced. She would have gladly stayed here cradled in his arms forever, but she must think of David.

"Where have you looked?" she asked as Lorenzo set her down on something soft. With a gasp, she realized it was the bed behind the bookshelves in the library.

He sat on its edge and chafed her wrists, bringing feeling back into her numb fingers. "Everywhere that I could think of. I told Kirby to have the men search everywhere else, especially the old wall that has fascinated David since you arrived. Gil is certain that David would not go out on the moors alone at night."

"He knows better than that." Wanting to relax back against the pillows, she sat straighter. "Lorenzo, what if he has—?"

"Let's not consider more disasters than we have. I assume all your guests have taken their leave."

"Save for Tilden and his mother and sister."

He stood. "If you would as lief be with them, I—"

"Do not trouble yourself on my behalf. Tilden hasn't." She raised her gaze past his dust-covered coat to his sorrowful face. "I never will be a part of that family, no matter what I do."

"And being a part of a family is important to you?"

She gulped back a clump of tears that filled her throat. "I have always wanted to be a part of a family, but each time I think I may be, something happens to destroy that. Lorenzo, what if—?"

He put his finger to her lips. "Gil and Kirby will find David. They always have in the past."

"But he never failed to meet Gil to arrange a prank before." She slid off the bed and paced to the door and back. "I should have . . ."

"Should have what? Valeria, it has become more than obvious that David has been having a wonderful time bamblusterating all of us to his heart's delight. He has been learning a lot about the Roman settlements in this area from me and has spent as much time as possible digging like a collier."

"I should have made certain he attended the party tonight. He is so angry about being sent to Oates's Hall when he has not finished inspecting every inch of Moorsea Manor. When he discovers that Tilden intends to package him off to school as soon as we are wed, he—I—" She hid her face in her hands and sobbed.

"Don't weep, my dear."

"I can't help it. When I think of him lost in some bog or hurt in the shadow of a hedgerow, I . . . I . . ."

When he put his arms around her, she pressed her face against his waistcoat. Gripping the satin, she let her tears fall. She could not be false any longer. She was scared and unhappy and utterly miserable. Her last words to her brother when he was brought back to her house near death had been that she would watch out for David until he was grown. Now he was missing.

A single finger under her chin drew back her head, and she stared up into Lorenzo's eyes which were so close to hers. He did not speak. She could not as his eyes came even closer. Her eyes closed when his lips brushed hers, as gentle as a brother's. She was not fooled, for there was a strange tension about him, about her, a tension of standing on a precipice and deciding whether to turn back or leap into the mists beyond.

She did not hesitate. Sweeping her hand up through his thick hair, she brought his mouth back to hers. His arms tightened around her, crushing her to him as he explored her lips with slow, deep strokes. When she gasped, surprised and delighted at the pleasure soaring through her, his tongue delved into her mouth, teasing her with its bold touch. She splayed her fingers across his back as he pressed her back onto the bed, holding there with the length of his body so that every ragged, eager breath was a separate, unbearably enticing caress. Her other hand curled around his nape as his lips wove a silken path along her face and across her throat. When his uneven breath warmed her ear, she trembled, and her hands clutched more tightly to his coat.

He found her lips with the ease of the fulfillment of a beloved fantasy come true. And it was. She had dreamed of this since she first had jested with him about needing to consider finding a wife for himself and he had kissed her on the cheek. That had been a shock. This was something absolutely different, satisfaction and longing for so much more all at once.

"What in the blazes—?"

Valeria came to her feet and stared at Tilden who stood at the end of the bookcase.

Sixteen

Lorenzo's arms did not release Valeria as Tilden crossed the room in a pair of steps. With a tug that Valeria feared would rip her arm right out of her shoulder, he pulled her away from Lorenzo.

"Moorsea, what are you doing with my future wife?"

"You know less about women than I do if you cannot see for yourself," Lorenzo replied with a coolness that Valeria had never heard in his voice.

Tilden reached under his coat and pulled out his evening glove. As he raised it, Valeria grasped his arm.

"Don't be a beef-head." When her voice quivered as she had in Lorenzo's arms, she saw Tilden's mouth work. She did not give him a chance to spout his anger. "Tilden, this is not the time for discussing anything but finding David."

"So that is why you two weren't talking?"

"Don't be absurd!"

Lorenzo put his hand on her arm and stepped between her and the irate baronet. "Oates, Valeria is correct. Discuss this we must, but not now. Can we count on you to help us find the boy?"

"Yes, you can," answered a higher pitched voice from by the bookshelves. Mary came around them and stared at the bed. She gulped, turned an unhealthy shade of red, but said, "Lord Moorsea, your footman is seeking you."

"Gil?"

"The young, long-legged one."

He nodded with a tight smile. "That's Gil. If you will excuse me."

"I have so far," Tilden grumbled.

"Valeria?" Lorenzo held out his hand.

She looked from him to her fiancé who was turning the glove over and over in his hand.

"Go with him," Tilden said stiffly, "and our betrothal is finished."

"You have no need for a wife now," she answered with a smile she hoped would beg his forgiveness as she reached for Lorenzo's hand. "I'm needed here."

"By Moorsea?" He laughed. "What need does he have for a wife when all he thinks of are his silly poems and his dirty relics?"

"That is not all I think of," Lorenzo said as he folded her hand in his, "as you should know from what you unfortunately intruded upon, Oates. Lady Fanning and I bid you a good evening and a good-bye. The pressing matter of her nephew's whereabouts may even now be resolved."

"Valeria—"

"Good-bye, Tilden," she said as she walked out of the library with Lorenzo.

When she trembled, Lorenzo whispered, "Don't worry. He'll be fine."

She was so pleased that he understood that she was more worried about David than her reputation which would be devastated as soon as what Tilden had seen was repeated through the *ton*. "How can he be fine? Without Tilden to buy off Lord Caldwell with his £8000, I don't know what we'll do."

"One problem at a time. Let's find out what Gil has to tell us."

When she nodded, Lorenzo gave her a bolstering smile. She could not return it, not until she was certain David was safe.

Gil ran up to them as they reached the stairs. "My lord, this was just delivered." He hesitated, then added, "For Lady Fanning."

She took the folded page that had been sealed with a crest

she did not recognize. She had not expected to receive a chiding message from one of her guests until the morrow.

"Gil, what about David? Have you found him?"

"No, my lady. This note—"

"Can wait. Where have you looked?"

"Everywhere, my lady. This note—"

"Lorenzo, how about the area beyond where the roof had collapsed in the old section?"

He shook his head. "It's been sealed for the past fortnight. I checked it myself."

Gil said, "My lady, if you will read the note—"

"Later!" She waved him to silence. "David was bored with the attics weeks ago. How about the cellars? He mentioned something about a room down there that he called a dungeon. Could he have gotten himself locked in there?"

"I can have it checked." He looked past her, and she saw Tilden Oates escorting his outraged sister and horrified mother out of the house. "Don't think about them now, Valeria."

"I know. David! Where could he be?"

"Why not read the note?" asked Gil. "The lad who delivered it said you would want to read it right away because young David's time might be short otherwise."

Valeria gasped as she ripped open the note. She did not waste time berating Gil for not telling her this before. The poor footman had tried. She had not listened, and now . . .

Valeria,

If you are looking for your spoiled nephew, I suggest you come to meet me at the bridge near the horseshoe turn leading down into Winlock-on-Sea. We will work out the terms for his release then. You have until midnight to meet me alone. Otherwise, my patience with this child will come to an end along with him.

It was signed Austin, Lord Caldwell, but she did not need to see the signature. Handing the note to Lorenzo, she looked at the clock. The minute hand had already begun its upward turn.

Lorenzo grasped her hand and shouted, "Gil, have the carriage brought at once."

"You can't come with me!" she cried. "Lord Caldwell said I must come alone."

"He is a high and mighty looby, if he thinks you will agree to such terms."

"But we have to protect David."

"Go and change into something dark. I think I have an idea that might be just the ticket to convince one arrogant viscount to give up his new habit of kidnaping."

"What is it?"

He smiled. "Change, and I'll explain on the way."

Lord Caldwell pulled his pocket watch from his waistcoat and peered at it. He swore and walked back to where his carriage waited in the shadows. Ignoring the thumping sounds from within, for the boy had not tired of trying to escape even though he had been tied up in the closed carriage for hours, he scanned the road. Mayhap he had miscalculated. Valeria might care no more about her nephew than her brother had cared about her when he sat at the card table and hoped that luck would come his way one more time.

He heard a crash behind him and whirled, pulling the pistol that he had hidden beneath his coat. He cursed again when he saw the door to the carriage was open wide. On the road, the bundled boy was fighting his bounds. Hearing a laugh from his coachman and the two men he had hired to help him tonight, he turned back to look along the road.

Slipping the pistol away, he noticed how his hands were shaking. Why hadn't Valeria just given in? He had thought she would be as weak as Paul Blair who had wisely ended his miserable life in that carriage accident.

He gave a shout to his coachman and the other men as he saw the flash of a lantern through the trees. This must be Valeria coming to rescue her nephew. No one else had traveled along this deserted road in the past hour. Hearing the rattle of carriage wheels on the uneven road, he smiled as he walked over to stand by the struggling boy.

With a signal to his men to be prepared, he crossed his arms in front of him, keeping one hand on the pistol under his coat. He put his foot on the lad and heard a mumbled oath shot at him. He smiled. Finally he was going to get his due from the Blair family.

His smile faded as the carriage stopped the length of a four-in-hand down the road and two people emerged. Dash it! Didn't Valeria understand that she was to come alone? He squared his shoulders as he realized she was coming with that pluckless fool Moorsea. He would have finished this at Moorsea Manor, but Moorsea's intrusion had reminded him of the many ears ready to eavesdrop on the confrontation. It was much better here where there were fewer witnesses. No matter what happened, his men would swear any vow he asked of them as long as he kept their palms bright with gold.

He grinned again as Moorsea offered Valeria his arm. Why had she come here with him instead of her fiancé? If she had brought Oates, there might have been a problem. Now . . . He chuckled with satisfaction.

Valeria's hand clenched on Lorenzo's arm as she heard Lord Caldwell's laugh. She flinched as she saw something move on the ground beside him, then gasped.

"Lorenzo, he's got David all trussed up," she whispered as they strolled toward the other carriage as if nothing were amiss. "That son of a sow has gone too far."

He patted her hand. "Hush. Having David safely secured in one place may be for the best right now, and we can keep an eye on him."

She glanced up at him. What she had mistaken for shyness was quiet resolve and self-assuredness that not even Lord Caldwell's villainy could undo. Only on one matter had she been right about Lorenzo Wolfe. He had depths that would endlessly surprise and delight her.

"Caldwell!" he called. "We are here as you requested."

The viscount sneered, "I asked Valeria to come alone."

"You have less respect for the lady than I had guessed if you would ask her to drive out alone in the middle of the night."

"Do nothing out of hand, Moorsea. I have three men who will stop any attempt you make at heroics."

"That is not what I intended." He stepped back and smiled at Valeria. "I am only escorting Lady Fanning here to free her nephew from your asinine attempts to intimidate her."

Valeria kept her head high as she edged forward a step, wishing Lorenzo had stayed next to her. He could not, not if they hoped for his plan to save both David and her. She saw the guns in the hands of the men on the carriage, and she suspected Lord Caldwell was armed as well. "This is a very odd way to court a lady, my lord."

"I have no need to court you, Valeria. I have your brother's agreement that you will marry me."

"My brother is dead for months now."

"His obligations did not die with him. He—" He yelped when David rolled out from under him, and his foot fell heavily to the road. Shifting, he put his boot on the boy's side again.

"Why don't you release David so we may discuss this rationally?"

"If I release the boy, you will scurry away like the frightened, cheating rabbits all you Blairs are."

"Cheating?" She laughed and saw his amazement. "My lord, if my brother had cheated at cards, he cheated only himself and his family. Mayhap you have confused his crimes with your own."

His voice came out in an incoherent growl, and Lorenzo whispered, "Do not push him too far. Not yet."

Valeria nodded, scanning the darkness around them. She hoped Lorenzo could see more than she.

Lord Caldwell snarled, "This has gone on long enough. Come with me, Valeria. I will give your nephew to Moorsea, because I have no wish for the little devil in my life."

"Neither David nor I will go with you." She opened her reticule and held out a slip of paper. "This acknowledges that £8000 will be delivered to your solicitor by month's end."

He knocked it out of her hand. "That is worthless. You don't have the money to even your brother's debts."

"I will by month's end."

"How?"

"That is none of your bread-and-butter." She would not reveal that Lorenzo had offered to sell some of his uncle's antiquities to Mr. Pettit to obtain her the money she needed. The thought of his generous offer strengthened her. "You will have your money, so return my nephew to me."

" 'Tis not only money that your brother owed me."

Her eyes widened. "But you asked only about—"

"Because I never guessed you would be able to obtain the money to repay your brother's financial debts to me. There is still the matter of the other chit he signed before he ended his miserable life."

Valeria took a step forward as David squirmed on the ground, mumbling something at the insult to his father. She froze when Lord Caldwell pulled something from under his coat. Seeing the slip of paper he held, she dared to breathe.

"Your brother signed this," Lord Caldwell said, "the last time we sat at the board of green cloth together. He had run out of funds, and the only way I would accept his signature on a debt was if he would agree to arrange my marriage to you, as your guardian refused—"

"You asked my uncle to marry her?" Lorenzo asked.

The viscount scowled. "Before she wed Fanning. The old goat refused, and I vowed then that, one day, Valeria, you would be my wife. No one makes me look like a ninnyhammer."

"No," he replied, "you seem to have accomplished that all by yourself."

Valeria almost laughed, although she never had felt less like laughing. Lorenzo wielded words like a knight's lance.

Her urge to laugh disappeared when Lord Caldwell turned his furious stare back on her.

"The facts are the facts. After your husband's death, I approached your brother. He said no as well until I persuaded him to agree to arrange your marriage to me if he lost. He lost that hand and then his life before he could do as he promised."

"That's absurd! I shall not marry you simply because of the turn of a card."

"It is a debt your brother owed me, and now you must even it."

"But why do you want to marry me? We have seldom met before this."

He scowled. "That is why. You are a part of the Polite World that would never allow me admittance because I lived in the shadow of my family's reputation. With you as my wife, I shall be able to thumb my nose at those who refused to open their doors to me." His laugh was bitter. "Including you, for you shall keep no door closed to me when we are man and wife."

Trying not to let him see her shudder of distaste, she said, "Marrying me shall not gain you admittance to the homes of the tulips of fashion. You miscalculated by ruining me first."

"You will be welcomed by those whom you have befriended in the past, and so will I."

"Do not be so certain of that."

"Enough of this pointless discussion. You have no choice, Valeria. If you wish to get your nephew back, you shall——"

A shout came from the top of the carriage. One of the men pointed along the road. With a gasp, Valeria stared at the twin of the apparent ghost that had appeared in the garden. This was not part of Lorenzo's plan. Or was it? When she heard his oath, she knew he was as shocked as she was. A horrifying howl erupted from the glowing ghost.

Lorenzo grabbed Valeria and pushed her back toward his carriage as Lord Caldwell shrieked. Water cascaded over the viscount, and he fell flat onto his face as he tried to reach his own carriage.

She cried out, "David!"

Looking back at Lord Caldwell's carriage, Valeria chuckled as more filthy water cascaded down on the men around it. They were blinded by the water, just as Lorenzo had planned, and did not see a shadowed form glide toward David or the flash of a honed knife.

David jumped to his feet and ran to her, loosened ropes hanging from him like discarded chains. She picked him up and tossed him into the carriage while the branches in the trees over Lord Caldwell's carriage shook as if giant squirrels scurried through them. Empty buckets struck the carriage before swift shadows raced away around the corner and toward Moorsea Manor. For the first time, Lorenzo's servants and his new household had worked in perfect unison.

Lorenzo held out his hand to help her into the carriage, but she heard Lord Caldwell shout, "Stop!"

Tossed almost as inelegantly into the carriage as David had been, Valeria pulled the door closed when Lorenzo was within. The carriage rocked wildly as it started up the rough road.

Lorenzo patted David on the shoulder. "See? I can learn from you, too."

The boy grinned. "I—"

A gun fired, then another.

Pushing them toward the floor, Lorenzo gasped, "The man is completely insane!"

The carriage halted along with Valeria's heart for a single beat. Had the shots hit the coachee? The door was thrown open, and she saw the driver's horrified face.

"He shot her, my lord!" he shouted.

"Her?" Valeria asked, but Lorenzo had already jumped out of the carriage. She followed and bit back her cry when she saw a crumpled form on the ground.

A glow came from the front of the breastplate, save for a dark spot that was spreading across it. She dropped to her knees and clasped the hand held out to her.

"Miss Urquhart!" she moaned. "Why did you come after us?"

"Thought you might need some help. Don't trust any of those Caldwells. Francis always said they were the devil's spawn." She tried to sit, but fell back heavily against the ground. "Is the lad all right?"

"Yes, David is safe."

"And the boy?"

"He's not hurt either." She looked at Lorenzo, who was taking the breastplate off so Miss Urquhart could breathe more easily. "We must get her back to Moorsea Manor and send for the doctor right away."

He nodded and motioned for the coachee to help him lift the old woman into the carriage.

David clambered out. "I can run for the doctor, Aunt Valeria. We aren't far from Winlock-on-Sea. I know where the doctor lives. Gil and I saw his sign when we went to the beach one day."

"Go!" she urged, glancing back at the other carriage which had not moved. "Go as fast as you can, and don't let anyone stop you. Tell the doctor we need him immediately."

"Is she going to be all right?"

"I hope so." She kissed his soft cheek. "I hope so!"

She watched as he vanished into the shadows before she turned to climb into the carriage beside Miss Urquhart. A hand on her arm halted her. When she saw Lord Caldwell, she shook off his hand.

"Begone!" she cried. "Take your deadly greed and go!"

"I want you to know. I did not fire that shot." His face was the color of the pale glow on the breastplate that lay, bloody and forgotten, on the road. "The men misunderstood my shout to stop you. I never intended that something like this would happen. It was just an accident."

"Just like when her brother died?" Lorenzo asked as he assisted Valeria into the carriage.

"I had nothing to do with that! It was an accident caused by too much port and slick stones on that bridge."

"Mayhap the authorities will have a different opinion

about that when it is considered that Paul Blair might have had his mind more on his driving if he had not been worrying about how you had persuaded him to gamble away his sister's inheritance."

"You can prove nothing."

"I need not. Two accidents, if one is to believe that firing on us and Miss Urquhart is an accident, plus kidnaping David? You took the wrong gamble on this, Caldwell. I doubt even £8000 will buy you out of this."

"Moorsea—"

He pulled the door closed and shouted for the carriage to make its best possible speed to Moorsea Manor. He feared, as he looked at the blood along the front of Miss Urquhart's gown, that it did not matter.

When the old woman gripped his hand, he was amazed with the strength she still had. "Don't let me die yet, my boy," she whispered.

"Of course not! We—"

"I have too much I must tell you. What I should have told you weeks before." She moaned as the carriage dropped into a chuckhole. "You and Valeria."

"There is no need to speak."

"Yes, there is! My boy, were you taught no manners? You don't talk back to your elders."

He had not thought he could smile, and he saw Valeria's lips twitch. Miss Urquhart's eccentricities were comfortingly dear now. "Tell us what you must."

"Not here! When we get back to Moorsea Manor. That's where it began." She winced. "That's where it must end."

Seventeen

Valeria feared that Miss Urquhart's words would turn out to be less than prophetic, because blood flowed from the wound in her side. Yet the old woman was still alive when they reached the gates of Moorsea Manor. As soon as they arrived at the manor house's front door, Valeria ordered the old woman to be taken to the bed in the library, which was closer than her own rooms.

The house was somber as the servants watched in silence while Miss Urquhart was carried by three strong stablemen up the stairs. Even Kirby, whose face was still dark with the dirt he had used to conceal him when he led Gil and two of the other footmen to the trees and dumped water on Lord Caldwell, was sober.

Kirby asked, "My lord, what can we do?"

"David went for the doctor," Lorenzo said. "Send the carriage to meet them. It will be faster than the doctor's pony cart."

His valet nodded, backing away as he stared at the slow procession climbing the stairs. Valeria offered him a tight smile before she gave orders to Mrs. Ditwiller to bring clean water and cloths and Miss Urquhart's nightdress.

Hurrying up the stairs, Valeria entered the library just as the men who had carried Miss Urquhart were leaving. She tried not to look at the blood on them, for she doubted if a person could lose this much blood and live. Yet, Miss Urquhart had survived the trip back to the manor house. Mayhap she would meet Death on her own terms, exactly as she had Life.

Lorenzo held out his hand to Valeria as she came around the bookshelves to see the old woman looking incredibly small and fragile on the grand bed. Taking his hand, she let him draw her within the curve of his arm. So much they needed to say to each other, so complicated their lives had become in just the past few hours, but that must wait until Miss Urquhart was tended to.

"Tell her to leave me alone," Miss Urquhart ordered when Mrs. Ditwiller hurried in with a pitcher of water and some rags. "I want to speak with you two alone."

"My lady?" the housekeeper asked.

"Just leave it here." She pointed at a nearby table that was not completely covered by books.

"I will speak with just you and the boy," Miss Urquhart said in her most imperious voice.

"Thank you, Mrs. Ditwiller," Valeria said.

The housekeeper gave her a sad smile and left.

"Come here, boy."

Lorenzo went to the bed. Even with his height, he looked like the boy Miss Urquhart always called him when he knelt beside its high mattress. "I'm here, Miss Urquhart."

"I want you to know the truth."

"The truth?"

She looked past him to Valeria and motioned for her to come closer to the bed. As Valeria did, she said, "You both must know the truth of what has almost destroyed your families. Francis was a good man, but he never was completely comfortable with the constricting ways of the peerage." She smiled. "Like you, boy. Yet, unlike you, he went often to London to enjoy its entertainments. There he fell in love with a beautiful young woman."

"You?" asked Valeria when the old woman paused.

Tears of pain filled Miss Urquhart's eyes for the first time. "How kind of you to say that, but you are sadly mistaken. He fell in love with your mother, my dear. He adored her first from afar, then he dared to approach her to discover she held a *tendre* in her heart for him as well. The only problem was that she had already been promised to another. He tried to talk her betrothed into allowing her to break her engagement, but the man refused." Her voice faltered. "Love can be a type of madness, don't you know? Francis challenged the man to a duel for your mother's hand and was the victor, killing his rival."

"Oh, my!" Valeria dropped onto a stool by the bed. "I had no idea. Nobody ever spoke of this to me."

Miss Urquhart patted her hand. "It was hushed up swiftly, and your mother was as swiftly married to another man, for your grandfather would not consider Francis's offer for her after the duel. Francis returned here in shame and cut himself off from everyone, even his beloved sister." She looked at Lorenzo and smiled with sympathy. "He missed your mother deeply, but he did not want her to suffer from the taint of his moment of insanity, too. He arranged for her marriage to your father and then, wanting to protect her from ever being connected to him again, did not attend the wedding." She grimaced and groaned, clutching the covers, but added, "Her letters to him went unanswered until she gave up and stopped writing."

Lorenzo whispered, "Thank you for telling us this, but you are straining yourself when you should be reserving your strength."

"But that is not the whole of the story."

Valeria watched in amazement as the old woman pushed herself up to sit against the pillows. She looked toward the door. How much longer could it take for the doctor to arrive? "Miss Urquhart, you shouldn't—"

"Don't you start telling me what I should or shouldn't do, too," she scolded, but her voice was growing weaker. Leaning back into the pillows, she said, "I have more to say."

"It can wait."

"I doubt that." She closed her eyes for so long that Valeria feared she would not open them again. Then, her voice once again stronger, she said, "Your mother loved Francis all her life, Valeria, and her letters to him never stopped. I don't know how she smuggled them out of her husband's house or how she arranged for Francis to be your guardian if something happened to her, but she did. And I hated her for it." Miss Urquhart opened her eyes and glared at Valeria. "And I wanted to hate you."

"But you have been so kind to me."

"Because you have treated me with respect that no one else felt I deserved because I was only Francis's mistress, not his wife. I did try to treat you with the contempt I always held for your mother, but I couldn't," she said, dabbing at her eyes. "You are a dear child, and I cannot be angry at you because Francis wanted to marry your mother. He never asked me to marry him. That made me angry because I believed he loved your mother more than he ever loved me."

"That's not true."

Valeria whirled about to see Earl standing behind them. For once, he was not carrying his candle, but the soft glow surrounded him. She wondered where it was coming from, for the room was dark beyond the bookshelves.

"How do you know that, Earl?" she asked, knowing that soothing Miss Urquhart's pain was more important than satisfying her own curiosity. "Did Lord Moorsea's uncle tell you something that will ease Miss Urquhart's heart?"

The old man smiled and stepped closer to the bed.

"Miss Urquhart!" cried Lorenzo as the old woman stared at Earl and swayed as if caught in a high wind off the sea.

Valeria grabbed a cloth from the table and dipped it in the pitcher. Wringing it out, she placed the cloth on the old woman's forehead. "Mayhap you should leave, Earl. This discussion can continue later when Miss Urquhart is better."

Miss Urquhart pushed aside Valeria's hand weakly and used Lorenzo's arm to steady herself against the pillows. She pointed at Earl and asked, "What are you doing here?"

Lorenzo said, "Do not distress yourself, Miss Urquhart. Earl, this is not a good time. You should leave."

The old man did not move as he gazed at Miss Urquhart with a broadening smile.

"If you would please—" Lorenzo put out his hand toward the old man. With a yelp, he pulled it back and shook it.

"What's wrong?" Valeria asked, tearing her gaze from Miss Urquhart.

"He's cold. Incredibly cold. I froze my hand when I touched him."

She whirled to see Earl reaching toward Miss Urquhart. As she moved to halt him, he waved her back.

"I do not want to hurt you, too, my dear child." He smiled at Lorenzo. "Forgive me, my boy. That was most unintentional." Not giving them a chance to answer, he turned to Miss Urquhart. "I waited for you," he said as he held out his hand. "Our time here was not the same, but I could not leave without you."

She raised her trembling fingers out to him. When she put her hand on his, Lorenzo gasped, because she did not pull it back. Instead the glow flowed from his hand into hers as if she was cupping a handful of sunshine. Color flowed back into her face, wiping away the lines engraved by pain.

"Who are you?" asked Lorenzo as he drew Valeria closer to him.

"I thought you'd recognized me when you spoke of the painting of me and your grandfather at the tavern in Winlock-on-Sea." He smiled broadly. "I am your late Uncle Francis."

"My *late* uncle?"

"A ghost?" whispered Valeria, grateful that Lorenzo's arm encircled her shoulders, because it was her only connection to what was real. This could not be real. Could it? "A real ghost?"

"Mayhap that is what I am. I have not really worried about what to call myself other than Earl, so you would not be suspicious of an old retainer no one else seemed to know about."

Valeria recalled how Miss Urquhart had mentioned soon after their arrival that she knew of no one named Earl in the house. "No one else saw you here?"

"Just you two and young David. Where is he?"

"Getting the doctor for Miss Urquhart."

"There's no need for a doctor now." He turned to smile at Miss Urquhart. "I knew I could not go on from here until you were ready to leave, Nina. So much I owe you for mending my heart when I thought it was forever shattered, for tolerating my peculiar obsession that my nephew seems to have inherited for the study of the past, for understanding when I never seemed to find a convenient time to ask you to be my wife." His smile faltered. "But, after hearing you just now, I see that I was wrong. You did not understand. You thought I loved someone else more than you."

"But you said you would never stop loving her," Miss Urquhart whispered.

"So I did." He drew her down from the bed.

When Lorenzo started to steady the old woman, he pulled back his hand and shook it again. He clasped Valeria's hand with it, and she shivered as the cold on his skin touched her. Folding his fingers between hers, she rubbed them gently, trying to warm them as she watched in stunned silence.

Tears billowed into her eyes as she heard Earl—How he must have enjoyed the jest of using his title for his name!— say, "And I never have stopped loving her, Nina." He gave Valeria a swift smile. "To see her daughter here and to know that she is happy makes me joyous beyond words. But, my dear Nina, the love I had for Valeria's mother was a young man's love. As unbearably intense as lightning and as fleeting. The memory of that flash remains with me, but it is only a memory. What warmed my heart for most of my days was the love I have for you, a mature man's love, no less passionate but more like sunshine, there every day until one takes it for granted even when it is overmastering any storm clouds that dare to try to intrude."

"I never knew."

"Forgive me for that, Nina." He took a step away from the bed and offered his arm. "Will you grant me the rest of eternity to atone for that?"

She gave him a coy glance and laughed. "The rest of eternity? You may come to regret that offer, Francis."

"If I do, at least, I will regret it with you." He put his hand over hers on his arm. "Are you ready to go with me?"

"Wherever you wish, my dear Francis."

The earl smiled. "I wish you happiness, Valeria. I tried to do my best for you."

"You did, especially when you kept Austin Caldwell from marrying me."

"I know the marriage I arranged to keep you safe from that cur might not have been what you dreamed of."

"My lord—"

"Francis, my dear."

She smiled as the tears fell from her eyes. "I wish to thank you for arranging that marriage, Francis. Albert was a good husband to me. He gave me the life I wanted then."

"Then?" Lorenzo asked as he turned her to face him. "Do you mean that you have changed your mind about your life in Town, Valeria?"

His uncle spoke before she could. "Lorenzo, I am glad I have had this chance to know you, brief though our time together has been. I am sorry that I was not able to help you understand much about women. As you can see, I still am learning myself. You will be an excellent successor to me, but take two bits of advice from your old uncle."

"Yes?"

"First of all, don't worry that I would be upset if you sell Mr. Pettit all of my collection. It will make him happy, and I suspect that you and Valeria will be starting a growing collection of your own soon that will be much more important to you than the dusty shards I gathered in the fields."

"I understand," he said, although his tone warned that he was as confused as Valeria was. "And the second bit of advice?"

"I think I will let you find out the rest on your own." He chuckled. "Ready, Nina?"

"I think so."

Valeria watched them walk around the bookshelves. She hurried after them, but when she reached the edge and peered around, no one was there. Looking back at the bed, she saw it was empty. She grasped a bookshelf and whispered, "What just happened here?"

"I'm not sure," Lorenzo said quietly.

"How are we going to explain about Miss Urquhart to everyone?"

"I'm not sure about that either." He took her hands and brought her back to him. "But one thing I am sure of. I have been waiting for you, too," he said, tipping her face back and brushing away her tears with his kisses. "The difference is that I never realized it until the moment when I thought I had lost you."

"And I thought I was lost to you forever, but I thought you wanted me out of your life."

"I thought I did, too. I was wrong, and I want to make certain that we don't make the mistakes our elders made. We need to gather our love about us and savor every moment we have together."

She leaned her head against his shoulder. "Believe it or not, I agree completely with you for once."

"Shall we try for twice?"

Again she looked up at him. "What do you mean?"

"I mean that I have been seeking a convenient arrangement for you from the first night we met."

"And?"

His thumb grazed her cheek as he smiled. "What can be more convenient for me than to have the woman I love here with me as my wife?"

"Your wife?" She wondered if her heart could contain all this joy or if it would explode into a glorious display like fireworks splashed across the sky.

"Will you stay with me, Valeria? Will you share my quiet days with the growing collection my uncle spoke of?"

"Collection? Of what?"

"Stay with me and make my nights worthy of great poetry, and you shall see that David is only the first child to fill these halls with pranks." He brushed her lips with sweet, swift fire. "Will you stay here with me as my wife?"

"And plan just a few gatherings?" she asked with a smile.

"Maybe just a few." His arm swept around her, pulling her even closer, as he asked, "Why don't you start with our wedding?"

"That sounds like the most convenient arrangement of all."

AUTHOR'S NOTE

I hope you enjoyed this story. If you would like to read other books with these characters, look for Lorenzo in *A Phantom Affair* and Valeria in *Rhyme and Reason,* both Zebra Regencies. My next Zebra Regency is *Lord Radcliffe's Season,* which is scheduled to be in stores in July, 1999. A woman who has a shattered heart and a man who has been shattered by the war with Napoleon might find healing if they dare to take the biggest risk of all—falling in love.

I enjoy hearing from my readers. You can write to me at:

VFRW
PO Box 350
Wayne, PA 19087-0350
E-mail me at jaferg@erols.com

My web site is: http://www.romcom.com/ferguson

ROMANCE FROM FERN MICHAELS